I0738195

KATY *of* CLAY

ALSO BY U.L. HARPER

The Secret Deaths of Arthur Lowe

In Blackness

In Blackness: The Reinvention of Man

KATY *of* CLAY

U.L. HARPER

The Body Politic Press
Tacoma, Washington

Publisher's Cataloging-in-Publication Data
Names: Harper, U. L. | Harper, Aronald Uriah Lejan.
Title: Katy of clay / U. L. Harper.
Description: Tacoma, WA : The Body Politic Press, 2021.

Identifiers: ISBN 9780578810294 (pbk.)
ISBN 9780578810300 (ebook)

Subjects: LCSH: Coming of age -- Fiction. | Identity – Fiction. |
Redemption -- Fiction. | Self-actualization (Psychology) -- Fiction. |
BISAC: FICTION / Coming of Age. | FICTION / General. |
FICTION / Family Life / General.
Classification: LCCPS3608.A774 K38 2021 | DDC 813 H37--dc23

To Brianna Rose Harper

Contents

Katy

The problem is that I don't remember what my mother looks like.

When I was small, it was my mother, Arcilla, who made time to fingerpaint and dance with me. She made our house a home. She said that one day I'd be in upper education practicing the kind of art I loved.

She was right.

This close to break, I can focus on this personal project I've been working on. I dabble with it in my spare time. I start it, tinker with it, restart it, tinker with it, but never complete it, just constantly frustrated by this portrait of what I hope turns out to be my mom.

While waiting for Tess to pick me up, I retrace the eyes with a graphite pencil, mostly buying time until the epiphany of what she looked like comes to me. It's like when you know someone's name but can't put a face to it. The name on the tip of your tongue is how I remember her face. It's not quite there.

I probably look a little like her, so I use myself as a model. I don't trace this photo of me. I still try to copy it. I try to duplicate my buzzed sides and ponytail. The ponytail I draw is more like a long piece of dung sprouting from the side of my head. Every time I get to this point, I need to start over. I'm not a perfectionist, but I don't want it to suck.

What I like about it is how the brown of the eyes flourish next to the more silver than black eyeliner. It's gothic, although I didn't mean for it to be. A weird, exciting, and inaccurate version of myself stares back at me. In this portrait, the character has puckered lips. It's as if I'm the mirror the portrait is going to kiss.

Then there's the relatively new sensation I'm quite sure is caused by stress—like rocks grinding along my spine. Hopefully, it goes away now that we're on break. My dad doesn't think it's stress. He says sensation of grinding rocks are symptoms. According to him, they're the same symptoms my mother had at the time of her death. In her last days, her supposed symptoms also included staying up late, mumbling to herself and spending a lot of time alone. The thing is, college students, like me, who deal with final projects, we mumble to ourselves like she did, and stay up late, like she did, and spend plenty of time alone laboring over projects. We're twenty going on twenty-one, and sometimes we feel lonely, no matter how many people we're around. Maybe my mom had symptoms of being basically lonely and creative before the heart attack took her life.

A knock at the door.

"Katy!"

It's Tess.

I shut the sketchbook, toss my pencils into their container, toss on my jacket, and swing my duffel bag around my shoulder. When I open the door, Tess is waiting for me, glee smothering her entire body—her tall, frizzy hair, her bony jawline, her overly thin neck and freckles, and her tip toes slightly bouncing. She's happy, sassy, and ready to get out of here.

She and I will drive two hours straight until we reach my father's house. For spring break, we typically go home to visit family and friends. If you're me, you go home and recognize the death of your mother, and *then* visit friends.

As much as I appreciate my friends, it's hard to not focus on my mother's death, her missing face. She died nine years ago tomorrow. Toward the end, she maniacally laughed in the basement, sometimes all night. Came up for air only to take me to school. I remember all of that and can't recall her face.

"I'll let you drive," Tess says, "if I get to play the music." She tosses me her car keys, and backpedals down the hall. We're down the hall and down the steps in a snap. Then we're in her car. She hooks up the music, connects her phone to the radio via sweet, modern technology, presses play, and I put the sedan that her guardian, Ms. Maxine, gave her for college, in reverse.

It's a straight shot to the freeway. Just like that, we're gone, as if we were never here.

She's tone-deaf when she sings, yet on the other hand, damned near perfect in her writing. She's an editor for the annual literary magazine the school puts out. She can't hear her inner voice, but says she hears another voice that tells stories, which to some people makes her seem closer to crazy than to graduating.

Miles, miles and miles between where I live and where I go to school is a lifetime worth of grass, cattle, and sky, on this nearly traffic-less, two-way highway.

"I have to be honest." She thumbs the screen on her phone. "I already miss school. Not school, but the whole, you know, the stuff around it."

"You mean sex."

"Oh." Her eyes bear down on her phone. "This is going to make you squeal."

"What?

"Don't let go of the wheel." She slaps the dashboard. "Leslie finally hooked up with Max. I *Knew* they would."

"Bound to happen. Only a matter of time."

Tess scrolls. She looks like she's searching for something, brows furrowed as she bites her bottom lip.

"Here we go," she says. "Cameron wishes you a happy spring break, and, oh, he wishes he could come."

Cameron is some guy I met a few weeks back at a friend's get-together who thinks he has a chance. He doesn't. Tess keeps scrolling.

She gasps.

"What?" I glance at her, as her hand cups her mouth. "What?"

She slowly thumbs, deeply reads something.

"Roger's mom is saying…" She drops the phone on the floorboard. "Say it."

Roger's my ex-boyfriend from home. We stopped being a thing in high school, so I haven't been with him in years. The three of us were close. Myself and Tess still communicate with his mother every here and there, mostly online. We stop by when we visit.

The look on Tess's face is of thorough confusion.

She rolls down her window, her mouth hanging open. "She says he shot himself."

"Like, he's okay?"

"No." She flings her hands in my direction, then turns her head. "He's not."

"He's in the hospital? Does it say?"

She lifts her phone from the floor, expands her thumb and index finger to make the screen wider. "They found him dead on the floor of his living room. Shot himself in the head. His mom wants everyone to know."

Tess turns off the background music. For miles we listen to the tires against the road, the muffled rumble of the engine, the wind bending over our vehicle.

Somewhere in me I knew Tess would say something like Roger killed himself or hurt himself. We've all known someone on the proverbial edge or someone who for some reason or another you feel they could hurt themselves; they aren't going to make it. Maybe they're into drugs or never seem quite right, never seem happy or they're too happy for too long; either way they don't seem adjusted. Roger was like that. I didn't think he'd kill himself. I did figure he had it in him to do so.

I picture him smiling at me on that first date, in that first year in high school. I rode his skateboard to the theater.

Roger had so much anxiety about school that he drank and smoked a lot. He started doing meth and selling meth. It's around when he really got into the meth when me and him stopped seeing each other. We never even broke up. I stopped taking his calls and he stopped trying to contact me. That was senior year.

Tess smacks the dashboard again.

I've been slowing and not realizing it. I press on the gas. "When did it happen?"

"Two days ago."

"*Shit.*"

She mumbles something under her breath, pretends to wipe her curly hair out of her eyes. It's what she does when she's heavily thinking or upset. More like she's upset whenever she's heavily thinking. She's like this before tests, before dates when she thinks she has to have sex, and, I guess, she's like this when she finds out a friend has committed suicide.

She unbuckles her seatbelt and turns in her seat so she's facing me. "Are you okay?"

"He was always going to kill himself."

"That's not fair."

"Am I wrong? Are you surprised? Honestly, are you surprised?"

She wipes her imaginary hair from her forehead. "*Yes,* I'm *definitely* surprised."

"I guess maybe it hasn't hit me yet."

"Doesn't explain why you'd say something like that."

"Don't take it that way."

"Okay, I'm sorry. I'll take it another way. What way is that? What way should I be taking it?"

Not ready to have this conversation, I focus on the road, make sure I'm going the speed limit, and take note of all the nature that is dying around me. The grass, the trees, the birds, my friends. Everything is dying.

We arrive at my dad's. I pull over, exit her car, open the back door, grab my duffel bag, and shut the door behind me. She's already walked around to the driver side.

"You can remember what she looked like if you want to," Tess says. "She was beautiful and pretty and I loved her, too."

She says it, not making eye contact. Then she's in the driver's seat. We don't say goodbye, don't make plans to meet later. Like someone who is lost, I walk away.

She's only going next door. After all, she's been my neighbor the entire time I've lived here. The first time I saw her, it was a week or so after Christmas. I had a jump rope that was too small that I didn't like all that much. Tess came outside with a rope way better than mine, although hers was too short, as well. We tied them together and never separated, even had the same friends through middle school and high school, even went off to college together.

I rummage through my bag and find the key to my home. It's small and cream-yellow with one of those upside-down V roofs. Inside, it's amazing how things don't change. There's our same leather couch we've had forever, faded, and frayed at the bottom of the armrests. The same flat-screen television. It's turned off, always off. I set my bag on the dining room table. From across the room is the kitchen—dishes stacked in the sink, probably for days or weeks. Like how lazy can someone get? Above the fireplace mantel are multiple pictures of my mother and father and myself. The problem is I don't remember the lady in the picture being my mom. She doesn't look like me. I don't look like my father. The times I asked my dad about the pictures, he implied I was on drugs. He acts as if me not remembering my mom's face is part of some running joke.

My father emerges from the kitchen. His silver slacks and work shirt are of professional status. If I didn't know him, I'd think he recently got off from his white-collar job. His shirt is *that* pressed. His slacks are *that* clean. Look at his shined shoes. I don't think he's worked a day in about five years. He claims he feels productive if he's well-dressed. He doesn't think productive is about actually being productive. To him it's more about *feeling* productive. To him, if he dresses the part, and people think he looks the part, then he's fulfilling that part.

He opens his arms. We embrace. There's something extra in his hug. Something abstract.

"Where were you, in the basement?" I ask.

"Got a special surprise for you."

"Really?"

For someone surprising me, he's not happy. I've seen him happy with surprises for my birthday or Christmas. This isn't it.

"I know you like to acknowledge her," I say. "Didn't expect you to go out and surprise me. Okay, then."

"You do more than remind me of her. You're better than her. You're better than me, too. You have the potential to be."

"Maybe, I guess. You're the one who keeps saying I have the same symptoms that took her life. I don't remember having symptoms of a heart attack. I don't think she had those symptoms either."

"You know who you're better than?" He rocks on his heels. "Roger. His mother had the message. I assume she got to you and your friends."

My hand goes over my mouth. "Am I better because I'm alive or because it was suicide?"

He cranes his head. "I don't have the proper language to truly express my thoughts on it. I'm sorry."

He also lacks the proper body language and tone of voice. I'm certainly his daughter. For me it might take a while for something like this to hit me. For him it could take months.

"Not sure how I'm supposed to feel," I say. "It's like, I don't know, maybe I saw it coming."

"You don't need to make sense of it."

"I guess not. Around here people die and to remember them we, what, eat turkey sandwiches and maybe watch TV. So, I'm going to go ahead and do that with you and then see about some more death somewhere." I cut myself off because I can picture Roger. It's odd how the mind recalls good times no differently than moments that didn't end so well.

"You don't need to be in a hurry to make sense of it," he says. "Your mother leaving us didn't settle on me until quite a while later. If you're going to grieve, it's not always in the now."

"I've never seen you grieve."

"I've never seen you have sex. I'm certain both have happened. Your mother was the left foot. I was the right. Now I mostly hobble around. You'll adjust without him."

"What's with the surprise downstairs?"

He throws on a grin. "It's interesting how you come to me, choose to talk about your friend dying, though you still brush it off. It's fine. You can deal with what you're dealing with in any way you like. Or don't deal with it. It's up to you."

"I know. I deal with me. You're busy dealing with you. I like that our relationship is constant, no matter who has died."

He says, "We act differently when we grieve."

This is how he grieves. You can't tell by looking or listening. You need faith.

"That surprise you got for me." I slap his shoulder. "I'm all about it."

"Maybe it's not quite your time."

"If it's the kind of surprise I need to be ready for, I've never been so ready."

He strolls toward the kitchen. "Let's get something to eat first, if you don't mind."

In the kitchen, he makes turkey sandwiches. I wash a bunch of dishes and set them out to be used. Back out at the dining room table, you can kind of feel my mother's absence. I try not to romanticize her. It gets downright stressful to keep her held so high. She's got a special place in my heart that I keep at arm's length. He's got her lifted so high, I don't know how he can keep his posture under all that weight after all this time.

He says, "Do you still have your mother's symptoms? You feel okay?"

I take a bite of my sandwich. "I'm not sure if I remember you trying to get her help."

He sets his half-eaten turkey sandwich on the table, circumventing the paper towel. The bald spot in his thinning grey hair glistens, reflects light from the window. "Doctors wouldn't see anything wrong with her."

"If there's going to be a symptom, it's that I don't remember what she looks like. I'm not kidding, I swear."

He shrugs. "What do you want me to do with that."

Suddenly he has a kind of acknowledgment in his body language, that shrug, an admission. An attempt. Oh my god, he's lying to me. He actually believes me that I don't remember her. Is that it?

The laugh I have for him is a piece of bad acting left in my body from high school drama class. "She died of a heart attack. She didn't even have heart attack symptoms, did she?"

"Do you still get the feeling of rocks grinding your back? Headaches?" He sits straight up, taps the table. "You feel manic sometimes?" He pushes himself away from the table and walks to the end of the kitchen where the stairs to the basement wait for us. "Finish your sandwich. Come down. I'll show you what I got for you."

We have some family history down there. Dumb stuff. Dusty clothing, washer, dryer, old furniture. Items from my childhood. Irreplaceable stuff. My old bike, boxes of replaced dishes and boxes of books. None of it could be mistaken for a surprise.

I follow him. He's always said he wants to convert the basement to something guests will find useful.

The steps creak more than I remember. At the bottom, it's colder than upstairs, no matter what. Every now and then there's a mystery breeze. Who knows where it comes from? Cobwebs hang from the exposed inner part of the ceiling; spiders tuck themselves away in crevices between wood beams and coping and rusted screws. The concrete floor is uneven, more so near the sump pump in the corner.

The shelf on the far wall holds figurines made of clay that are no taller than my arm. I like to think I draw and paint, while he makes things out of clay. They're creepy and detailed, as if pulled out of a scene and shrank. He's always been good at his craft, although I've never seen him practice. He'll toss his blazer to the side, put on his apron, and manipulate the clay with his hands. The newspaper he used to keep the clay off the floor is strewn about. He's more brilliant and talented than neat. The specific clay he uses smells a lot like dirty water.

He stands next to the laundry table, looks at me, then glances at something next to it, looks at me, then glances at that something again. He cups his mouth, removes his hand, and takes a breath. "What do you see?"

"A laundry table. Is it wet somewhere? I smell mildew. Is that mildew?"

Like the skinniest of bulls, he huffs through his nostrils—a disappointed sigh—and then he wipes underneath his nose with his index finger.

"What's wrong?" I know he won't tell me.

"You don't see what's here for you?"

I gaze at the spot next to the maple laundry table.

He mumbles to himself, "All the symptoms."

"I'm not going to go crazy the way Mom went crazy. I'm not going to, uh, see hallucinations like she did."

"When your mother left us—"

"*Died.* You can say she *died.*"

He does that head shake thing, like I wronged him. "Why don't you do yourself a favor and go mourn your friend, assuming you know how to do that. We'll meet later for dinner. Yes? No? Your decision."

"You're mad?"

"Let's get together for dinner in a few hours. Not going to make you."

"Okay, starting again. You said there's a surprise."

"You either can't see it or you're too scared to admit you do."

Is he crazy, or am I? "I'll be back in a few."

Not sure if I will.

Made From Clay

I knock on Tess's front door.

She opens it looking dumbfounded.

I say, "I wanted to apologize, in person, before you left." Greta invited close friends and family over. No doubt Tess will be going.

Tess wraps her arms around me. "It hurts, Katy."

"I know. I'm still coming to terms."

She lets go and stomps her foot. "Why did he do that?"

I follow her inside. She grabs a backpack from off her couch. The scent of fresh cookies wafts in from the kitchen, as does jazz music, both staples of Ms. Maxine trying to cheer her up. Tess's bag clanks when she tosses it over her shoulder.

Holding the backpack over her shoulder with one hand, she wipes imaginary hair out of her face. "You're coming?"

"I don't want to cry in front of you guys. It's too much."

"If you want to come, it's not embarrassing to cry." She puts her arm through the other strap. "I'm not embarrassed."

"I can cry by myself," I say, even though there's no way I'm going to cry right now or any time soon.

"It's not only you."

"I know it can look like I don't care, it might sound like I don't. This is what I look like caring."

"The older you get, the more you're like your dad. Let's just walk."

She high-steps past me and out of the house, down the steps and to the sidewalk.

Roger's place isn't far. Mine and Tess's houses are in this cul-de-sac. We make a left at the second street up, go two blocks, make another left, and turn down a gravel alley. Go all the way to the back and you'll see Roger's place.

"You okay?" she asks.

"Symptoms."

"Symptoms? Of what?"

"Might be going crazy. Oh, yeah, and then a heart attack."

She gives me a look like she agrees on the whole going crazy thing.

We arrive at the bottom of Roger's steps. To the right of us is his neighbor's wooden picket fence that has shrubs growing over it and our heads. To our left is a backyard with a large apple tree and apples scattered throughout the yard. Tess walks up Roger's rickety stairs. Neither of us grabs a handrail because we don't want splinters, the rail is so worn by weather. Before we get up to the top of the porch that wraps around to the side of the house like a wooden moat, his mother, Greta, opens the screen door. Her foot holds it open as she waves us in, ashes her cigarette, blows smoke out the side of her mouth and keeps waving, continuing to tuck her robe underneath itself.

"Come on in. I hope you like beer." She grins at us, puts the cigarette to her lips and sucks. She tries to get her hair to the side of her face by shaking her head, but her hair is so greasy, it barely moves. "It's been a while, hasn't it," she says.

Tess is the first to the top of the steps to meet Greta. "A few months," Tess says.

"A lot has happened in a few months hasn't it." Greta exhales, gives Tess stank eye.

Tess strolls inside.

Next to Greta, I hesitate to look at her, I'm so damned ashamed. Is his death maybe a little on me?

Greta playfully smacks me on the back of the head. "You can lift your head, ma'am. You didn't kill him. Not on purpose, at least. Just kidding. You didn't kill him." She gently grabs the ends of my fingers and escorts me inside. "He was erratic and a drug addict. If anything, it was my own damned fault, not yours."

How she says it, she's fishing. I'm not taking the bait. In no way am I letting her off the hook.

I maneuver toward Tess. Greta has gone out of her way for new carpet. Roger. He had made quite the mess, I bet.

A few people are here so far. There's two of Roger's good friends. Sam, who helps at the mechanic shop up the road, who, to me, is more of a handyman than a mechanic. His hands are super calloused. Always that black grease under his nails, always a cigarette between his fingers. A super nice and funny guy, dilated pupils, and all that. Late at night, you might see him on his bicycle, going nowhere, tweaking into the night. And then there's Lollar, who is so short and unattractive and such a tweaker, I have no idea how he's going to make it.

Sam nods to me as I join him and Lollar next to Tess.

Sam says, "We were supposed to pick Roger up and drink some beers over at Tony's. It was getting kind of dark, so *I* noticed his lights weren't on. Lollar peeked in the window and—"

"He was lying there on the floor," Lollar says. His beanie pulled down over his eyebrows.

"I knocked on the window," Sam says. "Sure enough, there Roger was. You could tell something was wrong. He's balled up on the living room floor. You could tell he was injured or something. Nobody sleeps in the shape of lint. He looked a lot like lint."

Sam eyes me. We haven't spoken for a long time. It's not hellos he's saying with those off-center eyes. He pauses to light a cigarette.

Tess takes off her backpack and sets it on the floor near the wall. "Don't smoke inside right now."

"Roger's door was unlocked." Sam stuffs a cigarette behind his ear. "We walked in, like we should have. Doesn't say anything or hear us. By no means were we quiet. We were like what the hell is going on?"

Lollar chimes in, "There was blood all over this place. Horrific. Know what I mean? I was staring at bloody footprints. I'm like what the hell?"

Sam says, "Roger sat there not saying anything or moving. It became obvious by all the blood on him that he wasn't going to say anything. Our boy didn't have any breath left."

"This is going to sound super insensitive," I say, making them all stop talking. "I thought he shot himself in the head. It doesn't sound like it."

"You know what's super insensitive?" Sam says. "He asked about you, about once every other week. I kept telling him, I don't talk to her. Nobody talks to her. I had to keep telling him that you and Tess… Y'all do whatever you do. Together."

"Wait, what?" What is he trying to make me feel guilty about?

"This is why we don't talk," Tess says. "If we were gay, it wouldn't be a problem. Get off it."

"Whoa," Sam adds. "No judgment."

"I talk to Greta all the time," I say. "Just not you guys."

"I heard my name!" Roger's mother calls from across the room.

"He was saying I don't talk to anybody," I shout to her.

"We text back and forth."

"That's not talking." Sam puts the unlit cigarette in his mouth, removes it and pretends to ash it. "That's cool, you eighty-six this guy from your life. You're not perfect. No more perfect than I am."

"I'm not better than anybody in this room," I tell him. "I have as many flaws as you do."

"Then why is it you act like you're better than him?"

"She didn't feel like being a meth head." Tess to the rescue.

"I didn't want to watch him destroy himself." Folding my arms, I stare at Sam, waiting for his comeback. "I don't have the skills or the will to love someone who is trying to kill themselves in the worst possible way."

Roger's father dropped Greta for similar reasons as why I stopped seeing Roger, is my guess. Tired of self-destruction. My opinion is that anxiety and addiction run in his family. My opinion is that tragedy runs in his family. In the future, scientists will be able to isolate a tragedy gene, stick it in dirt and sprout random, multitudes of bitter, already-rotting fruit. Roger could be used, posthumously, to breed these plants.

A kind of energy falls on me, and pulls my face taut. My heart speeds up. A small laugh escapes my lips. Those in front of me are stunned by my giggle. Can't help it. It's like someone doused me with nitrous oxide.

"What are you laughing about?" Tess says, her face close to mine.

"I'm not trying to. Trying *not* to."

Symptoms. Right now, it feels like symptoms of something. I manage to straighten my face. "Damn."

"Are you somehow blaming her for Roger dying when you guys didn't even call 911?" Again, Tess defends me better than I'm defending myself.

"Y'all stop that!" Greta yells. There are a few older, more serious adults now with her. "It's plain my fault. I allowed him to become a drug addict. I let him drop out of school. I let him, no offense, have friends like you guys. Beer's in the fridge. God damn it, stop blaming yourselves."

Somebody turns on heavy metal music.

Feels like blood is being pushed through my body via millions of the smallest, tickling icicles.

"Katy, are you okay?" Greta shouts to me from across the room and above the squeal of guitar and drums blasting at about two hundred beats a minute. "That clown smile of yours."

"I could burst!" I yell. Not sure if the words come out, I say it again. This time my mouth doesn't move. "Did you hear me?"

"Twice," Tess says, hands on her hips. "You all right?"

Lollar's tweaker jaw opens and closes, in his attempt to bite his shoulder off.

Sam claps his hands and rubs them together as if he's pulverizing rocks.

My insides are tickling me with light. Not willing to risk pissing anybody off anymore with my body language and laughter, I meander away from them. First, I find myself down the hall near Roger's room. It's weird down here. I find myself cackling. Don't need weird. Need out. Next thing I know I'm near the front door, then I'm at the front door, waving with a purposeless grin, like I'm appreciating somebody else's birthday. I'm out and across the wooden moat/front porch that wraps around the house. I venture back down the alley in a full sprint. I'm up the street, make a right, another right, then huffing the night air I arrive at my house.

In my house.

Nauseous, I run up the stairs to my old room. The rocks drag against one another at my spine. It's all too much, all symptoms of something.

I'm not crazy.

Doesn't mean something in me isn't.

I've been at my desk for about an hour, feeling myself breathe, listening to myself breathe, coming to terms with the mechanism of my body. I'm not sick, but I'm not healthy.

I dig in my bag to get my things for drawing. It's odd for my hands to shake like this. My pencils and pastels are in separate boxes, these squares that lift apart and it's almost a surprise to see my tools waiting for me. I swing them over to the desk and set them at the top. I reach back into my bag and grab my sketchbook. I lost my favorite sketchbook with Roger years ago. My dad gave me that one. The leather was so nice and felt like nothing else. Using it with Roger, for a while it made sense. I would draw, and separately, his tweaker self would draw. It worked. One day I forgot it at his place and never got around to going back. We stopped talking. So, Roger kept my favorite stuff.

Newer sketchbook in hand, I sit on my bed. It's my work that'll make me better, sane.

I scooch into my seat at my old desk. With a pencil, I start with my face.

What if out of nowhere I could draw my mom's face? Mom, what does your face look like? Thinking about my mom calms me. I don't feel so symptomatic.

My dad is somewhere sulking about Mom. There's this time she yelled at me for dropping a glass bowl, a gift from a good friend of hers. I scribble the remembered creases from her angry forehead into the character in front of me. It's a new touch. The lips of this pretty version are full. I draw what I think are her lips, next to a version of my dimples. Dimples aren't easy. At the bottom of the page I save space for the neck, which I always get wrong.

What's that? A muffled bang comes from where I think is the basement. Listening for commotion, I gaze at the door jamb and the worn-out, cream-color paint, the splintered wood piercing it. The bedroom's wallpaper peels and curls and fades. A crack cuts through the water spot in the corner of the ceiling. I've known how small this room was since I was tiny. The queen-sized bed is too big for it. The only real walking space is between the bed and my closet. My closet door is basically a window, a beige trim for a frame. It's black, partially rusted handle doesn't lock anymore.

Pulling the closet door open gives me a better view of the boxes of artwork I have stored. From the far left to the far right are boxes of stored drawings and paintings. Back in the day I'd create something—a picture or some craft. Instead of setting it aside, my mom found space for it. At first, she saved them for herself in their closet. The art became too much so we stuck it in the basement. It's not until after Mom died and I left for school that Dad pushed a lot of it up the stairs and into my closet, kind of a perfect landing spot. There's no way he kept everything. Wouldn't have fit.

You can see through the glass double-doors of my closet and bask in the history created on the other side, from my mind to the paper or whatever. Who I've been for most of the last few decades is on a shelf in crayon, in marker, in pastels; erased and redrawn, smeared and touched-up. It's not perfect, although it's perfectly me.

On the floor at the left end of the closet is an unorganized pile of curled paper, of assorted colors and types. On the shelf, brushing up against the left wall is a white box—the kind you might store tax files in. To the right of it is another white box, followed by the same kind of box, followed by another. Resting on top of each box, smothering each of them is my newer artwork that might as well have fluttered out of the ceiling, how they've tumbled on top of one another. A bunch of it has fallen onto the floor. I kick some to the side so I can get to the boxes. I want the history lessons inside.

A solid thunk comes from downstairs. I hope he didn't hurt himself. Leaving everything where it is, I bolt out of my room and down the stairs to the living room. I turn the corner and find my way through the kitchen. I call him a few times. At the bottom of the basement stairs, what's in front of me is outrageous.

"Can you see it now?" he says.

"Yes. Yes, I... *Can.*"

"I've had this surprise for you here for years." He places the palm of his hand on a life-sized clay sculpture of what looks like a woman with long hair part way down her back. The sculpture is so detailed that the hair is shaped into individual strands, layers upon layers. It faces the far wall, with one of the hands reaching for the ceiling. It has reddish-orange clay spliced with faint blotches of blue clay, the same kind of clay he always works with. The tiniest of black dots all over it reminds me of zit heads. The lighting isn't amazing, how several rows of fluorescent lighting blinks and buzzes, but still holds enough accurate color. Just enough. I'm looking through the light and at the sculpture's profile, stepping towards the profile. It's smooth and detailed. The ends of the fingernails are slightly lifted from the fingers themselves, it's so detailed. The creases, the strands of hair, so many of them. It's so detailed.

He steps to the side so I can get closer to it.

"You did this?"

He answers, "Yes."

The sculpture sits less than a foot from the laundry table, fitted in a real and loose black dress all the way down near the ankles. Elastic allows the dress to hug the waist. A sculpture in real clothes. The reddish-orange ankles are exposed like flesh. This monolith is in well-worn black flats. What if this is supposed to be my mother? Seeing she's all he's ever probably thinking about... Why is her face blank? Like it's been scraped off and smoothed out.

"Why did you put clothes on it?"

He smirks.

Not sure what this expression means right now.

"How long have you had it?"

"Since your mother left," he says, and how he looks at me, he's waiting for some kind of response.

In my current state, with how my body feels, it's hard to gather myself and think. Yet he's been hiding this piece of work for all this time?

I place my hand on his sculpture. It's dry yet soft, like grimy model magic. Can't stop staring at the blank face. "Where've you been keeping it?"

"I've kept it right here. The whole time." Again, he's gazing at me in an odd way. Looking for a response, is that it?

"I'd have seen it. How did you—?" Rocks grind at my spine. The colors in the room become smooth. Now, look at the sculpture. It emits the vibe of walking into an anxious room, like stepping into the middle of a crowd at a concert. His sculpture is nothing but that feeling, nothing but that vibe.

"Is that supposed to be her?"

"It is what it became." He shuts his eyes, dips his head, and then lifts his eyes open again. "There was a time when people created people out of the very earth we now destroy. There was a time when if you inspired the world, it would adhere to you. You could inspire the things around you. The *things*."

"What are you *possibly* talking about?"

"It's new for you to hear, I know." He's waving his hands as if something is stuck to them, he's so animated with his words. "It doesn't make it not true. I'm speaking of the nature of both me and you. I want you to think back to a specific sketchbook I gave you, a specific tool I brought into this world."

I do remember a notebook he gave me. The one I left at Roger's.

He says, "You can be better than your mother."

"Why *say* that? Why say *that*?" Because of the symptoms, I'm breathing so hard, my lungs might burst.

Then he stares at me, just *stares* at me, in something approaching both determination and anger. "Those figurines over there, I shaped you, with my hands, out of that same clay. I thought I'd have more time to explain. Looking at you, I don't. You need to know, I shaped you, my Katy, quite literally, out of the oldest of clay."

It's hard to listen to him. The symptoms are so intense, I can't focus. I'm barely in control of my body; my body is merely acting out, reacting, it seems. He said I'm made out of clay. It must be code for something he did to me. Are those what his odd looks were about? He said, clay, and look at my hand, it doesn't look too different than the figurines, not too different than the life-sized sculpture. My hand, which is now basically a portion of a clay sculpture that's made of me—it's so detailed, the fingernails so detailed, the elbow and the slight bend of the wrist, so detailed. What you do when something unthinkable happens to you, is you close your eyes and wait for it to stop. It doesn't hurt, so imagine things are normal, and then, "*Fuck, fuck, fuck*. What is this!"

"I don't believe there's anything I can say to make you understand what it means to have your creative energy," he says.

My breathing quickens, and then thins. "Can you make it stop?"

He shakes his head. "You'll come out of it, alone, like a butterfly. The energy—"

"What *fucking* energy?"

"Those bodily sensations, Katy. The sensations. The symptoms. The energy."

The rocks grinding my spine, the tingling from within.

"The clay you're made of—now listen to me—the clay your made of, that your mother was made from, it's still in the DNA of everything we see and feel and live with. You're made of it, so you talk to it, even if you don't know it. You need to accept it. You need to master it and the creative energy that comes to it."

"But—"

"Those like me and you, we still shape the world from the things around us—"

"But you're not making any sense," I say, staring at my hand that's now, from what I can tell, an object.

"You act like we didn't create the entire world we live in, even the weather and modes of death. We invent new ways, right from our hands." He taps me on the head. "This truth is one of the few tools I can give you."

"Okay," I say, trying to relax, hoping it'll get him to stop talking. Just. Think. Just. What the hell?

For a second, it's quiet.

For a second, I don't think either one of us breathes.

Then he says, "You're between two places. Because that sculpture is not in this house. Do you understand?"

How would anybody understand this?

Still, something, damn it, an energy entices me towards the life-sized sculpture. It's the craziest shit, because I can feel what he just told me. I feel body heat. This close to it, it's like being next to a sleeping beast. You can tell when something is alive. No, asleep. The vibe, the anxiety. You can tell when you're next to a person compared to a wall or a pole or even a sculpture. It's alive. I swear the head moves, if only a little. The fingers twitch. It's alive. Isn't it alive?

"You need to get to Sunderland," he says.

"Is it alive?"

"Katy." His eyes are wide, his nose flares.

I don't think I've ever seen my dad ecstatic like this.

"Why won't you help me?" I ask him, plead to him.

"My Katy, you need to get to Sunderland."

Sunderland is at the edge of the state. It's where my parents met, where we went for family vacations. It makes no sense for him to tell me to go there right now.

The rocks grinding at my spine, the tickling from the inside, it's all working to get me to use my hands, to use my energy or whatever is shooting off in me. It's a calling. With my useable hand I lean for the sculpture's blank face, gaze deep into it. It's alive, right? Can it somehow see me? And then there's something that I dare accept. Is it my energy making this thing alive? I stare at the blank face. With my nail I make somewhat oval incisions for the eyes. It's difficult to do with one hand. I need to make the eyes deeper. And I can feel that creative energy. It's not just a feeling. There's life in my fingertips.

With my nails, I cut, I shape. With my last good hand stiffening, it's nearly impossible. I pinch the clay to shape the brows.

My dad, he stares at me in awe, with pride.

What would my high cheekbones look like on this? My nose. Would a narrower nose fit better? With a fingernail I scrape creases into this clay forehead. Taking a step back, it looks like I vandalized it. A random wave of glee floods my belly. The smell of trees and rainwater fluttering off this clay. The rocks grinding at my spine. I'm stiff, like a piece of wood has been inserted into my arms, in my legs, in my belly. There's wood inside of me.

Again, I look myself up and down, really focus, despite all that is happening, I truly focus. As a reaction, I smile and laugh at my body turning into dried clay, from my elbows down to my fingers, dried clay flaking off me and fluttering to the floor. For a second, I don't feel much different than this life-sized sculpture he says has always been down here.

The symptoms. He's seen this coming. For a long time.

My breath tickles as it expels itself from my lungs. It says, "Is this like what happened to my mom?"

He places his hand on my forehead. "Listen to me. Listen—"

"Daddy."

"The clay you're made from, it's very much like a door. You are a door that's ready to open, all on its own. We're all capable of opening doors for ourselves, understand? Don't be scared to be you, no matter how much you learn, like or don't like. You need to go. On your own. And you will." He pets my face, and then nudges me away from the sculpture. "Stay on Thirteenth Street, to begin. After that, find your way to Sunderland. I will meet you there. Your energy will get you to the other side. Mine will get you home."

Everything becomes stiff, like a shell shaping around me, in the shape of me.

He says, "You need to trust me and do as I say."

"Dad?"

"Relax. It's fine." He lays his hand flat on the life-sized sculpture. "It's fine. You're going to be perfectly fine. It doesn't mean I don't want you aware that the raw energy of violence, it shares our space, so you'll find people there. Suffering." He closes his eyes and slowly shakes his head. "Always dying."

"Wait, what? What about people dying?" I can't move. I'm not like a sculpture. I *am* one. "What the fuck! Who is dying?"

He chuckles. "It could be that Roger is there."

My dad casually walks over to the fold-up chair, grabs his silver blazer, and throws it over his shoulder. He walks up the stairs, looks back in my direction, though not at me. I try to reach out. I'm stuck with my arms outstretched. I try to call to him. Nothing comes from my mouth. There's no sound in this clay shell.

Vision in both my eyes fade.

He knew this would happen to me. It happened to my mother. She and I had the same symptoms.

Why didn't my father tell me I was made from clay?

Why *wouldn't* he tell me?

Why didn't he tell me?

Tess

I t didn't surprise Tess to see Katy's half-smile as she watched Katy sneak out of Roger's house. She knew Katy didn't want to be at the gathering anyway. So, catch up to her later.

Tess stuck her fingers in her ears to block the higher decibels of the heavy metal music. "Can we get that turned off?"

"I don't know what they're thinking." Sam acknowledged her and the obnoxious music by smacking his hands together. She knew Sam didn't mind the music. Sam loved this band. "Katy didn't need to act how she was acting," Sam said.

"It didn't help for you to say she ditched Roger to be with me," Tess said. "Yeah, that's what you guys were getting at?" It wouldn't have been a problem for her and Katy to get together. Although they hadn't talked about it, it's not as if it hadn't crossed Tess's mind.

"Katy had an emoji smile," Lollar added, grinning through his yellowed teeth. "Not her normal smile. I'll leave it at that."

The amount of bad judgment in the room had her thinking overly negative about the people in it. They all had the chance to go to school, to become something, to do something meaningful. Her friends decided to do meth instead. Now somebody died. Wouldn't be the last one of them either.

She pictured Roger lying on this floor, contorted, alone, in the dark, bleeding, and lifeless. When she thought in this way, a mental switch flipped. With the switch on, the writer in her tended to think in narration. *Nothing else could be taken from Roger. They had already taken his joy, most of his family, light, and finally his life. Wouldn't it have been more efficient to start with his life?* It wasn't until she found a reason to write the voice down that she considered it useful. Her characters narrated to her, and for her.

"I'm the one who called Greta," Lollar said, swaying and pointing at Sam. "That jackass made a sandwich."

Sam shrugged. "Was hungry."

She had to look away from the people she had called friends for so long. For too long. "You guys killed him."

Sam looked confused. "We walked in and he was like that."

"You guys saw him every day. Nobody saw this coming?"

Lollar ripped the beanie from his head and stuffed it under his arm. "I feel like shit, how we dealt with it, okay. He used," he lowered his voice, "Greta's .22 to shoot himself in the back of the head. We found that out. Ask her. I don't see why you act like you weren't his friend."

"That's my point." She sniffed, ready to let the tears fall. "Was I being a friend at all? We, all of us, knew he had problems. We ignored it. Is that being a friend?"

Lollar stopped swaying. "We know we're fucked up. Roger was fucked up, too. Life goes on."

In war with yourself there will be casualties. Accept it and move on.

Tess gazed across the room at Greta. Knowing Greta, she would grieve in her own way or already had. She invited everyone to her house, the place where Roger died, to have these conversations. Tess didn't want or need the conversations. These weren't the people to grieve with, come to find out.

Sam said, "We didn't put the bullet that got lodged in his head there. It's possible that if you cared for him so much you would have gone to school close by and had been around. Maybe you could have stopped by and helped him. He didn't die right away. Who knows how long he had wandered the house? Blood was everywhere. All over the walls, in the kitchen. He shot himself in her room. I bet you could have done something different for him or better, if you would've been anywhere close."

Tess took a step back from them, disgusted. "Whatever is the matter with Katy, it's not as wrong as what's the matter with you guys. She wouldn't show up to a suicide and grab a sandwich from the fridge."

"She wouldn't show up," Sam added. "We did. I thought he was hurt. Not *that* hurt."

Katy was right. These weren't people you could cry in front of. She wouldn't allow herself to shed a single tear in front of them. "I'm going to go find Katy."

"What?" Sam said, furrowing his brows.

"I'm going to go find Katy. Is that okay by you?"

"Sorry. Whatever. Go get your girlfriend."

She headed for the door, ignored Greta and her friends who all stood near the threshold. To her surprise, Greta didn't try to stop her. Tess carefully made her way down the steps, not willing to fall on the misshapen structure. As she strolled up the alley, head in hand, the sound of heavy metal music blared.

Tess knew Maxine had gone to sleep. Instead of going inside after returning from Roger's place, she unlocked the door, but remained outside. She tossed her backpack on the porch, sat on the steps, and pondered Katy and Roger and how everything became neglected and trash. Roger wound up being the exact kind of person to shoot himself in the head. Their friends didn't know how to show they cared. Nobody knew how to show love for someone. Or they didn't love.

She found her way into Maxine's rocking chair. Next to it was the fold-up chair Katy would sit in if she were present. Tess rocked back and forth, back and forth, kept the balls of her feet to the wooden porch. How would she talk to Katy? The gentle rocking in Maxine's chair did not ebb her anxiousness. She loved Katy, but if Katy had shown a little give-a-damn to Roger, a little maintenance, he might not have been dead.

So, she rocked.

In middle school, she and Katy used to sit right here on her front porch and stare out at the street. They didn't talk as they paced and jumped and bounced and rocked and sat around in the vibe between them. They didn't need to talk about the vibe. During that time, Tess thought she had a crush on Katy. For the longest time it felt as if Katy knew about it, too. Then Tess met Izayah. Whatever she felt for him—a good thing—was different than what she felt for Katy. Izayah wound up being Tess's first kiss. Katy might have been her first crush.

Movement from the corner of her eye caused her to turn her head. Katy was strolling, possibly a little drunk, from her dad's house. She stopped on the grass island in the middle of the cul-de-sac.

"Katy, we should talk," Tess shouted.

The closer Katy got, the more it didn't look like Katy. The woman was too tall, and she didn't walk with Katy's gait. Katy clomped when she walked. This person twisted off the balls of her feet, swayed from the left and right with each step. That and she wore clothes Tess had never seen on Katy, a dress out of 1950's television. The woman's long hair should have been in a ponytail to make the look perfect. The lady stopped on the island with her hands out in front of her, turned 180 degrees and fell on her ass.

Drunk, of course.

Tess jumped off the porch, and in no moment at all was on the island, hovering above the lady who had her back to her. Tess leapt back when the lady stared up at her, faceless. No eyes, no nose, no eyebrows. No color. The hair could have been a wig. Tess drew up every ounce of courage and stepped all the way around to the front of the woman, peered in at her. People had faces so this was something different. A mask? The lady pushed herself to her feet, held her hand out.

Tess backed away, unsure of what she was looking at. She couldn't get a good enough look, but the woman had no face. She had no face!

"You need help?" Tess asked, her voice trembling.

The faceless woman nodded.

"Were you coming to my Ms. Maxine's house or next door?"

The woman nodded.

"Do you think you know me or Ms. Maxine?"

The faceless woman nodded.

"No, you don't." She deeply gazed at the woman, feeling the urge to run creep up on her, though there was nowhere to go. Something had to have happened to this woman. In the badly lit cul-de-sac, Tess couldn't see how in the world this person did what she had done to her face. It could have been that somebody else did this to her, again, a kind of mask.

Deformed?

"Are you running from somebody?"

The woman shook her head. Not a shake in response to the questions, but more a sign of the silliness of Tess's questions.

Uneasy, Tess maneuvered around the woman, started back home. She could be of no help. "The mask is…too weird. I'll call someone to help you."

The police. The woman could have been super drunk. The stumbling.

Tess jogged to her porch, escaping, worried the woman would follow. Tess sat in the chair and rocked, her chest stiff in anticipation of the faceless woman following her. She wiped her hair from her forehead.

Screw this.

Right on time, the woman stepped out of the shadow and into the dim light of Tess's front porch, stumbling. The woman couldn't have been wearing a mask. Tess felt herself rise to her feet and shuffle to the door.

From the lady's neck to her blank forehead, all one piece of awkward flesh.

The woman backed away, held her finger in the air, like, hold on. She began to dance like Tess and Katy once did as kids. They made up the dance with Katy's mom. In all actuality, the person wore something Katy's mom used to wear. The thing is Katy's mother had died years ago of a heart attack.

"Am I supposed to know you?"

The faceless woman shrugged, held her index finger up, gesturing to hold on for a minute. The faceless woman placed her hands on her hips and paced in a circle.

Tess grabbed the door handle, fumbled with it, her hands shook so much. She got a grip and pushed it open. Hurrying inside, she almost tripped on the rug. She recovered in time to twist herself around and slam the door shut. She locked the deadbolt and chain before twisting the lock on the knob. She closed her eyes and focused on making a good decision. But there was no good decision to make. What kind of an asshole called the police on a faceless woman?

Well, the woman must have been able to see a little.

The gentlest of knocks on the door.

The faceless woman, Tess heard her step to the far side of the wooden, hollow porch. Tess looked around the room, hoping Ms. Maxine wouldn't wake. Adrenaline arrived with fear of Maxine's safety. *Okay, call the police.* They didn't have a house phone, and she left her backpack with her phone outside on the porch.

Tess sensed the faceless woman looking in the window next to the door. Faceless tapped on the window. Said nothing. Tapped. The soft steps outside crept backward. Tess looked through the peephole, hoping the woman had walked off the porch. She hadn't. Or was she an it? It hadn't. It stood on the edge of the top step, holding its hand where its mouth should have been. It swung itself around and scanned the neighborhood.

As Faceless turned her back on Tess, Tess turned her back on Faceless. *A person with no identity has nothing to say, having come from nowhere. The faceless have nowhere to go, but they can still find a place in your heart.* No familiar situation involved a person with no face claiming to know her. She resembled, if she had a face, Katy's mother?

"There somebody there with you?" Tess heard Maxine from upstairs.

"A drunk friend of mine, Ms. M. I got this."

"Please do get it. The middle of the night, gasping and panting around. Damned near sounds like you're having sex down there."

The new knock came in so soft that Tess barely heard it.

Don't look.

Tess backpedaled up the stairs, keeping her eyes on the front door. She tiptoed to the far window of her bedroom and looked down at the faceless person on the porch steps. Every few minutes she looked out the window to see if Faceless was still there. One time it gazed up at her, looking like an ill-conceived Mr. Potato Head figure.

Tess fell asleep.

She woke at dawn. Faceless still sat on the porch, sitting with her head between her legs.

A few blocks up on the main road, the frequency of traffic had increased. What would happen when the neighbors left for work, when the kids came out to play? They'd see Faceless on the porch. Then what? What about when Maxine left the house?

Where the hell was Katy?

Tess made her way downstairs and gently knocked on the front door.

Faceless knocked back, equally as soft.

"Go to the side yard and wait for me there," Tess told her, and listened to her leave the porch.

A moment later, Faceless arrived at the side yard. Tess lifted the window open and told Faceless to sit with her back facing the road. This way no one would freak out if they saw her.

She must have come from somewhere close. Get her back to where she came from, don't involve police, and keep neighbors and everyone out of it.

Tess peered out at the face. Why did this happen to this person? With it being brighter outside, although a screen sat between them, Tess could clearly see this person had no face. In the added light of the morning, she looked every bit like Katy's mother, minus the face. She knew it but now couldn't deny it.

Tess made a mad dash to the front door, unlocked it, and swung it open. She kicked open the screen and grabbed her backpack with her cell phone in it from right outside. After shutting the door and locking it, she called Katy. No answer. She called again. No answer.

She ventured back to the window.

The lady gestured to Katy's house, like a crossing guard signaling for individuals to cross.

Did she want Tess to follow her to Katy's? "You mean go next door? Now?"

Faceless nodded, with vigor.

"You for sure know them," Tess said referring to Katy and her father.

Faceless nodded.

Ms. Maxine rustled around upstairs. She'd be coming down any moment.

Faceless took a few steps in the direction of Katy's house, smacked her thigh the way someone might signal for a dog to come.

"I'm just going to make sure you get to where I think you're going and that somebody's there. That's the best I can do."

Tess made sure she had her keys, her phone, and exited her house to join this faceless person. If they were going to Katy's, then her father had to have answers.

Tess hadn't been inside Katy's place in quite a while. Dust lay underneath the television and on the back of the leather couch, in the cracks of the seats at the dining room table. The gray, thicker dust, meant neglect.

Pessimism clouded Tess's thinking, as it became clear that not only was Katy not here, neither was her father. Faceless seemed to have a destination.

Curiosity brought Tess to the top of the stairs, and then into Katy's room, following Faceless. What was going on here? But, no, really what the hell was going on?

Katy's art bag lay on her bed, her old artwork scattered all over the floor. No good place to step. A stuffy room needing airing out. Tess picked up some of the artwork, as did the faceless one. Tess slowed her motion, as she pondered how they both saw the importance of Katy's work. These were much older pictures. Sheet after sheet of a man with two heads that Katy might be embarrassed to have completed. The style, although clearly older, reminded Tess of the pieces Katy recently worked on. At school, she and Katy had discussed her pictures on more than a few occasions. Katy could never get her mother's face quite right.

The faceless one found a pen in an old coffee mug on Katy's desk. The cup brimmed with numerous kinds of pencils and pens. Yellow sticky notes at the side of the mug. Faceless sat. Every movement she more resembled Katy's mom. The pauses between thoughts, the sudden bursts of action. Faceless hovered the pen above the loose drawing paper, and then scribbled as if she were behind deadline on an article.

Through writing is how they could communicate.

Faceless handed Tess the sheet of paper, simply a woman with no face with the body and mannerisms of Katy's dead mother.

"I don't think I have a lot of time," Faceless wrote. "Can you please, at least pretend you believe me?"

Not sure how to respond, Tess handed the paper back to it.

"I'm looking for my daughter," Faceless wrote. "I miss her."

Tess contemplated what Faceless had wrote. She couldn't conclude this thing was Katy's mother. Not possible. However, the honesty of it confused her. Although it wasn't Katy's mother, it certainly thought of herself as Katy's mother.

Tess lifted her palms in the air, and then handed the paper back to Faceless.

"You believe me," Faceless wrote.

"I don't get what's happening," Tess said. "What's happened to your face?"

"They didn't bother to finish shaping me, not completely. I should apologize for my appearance," she said on the sheet of paper.

"What the hell?" Tess chuckled, a nervous reaction. "Well, why'd they forget your face?" The placation came out sounding a bit like a misplaced joke, she thought. For a second, Tess concluded she had imagined what Katy's mother had walked like and looked like, it had been such a long time ago. This person-thing in front of her, well, who knew what was going on with it? Super interesting and fucked up but nothing else. It's just that it seemed so honest and sad, such an authentic sadness. Sadness held more truth than any skepticism could.

"They didn't forget my face," Faceless wrote. "They did it wrong. I'm a mistake."

Tess thought about that statement and handed the paper back. She imagined persons shaping, sculpting, being like Katy when she worked on her personal project, and not being able to figure out the face. She handed the paper back to Faceless, confused and inspired; what if...just what if...

Faceless wrote, "In the basement, you'll see all the clay Katy's father used to shape me into me. I want you to think of clay but not as clay," she wrote. "It's more than how it sounds. We're not golem, if you know that idea."

Tess wiped hair from her face, held the recent note given to her, and exhaled in relief, thinking that, just maybe…

Faceless patted the bed behind her, suggesting Tess sit.

Tess sat on the end of the bed immersed in this person-thing, in awe at the idea of what it could be. Her creative mind wanted every bit of this awkwardness to be free of lies and speculation, so she focused on what she could see, refrained from asking questions. Let this crazy be crazy for a moment.

Tess scooted close enough to focus on the effortless scribing Faceless did. Faceless hunched over the paper, writing fast, neat, in cursive, and in a straight line. Of everything awkward happening, the cursive writing in a straight line is what Tess found the most incredible.

The piece of paper came back to Tess: "I have memories of when you were small. I remember that little dance you guys did in the basement. You didn't know I was alive, but I was there, invisible to you."

Holding the paper to her chest, Tess gasped, remembering those days in the basement making up dances with Katy. How Faceless could know such a thing didn't need to be explained. The person-thing's honesty would have to be as good as anything unproven, if for only this once.

Tess reached out, and with every bit of imagined courage, she touched the blank face, thumbed where the cheeks should have been. She paused at the inhumanity in how it felt. She continued petting it; as unreal as it had been, it also represented a forgotten distant memory. Tess was convinced that some of her personal moments, her personal history was somehow stored in it, lending it credibility. When she pulled her fingers away from the cheeks, her fingerprints remained.

Tess stepped to the side of her thoughts—an incredibly light step, despite the fear.

Faceless quickly scribbled on a fresh sheet of paper. "If you call what I'm made from magic, you won't be wrong."

Tess read the new line in the note and dropped her hands to her sides, disarmed. For this moment, she'd believe magic was real. For now, she'd allow it.

Faceless gestured for Tess to return the sheet of paper, which Tess did without hesitation. Faceless then jotted down something fresh and showed Tess.

"The truth is," it started, "if you go back far enough, everyone was created like me. They imagined who they were. The truth might be that, in a way, everyone is magic."

Tess closed her eyes, deeply wanting to believe she had magic in her. There weren't any facts in the thought process, she knew that much. The lack of facts is exactly why she had no choice but to believe.

"Is it the magic that made you come back?"

Faceless sat motionless for a second, picked up the writing utensil and wrote: "It's because of Katy we're talking. It's her creativity that made me alive this time. She filled her energy into me, I don't think purposely."

Before Tess finished reading, Faceless gestured to give the paper back.

Faceless snatched the paper and faced the wall, cursive wrote in that straight line of hers. She lifted the line-less paper in the air for Tess to see. "I don't know where my daughter is!" She shook the paper, as if it was a white flag. "I don't know where my daughter is!" She punched the air, the piece of paper now balled tightly in her fist. "I don't know where my daughter is!" And then, "Can you help me?"

Tess peered in at the note. "Help you find her?"

She wanted help finding her daughter, no different than any mother who hadn't seen their child for who knew how long? "I can look for her," Tess said.

Faceless intertwined her fingers, sat at the desk with her back straight, like a perfect student. She nodded, as if finishing a conversation with herself, and then she wrote something on the sheet of paper.

Faceless handed it to Tess.

"I don't want to be found in a chair like I was confused." Faceless pointed to the floor.

As Faceless stood, Tess gave her some space, moved away from the bed and toward the door.

Faceless bowed, something Katy's mother used to do for her and Katy when she introduced them to imaginary audiences in their bedroom when they were children. She dragged her feet passed Tess and exited the room.

Tess didn't immediately follow. First, she jetted down the hall to Katy's father's room. There were certainly signs he had vacated. His drawers were open and a few of them had been emptied. Although the bed had sheets on it, it didn't have blankets or pillows. Why would he leave like that?

It could have been that Katy left with her father, though she didn't believe it. Where the hell would they go without Katy's things?

She skipped steps on her way downstairs, turned the corner, crossed the dining room, and made it through the kitchen where the window of the back door allowed her to see outside. She didn't see Faceless. Once at the bottom of the basement staircase, she saw Faceless standing in front of the laundry table. She broke out into that familiar childhood dance. Faceless wasn't going to see Katy before she, what, died? Disappeared? What was happening here. But, no, really, what exactly was happening? Certain she couldn't let Katy's mother, or anything that might have been Katy's mother, be alone, Tess joined in, familiar with the routine, and the empathy that went into the communication. Who didn't? She didn't want to be found by whom upstairs in Katy's chair? Katy's father? Faceless needed dignity. Dancing gave her that. Dancing in your last moments prior to death is something Katy's mom would do, something Arcilla would do.

You need to dance till the very end. To the last moment, you need to laugh, no matter what face you're wearing, no matter what master you serve, despite the longing and misery, you need to dance. No matter how short and edited your history, just dance if the mood is lucky enough to be there, celebrate having been alive and having your life's worth of moments, just dance. Just dance. Just dance.

Tess dug up confidence from her gut and took the lead in this dance. Arcilla's joy wasn't in her face, instead it was in her movements. Happy, child-like feet and hands. Child-like hips and swinging of elbows. She clapped and jumped.

Arcilla's movements slowed. They slowed to the point to where she looked in pain or was avoiding pain. Her head became stiffened clay. Her feet were rocks dragging across the floor. Dust fell from her body, until she stood still, no different than one of Katy's father's small sculptures in the corner.

Feeling like she had witnessed a type of crime, Tess rushed up the stairs, darted through the house, across Katy's lawn, over the island in the cul-de-sac, and then leapt onto her porch steps. She scurried inside and locked the door behind her.

"Is that you?" Maxine called from upstairs. "Where'd you go?"

Tess gathered herself, not finding the nerve to answer.

Roger's Suicide

peel a mud mask off my entire body. If I had turned to clay, that's what I peel off. I flick away the reddish-orange pieces of what seems like soft dirt. After a bit, it's a lot like dust tumbling into nowhere, and then gone. If dirt were steam.

My dad said I might find Roger, because this place is full of death. Suffering, he said.

Where am I?

The life-sized sculpture is gone. Weird things happen. That sculpture my dad showed me was weirder than that. I finish dusting myself off. According to my dad, I'm in another world. The problem is nothing has changed, outside of the fact that I don't know how much time has past. This is what happened to my mother, this displacement of time. However, I had a horrible dream of going through a time of sustained thoughtless falling through darkness. Only a dream. I know I was falling. I know there was deep, soothing blackness.

I peel and crumble away the last of this clay off of my neck, from off the top of my forehead. It flutters to the floor in that small, mysterious breeze that's typical in my basement. I'm made of the dust tumbling to the floor. The breeze carries the slight scent of mildew. I wave at it, so it doesn't stick to my leggings, flats or thin sweater.

I don't feel made from clay. I don't feel like my own personal door to another world. In fact, it doesn't appear I've gone anywhere.

I jog up the stairs to the kitchen, from there into the dining room. I take my phone out of the back pocket of my shorts. It says not too long has past by since I left Roger's. Feels like a bunch of time has gone by, though. Not that it matters. It'd be nice to find Tess, because, damn, she's the only one who will listen to me about what is happening. Chances are she's still at Greta's.

Heading from the cul-de-sac, I travel a block underneath a quiet and clear night sky. On the next block, the sky is suddenly a sunny blue. It's impossible for this to happen and it's happened anyway. Breathe slowly and keep moving your feet to Greta's. Find somebody. Confirm all of this. Why didn't he tell me I'm made of clay? In the meantime, it's simply a perfect living painting of the afternoon. It's a deeper sky, a farther sky, a sky closer to heaven, I suppose. You stare at it. You ponder everything on it. I'm not dead. I'm in another place. The surprise that something, that some place like this exists makes you want to scream, but there's no panic. No need for that.

I shout to myself anyway, and then I double over in a scream until my mouth is dry. No need to panic. I find myself turning in a circle, not sure how to make this work or how to be or where to go because Tess isn't here, is she?

He said this happening to me is, in a way, my rite of passage. He meant to say inevitable. Being here was going to happen when I matured, no matter what.

I drag my feet along, trying to put everything he said to me in one place in my brain. He said I might find Roger. Roger killed himself. He killed himself and maybe ended up in a place where the time of day changed in a matter of a few feet. I pat the ground. There's nothing special or different about it. I shout as loud as I can. I kick a rock, for no other reason than to see how it reacts to being kicked. It appears the rules of physics are the same, although quite clearly, they're not.

I do start for Greta's, for Roger's. Where else do you go? What is there? Worst case scenario is I find Roger and something is wrong with him. Maybe what I'm experiencing is just me seeing things weird, hearing things weird, feeling things weird. I hope my head is just all messed up. This is why my mother stayed in basement when her symptoms got out of control.

I know I'm not crazy, but I hope I am. 'Cause…

By the time I turn the corner, a different afternoon sky is overhead. This one has strips of incredibly high clouds. I've known this street forever, so there are qualities about it I've never seen standout. Example—there's concrete that's uneven and cracked into fissures shaped like lightning. There are more trees than I remember, in the front yards and on the sidewalk outside the front yards. Barking comes from somewhere in the distance. I know a few people in the addresses on either side of me. The homes look different. Newer?

A cream-colored car drives my direction, a young guy behind the wheel. One of those old American cars. Those old bench seats that have never been okay, and it has red interior. He's my age. Never seen him. Nobody my age would buy this car let alone drive it. Too big. Too much gas. If it happened, it'd need to be in another world.

The car pulls up next to me at the stop sign. The front fender says Galaxie, in cursive. The driver's hair is slicked back. He has the expression on his face that says his mind is busy. If I had to draw him, I'd make his eyebrows thicker and bent to make him as menacing as he seems. One hand on the wheel, his eyes search for something. The white T-shirt should be an undershirt, despite it being creased. The word "greaser" comes to mind.

I raise my hands in the air and wave them, like, S.O.S.

He turns his head in my direction. I give the universal sign to roll down the window. He leans over and rolls down the passenger window. "Hey." His eyebrows lift. "Need a lift?"

"I hadn't thought of it."

He unlocks the passenger door. "Come on, where you goin?"

"Is this… Is this your normal world?"

He looks at me, first concerned, then worried. "I'll see you 'round." He rolls up the window and screeches through the stop sign.

I get to Greta's mini side road, the gravel and all of it. It's as I remember. Kicking the rocks, dirt flies everywhere. Somehow it feels later in the day than it did a few hundred feet back at the street corner. It's evening. The sun is now at the horizon; I can't see it from my position. It took six blocks to be in three different parts of the day, to see three different skies. It's fantastic.

Nobody answers when I knock on Greta's door. I knock again, this time harder. I put my ear to the door. Somebody's coming, so I back away.

Someone on the other side twists the knob. The door comes ajar. Right in front of me is my ex-boyfriend, Roger, the one who killed himself. The smile he gives is all joy. He reaches out with both hands, grabs me by the shoulders and pulls me into him. The embrace is like none he's given me. I wrap my arms around him. For a while we hold each other.

He lets go and says, "You're on break?"

There's nothing to do but stare at him. I need to make sure I'm really seeing him and he's not going to fade like the night sky a few blocks back. I know he's dead. I reach out and rest my hand on his arm, curious at what will happen. I squeeze. It's Roger, still Roger, stays

Roger. A flood enters my chest, because I know he's dead. I don't know where I am, although I understand where I am. There is suffering.

"Katy, what's the deal?"

"Not sure."

"What's up then. You're in town for what?"

"I think on my way down it became about you. I bet somehow all of this is about you."

"Oh, is it, now?"

He's dead and doesn't know it. "Every day I don't call you, it's a mistake," I tell him.

"We're not a thing. I know that."

"I know you know."

"It's been a long time. Had time to navigate through things. It is what it is."

"Should I come in?"

He steps to the side to let me through.

It's his place, minus Greta. For all intents and purposes, there's nothing unique about it. He's happier than usual, assuming it's really him.

He says, "I say some wild, wild stuff. What I'm about to say is going to sound crazy."

"I bet it is."

"I specifically remember killing myself. I don't want to freak you out. Things aren't right."

He hurries to his spot on the couch. I sit on the opposite end.

"What do you mean thinks aren't right?"

"It's hard to explain," he says. "I'm not talking about a dream or imagining it. I killed myself. That's what it feels like. Am I nuts or what?"

"Why did you kill yourself?"

"I don't know." He focuses on the ceiling, really peers in at it. "I guess I always kind of think about it. Mentally, I think I did something to make killing myself a thing."

"I don't know if any of those are reasons. That's it? No other reason?"

He refocuses on the stucco ceiling. "You never sound like you care."

"If I knew what caring looked and sounded like to you, I'd make sure you heard it and saw it."

"Whatever about all that. I know we're not a thing," he says. "Go ahead and keep being you. I'm fine."

But he killed himself, so he's not fine.

He says, "You think I'm on something? You're looking at me like I'm on something."

I lean forward. It's important to say the right thing. "Not too long ago I told Tess it made sense for you to kill yourself."

"You think I'm suicidal?"

"I really think you killed yourself."

He stands, bends over so he can see down the hall to his room. He stuffs his hands in his pockets, like, what now? "Why would you say something like that?"

He walks away from me, toward the dining room.

I wait for him to do something to shock me. I follow him through the dining room with my toes curled. I follow him into the kitchen, picture myself running out the front door. I'm sure I'd come right back. I can smell the normal Roger, the one who only bathed once a week who carried the smell of cigarette smoke on his clothes.

I follow him to his small kitchen. It's too small for both of us to be in here. The counter space is no larger than my outstretched arms and the fridge is smaller and older than most modern ones. It's sickness-yellow and faded brown at the edges. There's never much food in it. Condiments and that sort of thing. I don't see inside, rather I'm working from memory. The cupboards are smaller than most and don't have doors.

Roger digs into the large, front pocket of his backpack lying on the floor and takes out a super-small sandwich baggy of what to me looks like heroin. I know nothing about it. Still, to me, it's heroin. It's careless to have it in there. His posture and demeanor have switched since several feet ago. He's quiet.

"You could mind your own business." It's as if he's speaking from one side of his mouth. His breathing is different than moments ago. He's as nervous as I am.

"What's wrong?" I grab his shoulder, try to get him to stop moving, try to get him to look at me, to talk to me.

"This is that memory," he says. "How are you in it?"

Roger stomps back the way he came, baggy in hand. He makes a hard left up the hallway, heads past Greta's room and to his bedroom. If he's going to do whatever's in the baggie, I don't want to be with him when he does. I'd rather wait for him right here in the hallway. The carpet is so dirty. Greta let it all go to shit. Roger let everything go to shit. He went to shit. Is he going to kill himself?

Can I stop it?

How did he do it? Gunshot. Tess read me that message.

A while later, when he comes out of his room, his eyes wander, despite him heading my direction. He's in control of his body, not his mind. His shoes are off. He's high as fuck.

"Are you still here?" he says. It's less a question than intimidation. "You going to stand there and watch me kill myself? Going to be gone all this time and then come back right when I'm about to put a bullet in my head?"

"I can leave." It might seem like a threat. It's not. It's an offer to respect his dignity.

His face sinks. "Don't leave me," he pleads as he passes me in the hallway. He ducks into his mother's room.

By the time I catch up in the room, he's slid open the sliding mirror door of his mother's closet. He rummages through it, emerges with a small .22 pistol. It's a similar gun that my dad used to take me shooting. My dad said it's a good gun to learn to protect myself with.

His nose bleeds, a side-effect of snorting that shit. As he stares into the mirror-door, he has his head lifted with pride. Lowering his head, he grins, shows teeth. He's angry, lips puckered in an O. His eyes go wide, and it's a playful, joking face.

He says, "I don't know if I want to die happy or sad or what."

"Why…?"

Because his right hand holds the baggie, he shoves the gun against the back of his head with his left hand, his bad hand. "You're not even trying to stop me," he says.

"*You're* not trying to stop you."

"A friend puts a gun to his head, he's high, you haven't seen him for a while. Most people would try to not let this happen. Thanks for giving me my space, *Katy*." How he says my name, it's as if he's trying to bring something up in his throat. "Not you, Katy! *Katy*."

"Roger…"

He presses the gun hard against the back of his head.

I try to pull his hand away from his head. Although I manage to adjust his angle, he returns to his original position. The pop of the weapon makes my heart leap.

He drops the baggie, but he doesn't quite fall to the floor. It looks like he's having a heart attack. The blood flows down the back of his neck and saturates his shirt, all the while he hunches forward struggling to breathe. Ignoring my presence, he limps a step or so to the doorway and, for a moment, holds himself up. Finally, he stumbles across the hall to the bathroom. The trail of blood is from inside the room, across the bedroom threshold, across the hallway and into the bathroom. The blood is splotched and smeared, and it's the beginning of how he died.

In the bathroom mirror, barely holding himself up, he examines his facial expressions again. A smile doesn't quite materialize. His anger face stops at sorrow. His mouth hangs, and he falls backward, catching himself on the door. By this time, the blood saturates his shirt from his chest to his waist. I go to catch him. He stumbles out of my arms. An awkward, unnatural momentum carries him out of the bathroom, a tug, like something pulls him out of my arms. The front of him is like a bloody towel. There's so much blood in his mouth, his words are reduced to weak attempts at spitting.

He limps and stumbles to the living room and tries to stay upright. He gives up and falls to the floor. What I do is watch. I don't touch him, don't say anything.

I'm watching him and thinking of my mother and how she was no less alone when she died than he is now. I pat myself down in search of the hole inside of me that needs filling. There's still nothing to say to him. He's wounded and is going to die, no question he's going to die. In a way, he's dying because when I left him, I took off with part of his heart, because that's what we had, each other's heart. You can't give it back. That's how it works.

Helpless is everything in your body yelling at you to do something, although there's nothing to do. He's already dead.

"I'm not leaving," I say. From a few feet away, I stare at him, hope that when we make eye contact we understand each other. I might be as scared as he is, might be as guilty as he is dead.

Roger is motionless.

Roger is up, dragging himself step by step to the kitchen.

I raise my voice. "What do you need from me?"

Everything he touches has his bloody streaks.

Everyone around you who is dying, you want to make them comfortable, but you're just watching. Roger said he has a memory of shooting himself in the head. So, this is at least the third time he's gone through this.

In the kitchen, all he does is struggle to hold himself up. He coughs and spits up on the kitchen counter, long strands of bloody saliva drip and stack on it.

He lacks the will or strength to come back in my direction. Crawling back to the living room takes him the better part of fifteen minutes. In that time, he smears a second lane of blood. I step to the side, not wanting him to touch me. I don't know where he's going until he struggles to his feet, stumbles, braces himself on the wall. It's right there. He's looking for his phone that's on the floor near the far end of the couch. That's why he had gone back to the kitchen and dining room. It's right there. He drags himself forward, trips over his feet, stumbles, and then crashes on the floor and stops moving.

This is how he died, reaching for his phone.

For a while, he's breathless, he's motionless. Nothing about him has not stopped, and I'm paralyzed, as still as his couch.

In not too long Greta will piece together that he used her gun to shoot himself. She'll announce it on social media. I've been thinking Roger killed himself because he was on drugs, because he had no support for his anxiety, and because I abandoned him. Sure, it's all of that, but it can't be the only reason.

The trail of blood disappears, like it was never there. Roger pushes himself up off the floor, minus the blood. How he looks at me, stunned and disbelieving; he's having a silent conversation with himself, inching toward the couch. "Are you dead, too?" he asks.

"I'm not sure what's happening."

"I'm a ghost?"

"God, I don't know." Nothing worse can happen to someone. No, nothing worse.

"This keeps happening."

"How many times?"

He says, "I don't know. I'm not *remembering* it. I'm *reliving* it."

"How many times?"

"It's over and over and over again."

"You can't walk out?"

"I can't."

"Why not?"

He slaps his forehead. "How would I know? It's going to keep happening?"

"No. *Hell* no. We'll figure something out."

Focusing on the room, it's as if the events leading to his death never happened. There has to be a way to stop this from recurring.

Roger whips his hands into fists, stares down the way to his kitchen. "It hurts every time. Katy, it hurts every time."

No different than before, he heads to the kitchen and his backpack. From over here I see him grab the baggie from out of it. Unlike before, he's yelling and cursing. He'll get high in his room, walk down the hall, get his mother's .22 and shoot himself in the head.

He walks by me and into the hall. I watch him enter his room. Not too long later, he exits. Here he comes, strolling down the hall, head raised. He gazes at me as he ducks into his mother's room. After a few minutes of him shuffling in her closet, it goes quiet. During this quiet time, I know he's making faces in the mirror. Then there's the pop of the gun.

The next time he killed himself, I said nothing. I barely moved, as I tried to figure out the etiquette of watching a suicide. Nothing about you accepts it. Your mind remains in denial, your body physically shakes when you hear the shot and see the blood and watch him stumble and crawl, and you're helpless in it all. Guilt is triggered by the anxiety of watching him. Like I said, you shake and avert your eyes. You leave him alone.

In the current moment, he calls me into his mother's room, pleads with me to make it stop. The best I can do is make sure he knows he won't be in the house alone. I mutter to myself, talk myself into staying. I scurry into the kitchen before he shoots himself again. You can't keep seeing something like that. The moment is sheer disgust. I picture myself going through what he's been going through. How would I react? What would be the circumstances that got me to put a gun to my head?

"We're going to get you out of here," I yell to him.

"I don't think so," he fires back. "It's probably mostly fine. Living through multiple successful suicides grows you as a person!"

Although I know he's in pain, his voice, from this distance, sounds transparent with humor. I rush toward his mother's room, find him dragging himself across the hallway to the bathroom. I tell him, "You don't need to lie to me. This sucks."

"Then how do I get out?"

I'm not willing to tell him I can't stay here forever and watch him do this to himself. Being made from clay comes with the privilege of knowing I can walk away. When I get to Sunderland and my dad, I don't know if I'll make it back. But how can I leave? I can't leave forever, knowing he's reliving this shitty moment. I should have answered his calls way back then. I should have told him how I couldn't let someone I emotionally relied on make me into their crutch. I'm not made that way.

Explain to me how love is not a trap made of guilt. Explain to me how it's better to have loved than not. Once someone is determined to hurt themselves, if you choose them, they're going to take you down their road. They don't have a choice but to hold your hand inside a house they locked from the inside and set on fire.

After every cycle—that's what we're going to call it after he kills himself, a cycle—he has a few minutes when we can talk.

Again, he finds his way to the couch, this time he hides his face in his hands. "You don't have to stay," he says.

"What happens if you turn and run out the front door, right now? What happens if you do that?"

He drops his hands in his lap. "It's like gravity makes me do things. I *have* to kill myself."

He gets up and heads for the kitchen. "Here we go again."

"I'm coming in this time."

"You don't want to see that shit. Stay out here."

"It's fine. Pretend it's like me watching you go to the bathroom."

He takes an exaggerated breath. "Let's go."

We get the heroin from the kitchen and head back to his room.

"How'd you get into heroin?" I ask.

"It's meth."

"Oh. Lollar? Sam?"

"We went from skateboarding to drinking and smoking to meeting weird people. When I say weird people, I mean people like us." He chuckles, pushes his bedroom door open. "Suddenly we're selling drugs, doing them, in a short amount of time, too. Then, boom, you left."

"So, you were doing it before I left?"

"Way before you left."

Small talk helps. Talking about us is a great distraction. His room is a mess. His bed has no sheets. The blinds to his windows are on the floor on top of piles of clothes.

I kick some random clothing to the side. "Your room is all messed up."

"I got pissed one day and was like screw it. To let you know… To let you know, it's not because of you that I killed myself."

He sits on the end of his bed, searches near his feet and finds a children's book. Roger dumps the meth on the book. The meth is small, pink rocks he cuts down even smaller with a debit card he finds underneath clothes and loose paper.

"Did you want to do some?" he asks, while chopping.

"I'm good."

"Kidding."

Trembling, he gaks it up right off the book. Facing his bare, beige wall, he jerks his head back, inhaling the room with his nose flared. It wasn't only the gunshot that killed him. How does meth help with anxiety?

In his bedroom's rubble is a facedown, black, spiral-bound notebook. Oh damn. It's my notebook, the one I left and forgot, the one my dad gave me. I trudge through clothes and pick it up. Inside the notebook is my sketch—the face, I'll call it. I left it the day we were going to have sex but didn't. More like *I* decided not to. I was so distracted, I forgot it, didn't have the nerve to ask to get it back. My dad was always trying to get me to practice. A few feet away is a dresser drawer turned upside down. Inside of it is where he might have kept my notebook, along with those old wallets and duct tape, throwing darts, screws, bent nails, and the screwdriver on top of a pile of clothing along the wall.

Hands on his thighs, he stands. "I think at some point, you know if you have a future or not. I had that mental thing."

I step through the minefield of dirty clothes leading to the doorway. "What are you talking about?"

"Sometimes I'd picture you running from me and me catching you and, I don't know, trying to friggin' rip, I don't know, rip off your clothes and stuff. I'd think it. Feel guilty. A mental thing."

"Well… Well, that's crazy."

"Normal for me. Crazy for somebody else. Normal for me."

"What do you mean 'rip off my clothes?'"

He shuts his eyes. "I'd think of your clothes as an outside layer that could be peeled. The idea of you struggling while I sank my teeth into you, I don't know if turned on is the right way to put it."

"Sexually?"

"It's weird to have that kind of stuff in my head."

"Only me?"

He ponders something. "I've cared for other people."

He's telling me about remnants of drug use, and who knows what else? He has this stuff in his head that he didn't put there. He doesn't want it.

Roger smacks his hands together. "Let's do this."

I move to the side, walk with him down the hall, like we're getting married, but at the end of the aisle, instead of a wedding ring is a .22 pistol and a bullet. In his mother's room, he's in the closet looking for the gun. We both know where it is by now. It's that he has to go through certain motions.

On his mother's nightstand are opened envelopes and bills. I pick up the topless black pen. Holding the pen makes me a bit more at ease. Drawing is thinking, is meditating. My shoulders loosen. How my dad put it, this notebook, my old sketchbook, he made it from clay, and it took a while for me to recognize it. In a way, I made the sketchbook real. I don't have much of a reason to not believe it anymore. I still don't believe all of it. It's like you have faith in what you see yourself do, not what someone tells you that you can do.

I doodle, a sort of freedom. I can doodle with this, something to do that will help me figure things out. Damn, we need to get him out, don't we?

"I was depressed, and I missed you," he says. He has the gun, realizes the baggie is in his good hand and steps back to view himself in the mirror. "Something deep inside of me said screw it. I was like, I'm out."

Roger shoots himself in the back of the head. Now I realize the bullet doesn't exit his thick skull. It's lodged in it somewhere, somehow having missed his brain. Still, it's killing him.

He grunts, crawling to the bathroom. "Could you go meet me on the couch?" he says, still grunting. "It's embarrassing." He grunts. "Be there in a bit."

Having seen this happen so many times makes it easier to do as he says.

He eventually wanders over to the kitchen counter, searches for his phone that he knows damn well is in the living room. It takes him a while, but he makes a long, crawling bloody trail to it. I try to hand his phone to him. He's like, no, I got this. Leave it there.

And he dies.

I wait.

Instead of talking, I draw. I sketch him on the couch next to me, sketch how he slouches with the expression of a thief who knows he's about to be caught. I'm slow with each feathered line. I use my palm to balance the weight of the pen. Beyond us is the dining room table, and even farther back, to the opposite side of the dining room, is the kitchen doorway. The maple table they use for an island in the kitchen is a barrier to the sink.

He acknowledges he's modeling for my drawing by lifting his brows and twiddling his fingers. "Should I strip down?"

"Oh, please, please don't."

Roger chuckles.

He pushes himself up. "I'll be right back. Going to go blast myself in the head again. Sucks."

"I'll be right here."

"Okay."

"You wanted to eat me?" I ask. Raise your hand if a close friend of yours admitted to wanting to eat you.

"Imagined it," he says. "I swear I'm not an animal."

He drags his feet to the kitchen to get his drugs. I eye him, sketch him while he walks away, eye him and sketch, eye him and sketch, all the while bracing myself for him to enter his mother's room and shoot himself. I'll wait here for the pop of the gun.

After he shoots himself and eventually dies, he sits next to me on the couch. "You going to let me see what you got?" he asks, referring to what I'm drawing.

I haven't offered to show him because I can't imagine he'd be into art right now. Compared to what he's going through, whatever I'm drawing is nothing. The picture is of the inside of his house, in black ink. He holds out his hand as if he wants to shake. I place the sketchbook in his hand. He turns his back on me, walks back to his seat while gazing into the book. He sits, perplexed. He's not a judgmental person so I know he's going to say something polite or whatever about my work. Why say something negative to the only person you're ever going to see again?

"This is great," he says. "Have you always been able to do this?"

"What do you mean?"

"Have you always been able to draw like this?"

"I want to say, yeah. I don't usually do scenes. I struggle with faces."

"From now on do scenes. It's good."

"I had that one class. I could be better."

"This is great." Roger examines the room, then the pages. He examines a different part of the room, then, again, the pages. Turns around on the couch and stares at the dining room. Examines the pages. His eyes are on me. Holding my sketchbook open in his palm, he stands and takes a few steps toward me. "I'm glad you went to school. This is out-of-control-crazy, is what this is."

I've always been decent at drawing objects. He's amazed I can draw a couch and the dining room, the kitchen. He drops the sketchbook in my lap, before pouting toward the dining room and the kitchen. He's got to kill himself again. Looking at the picture, he's right, in a sense. I don't draw this smart, don't draw scenes as well as the one I've been doing.

The rocks grind at my back. There's something like an electrical current building inside of me. The symptoms. As my dad explained it, it's authentic creative energy. I can physically feel being creative.

The more I stare at the picture, the more the picture has something to it. How the black lines don't quite stay black, how they dig into the page. The room compressed onto these pages.

Roger finds his way to the kitchen, again to get his meth.

I draw a character, quickly, just so many lines scribbled together into the character's head. Is the character Roger? I'm not sure. When

I'm creating, I don't think in words, no definitions. It's only impulse, what I feel up and down my spine, like rocks grinding.

What I have looks like the work of someone desperately trying to stay sane, I must admit. It's not like anything I've done. Ever. There's something more present about it. I make the figure look as if it's walking toward his hallway entrance. Even if he can't imagine himself leaving, I can. Even if Roger can't imagine himself leaving, I can. That's what it'll look like when it's done. It'll be a sketch of him stepping out of this house.

He grabs the baggie, tosses it up, and snatches it out of the air.

On his way to the hallway, he steps into the same position as the drawing I just made of him. Yes, it's him. I imagined Roger taking these steps to leave the house, and now, is he making them? The real him does what the picture asks of him. The next drawing in the scene takes him past the hallway entrance. I frantically sketch, draw so fast and hard that I tear the pages in parts.

"Wait," I tell him. "Slow down. Slow down, asshole!"

He stops, I know it will be only briefly. But I do make something that resembles the living room door, resembles him moving to it. He blindly imitates my drawing, on my command, no words needed.

Go Roger, get there, get there!

The last, sloppy, mostly incoherent drawing is of him stepping outside his front door. Like the stills of an animation, step one, step two, step three, and then he's gone. Inside of me, it's like lightning. Stones grind at my spine. My blood spins at my joints. All the while, Roger steps right on outside. He's gone and free, and I did that shit.

Sketchbook under my arm, I follow him out the door, across the small, rundown porch, down these creaking steps, and onto the gravel of his alley. He keeps walking, picking up his pace with each step. I can't keep up with him. I can tell there's no blood on him, he's not in pain, and he's free. He leaps, lands and skids on heels, and turns to face me. I jog to him. With each step the symptoms fade back into me.

When I get to him, he squeezes and holds me tightly. I'm hugging a healthy Roger, like the Roger before he was dealing drugs and doing them. This is the Roger before cigarettes, before drinking too much. This is the guy who showed up at my house on a first date on a skateboard. I kiss him all over his face and mouth. He kisses me back because he thinks I saved him.

I drop the sketchbook on the ground to the side of us. I lean to pick it up, stare at it, open it, and gaze inside at the picture of him stepping outside. The whole picture is in that black pen and takes up the left and right side of the book. Roger can't take his eyes off it. I was in love with this Roger. He had a lot of fears, but not when holding me, not when talking to me.

He gazes at the sky, the sun, the blue. "What now?"

"Explore. I think the big in this place will be too big. It's moment by moment or else take everything too far."

The street is a few dozen feet away, the start of the real journey.

"Don't you feel weirdly alive?" I ask him.

"I feel healthy." He inhales, deeply. "How long since I've been healthy?"

I understand what he's saying. "Should I say it out loud or do you want to?"

"I definitely feel better off dead."

I've never felt this useful. I stopped his suffering. Have you ever stopped someone's suffering? Have you ever helped someone so much that they'll be better from that moment on? I did one of the few things I know how to do, draw, did it from the heart, and now he's better. He's healthy, and I'm not sure if I've ever felt this well either.

Zarieanna

Jessica wondered if it was possible for her anger and sadness this evening to have blown in through her bedroom window.

She shut the window, meandered to the lamp on the end table near her bed and clicked it off. The last time she felt this down was when Grandma Poe died a few years ago. The sadness seemed to be in the air. According to her father, the worst part about Grandma Poe dying was that she stored emotional history of elders who had an impact in her life. People were history containers. You could tell when parts of your history disappeared, he had told her. Now, at sixteen, she hadn't wavered in believing it, until this sadness entered her room through the window. All that emotion had not died with Poe.

As she crawled underneath the sheets, the despondency made the air so heavy that she had a hard time breathing. It reminded her that years ago in a different home and in a different, smaller bed, and still scared of the dark, she had yelled to her father through similar darkness. He never came to comfort her, in his attempt to make her more independent. It was Grandma Poe who consoled her every now and again. Grandma Poe always stayed until Jessica fell asleep. Now, Jessica lay on her back contemplating calling down the stairs for Grandma Poe. It would be satisfying to let her name split her lips, would be even more satisfying to be comforted.

The pleasant silence in Jessica's current house would let her sleep better, her father had said. In her experience in the month or so living here, the added quiet made it so she heard the smallest of things better: the wind blowing over the roof, wind seeping underneath the windowsill. Right now, she heard something she hadn't heard before. The creaking of the stairs as her dad slogged up them. A creepy bending of wood. Her dad must have had a few drinks. He didn't always walk this slow. The deep sadness that sat on her chest as if it was a blanket made her imagine Grandma Poe inching up the stairs to sit with her in the dark. Sudden anger piled on the sadness, helped her ball her hands into fists, helped her be brave in the dark, even at her age. The creaking of the steps stopped. She anticipated her dad would knock on the door.

Still lying on her bed, she held that blanket of sadness up to her neck. Tears fell down either side of her face and onto the pillow at the back of her head. She knew her father had been in the dumps about mom, about needing to move to this house to get a fresh start. Everybody had some conflict to think about.

Behind her bedroom door, to Jessica's shock, she heard a girl crying. A girl. Jessica quickly sat up, flicked on the end table light. Outside the door, a wicked sound of somebody trying to contain grief. Jessica tossed off the sheets and leaped out of bed, rested her feet on the cold, wood floor. She listened closer and, yes, some girl was pressing on her door, no way around it.

The knob turned. That girl pushed the door open. In strolled a young woman in her twenties. The woman wore a blue nightgown with short sleeves. She, too, was barefoot, with blood on her feet— hints of mud on her toes, her hair in knots, makeup wet from tears and smeared across her face. The young woman had blood all down her arms. Jessica screamed for her father, for her Grandma Poe. As the young woman slid past her, she almost disappeared into the air. This is what made it a thing, a creature, a ghost. How it faded unless Jessica looked at it directly.

The ghost sobbed and coughed, almost choked on its tears.

Her dad might not make it upstairs to her, because, well, she should work out whatever had scared her, he probably figured, despite her screams.

As the ghost sat on the edge of Jessica's long windowsill, Jessica ran downstairs, and barged into her father's room to wake him. She repeatedly slapped the wall trying to flip on his light. He was already wide awake.

"What's going on?" he asked with urgency and judgment.

"There's a ghost in my room."

He stared at her.

"There's a ghost in my room." She labored to speak in an even tone, so he'd take her seriously. Still, her bottom lip wavered, and her sweats were twisted backward, her face wet with tears. "It's bleeding and sitting in my room right now."

"What happens when I go up there and don't find anything? Are you going to keep crying or come to terms with whatever it is you need to come to terms with?"

"It's a girl older than me. It's barefoot. And it's bleeding."

Hoping he wasn't right, and she had imagined the whole thing, her knees knocked and her body shook, anticipating seeing the bleeding young woman again.

"Shit," he said, "fine. At some point you need to stop being a child. Shit."

Her father slipped on his slippers and made his way up the stairs in his boxer shorts and white T-shirt. Jessica followed a few steps behind him, uncertain of what was supposed to happen or what could happen.

Once to her room, her father walked inside with the confidence of an unrivaled academic. A second later he gasped and fell to the floor. Jessica stood behind her fallen father, gazed over him at what he had seen that caused him to collapse. The ghost had gone nowhere. Its eyes stared back at her, though not at *her*. It's as if the ghost gazed off into the darkness of some deep, dark wood—squinting, trying to adjust her eyes. Jessica stepped to the left to avoid the ghost's eye contact. It didn't seem to know she was in the room. When Jessica took a few steps to the right—mainly to test if the ghost was looking at her—its eyes did not follow her movements.

The young woman had slashed her wrists. The look on the ghost's face was a mix of fear, pain, and complacency, but the body language, Jessica thought, that right there was sadness and residue from violence. Jessica trembled, not from seeing the ghost, but from the emotion it gave off. What she thought had come in through the window earlier, it was in fact the emotions of this ghost.

Jessica's instincts told her to streak out of the house. Her intellect wanted to gather her dad before she did so. She bent over to grab her father. She wasn't strong enough to do anything with him. The visual of the ghost isn't what actually collapsed him, was it? He wasn't prepared to absorb the wall of anger and sadness he had stepped into. Dropped him like a left hook.

The ghost slouched, tried to sit up. Slouched again. What was it doing? Jessica rocked in place, in a terrified struggle to not think about hurting herself.

Her dad came to on his own and pushed himself to his feet. He grabbed her collar in his fist and yanked her out of the room. She followed him downstairs, skipped multiple steps at a time. She got outside in a huff, keeping her eyes on her father who kept glancing at her, as if guilty, she thought.

For nearly an hour, from outside, they watched the ghost in her bedroom window. At certain angles it wasn't present, but from other angles it sat there hunched over with its back to them. The concerned frown of her father matched Jessica's shock of being left speechless, outside in the cold.

"I felt her in the room," Jessica mumbled.

"Yeah. Me, too."

"Do we need to talk to her?"

"God, no. It leaves or we do."

The sky turned baby blue. The young woman vanished from every angle.

A month later during spring break, Jessica was again in bed. Ever since the night of the ghost, she went to sleep with sounds of nature on a low volume, keeping her bedroom door and window closed. If her father hadn't seen the ghost, he might not have believed it happened. Instead, he was affected enough by the ghost and its lingering presence that he was selling the house. According to him, they could move out before the house was sold.

From Jessica's perspective, if the ghost came back, it wouldn't hurt them—because did ghosts hurt people—and it hadn't come back. Still, her dad was so rattled that he said he'd leave the state for the right opportunity, the first opportunity. If he moved, she wouldn't move with him, no matter where he ended up. She could live on her own, find some friends to make it happen. She thought of this while pulling the blankets up to her chin. Through her speakers it rained in the forest. The ocean washed up on the shore.

Those heavy, inconsistent steps of the bleeding ghost of the young woman crept up the stairs. Jessica balled the blankets into her palms. The sadness filtered into the room. That's how she knew for certain the ghost had returned. The doorknob turned and in walked the young lady, her arms bleeding. The sadness felt like every future failure had congregated in Jessica's gut. Guilt swelled around thoughts of her father. Real guilt, not that she had wronged him, but that she had always been in a constant state of wronging him, to the point to where he wanted her upstairs, so he didn't need to see her stupid face at night. Why didn't she already leave? Pack and go. Why wait?

The ghost sat on the windowsill, hunched over. This time Jessica didn't leave the room. Although she and the ghost were a few feet apart, the ghost still stared off into the distance. It slouched, and despite it already being dead, it died right there in front of her. Jessica could only see it from certain angles. Then she couldn't see it at all. Again, it left its sadness and anger behind.

Two evenings later Jessica came back from the coffee shop where she had met a few friends. On her front porch, she hesitated to go inside. It was like the air in the house was toxic. Not all the sadness she felt when the ghost visited had gone away. She and her father had been living in a constant state of sadness and worthlessness that filled her up. Depression for breakfast, lunch, and dinner. If her dad got them to move, oh, she'd go, now, for sure.

Looking to not appear depressed, she had put her hair up, something she rarely did. A few of her friends she had gone out with this evening had complimented her necklace and positive new look. Great to get compliments. David said she smelled good. Jessica wore boots and one of three body dresses instead of comfortable running shoes and jeans. She had on makeup, all to feel alive.

As she stuck her key in the door, behind her a male voice cleared his throat.

"Hello, I didn't want to bother you."

Yet he had.

"Um," he said, stepping closer. "I don't live far from here."

"Can I help you with something?"

"It's awkward talking to young people if you don't know them. You're younger than my daughter."

"What do you need?"

"Maybe you know her? Katy?"

Having no idea who he was talking about, Jessica turned the key.

"Hang on there. Is Zarieanna here right now?"

She had never seen this man in the neighborhood. If he wasn't so old, he'd seem like more of a threat. Not that he wasn't creepy with his gray slacks and blazer. The collared shirt. She didn't think he was coming from work or anything like that. Too old. Was he on foot?"

"I'm not trying to be rude," she started. "I don't know any Katy. There's no Zarieanna who lives here."

"I already know she's here. I'm asking if she's present right *now*."

At first, she thought he might be lost, like he got the wrong house, which made sense. Looking at him, he had a snide demeanor to him, as if he knew something nobody else could know. Was he talking about the ghost? Was the ghost Zarieanna?

Jessica withdrew the key from the door. "I don't know. Not sure."

He clasped his hands together at his chin. "She's got these, uh, cuts along her wrists. She's bleeding. Bad mood."

Hearing the description of the ghost made her want to flee, made her want to run inside and lock the door.

"You have to come back when my dad gets home," she said. On the one hand, she welcomed someone with knowledge of the situation.

On the other, this guy was wrong, not someone she should be speaking to without a witness. "Come back when my dad gets home."

"That's reasonable. When might that be?"

"Maybe an hour. An hour or so."

"Reasonable." He inched toward her porch. "I'll knock on the door in about an hour. I don't mean to scare you, however, when I come back, I'm going to have two heads growing out of my neck."

"*What?*"

"To let you know. An hour or so. I'll be back."

The man started down the street, his hands in his pockets, the streetlights glistening off his shined shoes.

Jessica lay on her bed in the fetal position, sheets pulled over her head, certain the outside world didn't need her if it wanted to prosper. Nobody needed her. According to her father, how both of them felt had less to do with them and more to do with the house. Although Jessica agreed with him, it didn't mean she was worth anything. It didn't mean he could love her anymore or at all. He was saying what he needed to say to appease his conscience.

She had her ocean sounds and other sounds of nature playing through her speakers. She woke her phone, which she had near her head underneath the blankets, to see if, somehow, she missed a call from her father. He should be home by now.

The weird man she spoke to earlier had something sinister about him. Him knowing about the ghost confused her. His shined shoes bothered her. And he presented the eeriest threat ever: he'd come back with two heads. He said it so matter-of-factly that she considered he might be telling the truth.

Her father called.

She pressed the button to answer and put him on speaker phone.

"Where are you?" she asked, half thinking he had abandoned her.

"Listen. We can't be in that house anymore. I can't be there, neither should you."

"Okay, so, where are you?"

"I'm at the motel downtown. The what do you call it?"

"Why?"

"Jessica, call someone or get on a bus. Something like that. Meet me here."

She said, "Pick me up."

"It's better if I don't." His voice cracked. "I don't know what I'll do if I'm there."

"You'll let me sit here alone?"

"If I'm there with you…" He took several deep breaths.

"Are you okay?"

"I don't know what I might do to you in that house."

Shocked by his statement, she stared at the phone and tried to imagine what he meant. She had thought of hurting herself, anyway— throwing herself into rush hour traffic, eating a ton of pills, something along those lines. None of these thoughts had come to her before the ghost showed itself. He was right. She had to get out of there. The oddest thing is how after acknowledging she had to get out of there, she still had to push herself to do so; she still didn't want to. The depression the ghost had left behind tricked her into staying in bed and getting worse.

"Dad, I'm coming. Getting ready to head out."

"My little girl. That's so good. I'm sorry I can't be the man to come get you."

"I get it."

Without question, nobody else should be put in their situation. Nobody else needed to enter what they called home.

"Someone came by earlier and said he knew about the ghost," she said.

"Baby, it doesn't matter. Get here. We'll figure it out from there."

"Okay."

"I love you," he said.

"I love you, too. Okay, bye." She hung up feeling a slight tingle of confidence, like waking up from sickness.

No use in packing. She slipped on her jeans, shoes, and jacket, turned off her speaker and skipped downstairs. She took a final glance around the house, a look at all their things. These were the worst days of her life. In a matter of feet, they'd be behind her.

On her first step forward, she swallowed a mouthful of insecurity. Her next step she swallowed little bits of guilt. Another step she felt deceived. The step prior to grabbing the front door handle, the sense of loss nearly overwhelmed her. She swung the door open, victorious.

A few feet in front of her and down the concrete porch steps stood that man with the shiny shoes and gray suit, the man who said his daughter was Katy. The man who knew the ghost in the house. He said he'd return with two heads on his neck, and he had. Two heads grew off his neck like misshapen oversized grapes on a vine; there was his neck and a small branch neck on either side, and from each branch, a head.

"Can I come inside?" he asked.

She didn't have words and couldn't move, paralyzed by desperate and fleeting thoughts and the sight in front of her. Through the dim porch lighting she saw that the head to her left had one eyebrow sitting above one eye. If it weren't for the second head, he'd be a cyclops. His mouths weren't as wide as they should have been. They would have been wide enough if connected. The two heads were balding in the same manner, string of hair for string of hair, as if duplicated; along the sides of his heads was a single row of thinning dark hair, looking planted or as if someone glued it on. The left side of his face relied on the right side for normal expression, and vice versa.

She couldn't imagine letting him in the house or near her.

He took a few small steps forward, his body now out of the shadows from the street. "Don't scream. Don't panic. You must have had this in your head. I told you."

She hadn't had the sight of him in her head. Nobody could or should imagine this. She found herself tapping her thigh, stutter-stepping in place at the door.

"Your neighbors will ask questions if I don't get inside."

She couldn't get words to form, between the confusion and the sadness. She fought tears yet couldn't justify not crying.

"If you let me in, together we can see that all that despair you have goes away. How does that sound?"

"How? How does any of this make sense?"

"If I can get her to feel better, and I usually do, then you will feel better with her."

"What if I don't let you in?" Because letting him in could turn out to be a horrible idea.

"I'll have my time with Zarieanna. I always do. If you leave, you'll need to hold on to whatever she has given you. I've seen it before. People move into this house, move out and later die from the devastating emotions they have. Don't you feel like killing yourself?"

She whispered, "Yes." Sobbed. "I want to kill myself."

"Then why wouldn't you let me in?"

She raised her index and middle finger and pointed them at his heads.

"Scared? I arrived like this so she would know who I am. It's how we met. You believe I can do what I say, correct? I warned you, I'd come back in an hour with two heads. No reason to surprise you. Wouldn't you be scared if I didn't tell you?" He chuckled. "Where is your father?"

"He… He's not coming home."

"I'm not so rude as to make you let me in. I'm being honest and fair with you, don't you agree?"

She nodded.

"May I come inside?"

She inched to the side.

When he grinned, the smile spanned both faces. His brows were dependent on each other and in sync. He had an ear on the outside of both heads, not on the inside of either. In a way, it was one head split in half. His neck was too long, extended to accommodate the heads.

Entering her house, his heads pulled together a little. Her head came up to his shoulders. If he decided to do something to her, she'd deserve it, since she invited him in. How would he make a ghost who killed herself feel better? How would he make a ghost who felt so horrible that its emotions were contagious, feel better?

"Other than wanting to kill yourself, how are you?" he asked. "You're brave by staying."

She couldn't stop crying, could barely look at him. "It's too much."

"I'm sure it is."

He sat on the couch, snapped his blazer collar.

She paced in front of the door and shut it.

"I was saying earlier that my daughter is around your age. A few years older. Twenties, I think."

He tapped the backrest of the couch, his heads turning in opposite directions to take in the sights of the room. He saw her place as a waiting room, she thought.

"Did you want something to drink?" she asked. "I have, uh, um, water?"

"Your mother isn't in any of these photos."

"She died years ago."

"Not only are you about my daughter's age, but she also lost her mother years ago. Do you mind me asking how she died?"

"Rare brain cancer."

"As if brain cancer isn't rare enough, she died from the rare of the rare."

Seeing his expression spread across both faces sent her pressing against the closed front door, not out of fear. Out of disgust. More disgusting than when they were outside moments ago. Something about him being so nonchalant with it, something about him pretending he didn't have multiple heads.

"I don't want to talk about my mom," she said.

"We're not. We're talking about my daughter. How she lost her mother like you lost yours. We don't live far from here. Or would you rather talk about my heads."

She could run out of this house and never come back. Her father or anybody else wouldn't believe what she was going through. Didn't matter. She could vacate her life right now. Cry all the way to the motel downtown. She could cry the rest of her life, feel like killing herself every day, the two-headed man claimed.

"How do you know—what name did you say—the name you called her? The ghost."

"Zarieanna. I'm not sure how to explain it. She's someone I help and continue to help."

"How do you help?"

"What time is it? Is it about that time? About this time is when she comes. Should we go upstairs?"

"I don't know how honest you sound." Her body tightened, feeling the physical effects of all the courage it took to say what she said. "How do you *help* her?"

"I promised her things and follow through with those promises."

"What kind of promises?"

"I promised her I would never leave her by herself for too long. I'd always come back to visit. I've promised her that what is happening is not her fault. To my credit, I've always come to visit. It'll be the same this time."

"She needs company?"

"That's precisely what she needs."

"What are you going to—?"

"Let's go up. Let's not miss her."

He pushed himself from the couch and trudged up the stairs. He knew this house as well as she did. He had been coming to see Zarieanna for who knew how long?

He stopped at the top of the staircase. "I know you're scared of me because of my appearance. You know, a lot of people think two heads are better than one. Throwing that out there."

Humor. She couldn't bring herself to smile. She thought about other recent moments that let her feel good. Not too long ago, David said she smelled good. She had forgotten about that and her lipstick, which she still had on. A voice in the back of her head gave a thank you to levity and how it opened her mind to receive a compliment she hadn't fully heard earlier. For less than a minute she had partial relief from the shitty vibe of this house.

He pushed her bedroom door open, stepped across the threshold. Jessica followed him through, stopping in the doorway, not willing to get too close to him.

He moved to the foot end of the bed. She closed the door behind her.

For a while she stood at the head of her bed, next to the door. She stared at him, partially formulating questions she was too scared and upset to ask. The sense of worthlessness and guilt ground on her pride, pissed her off at this point. She trembled, dissatisfied, and worried.

He sat on the edge of her bed, gazed across the room at the window and the windowsill that jutted out from underneath that window.

They heard it. The creaking of the steps. The creaking stopped at the same moment it always had. Footsteps crept forward, crept forward, until the doorknob slowly turned.

Jessica watched as Zarieanna stared locked eyes with the two-headed man and jumped to her feet from the windowsill. Blood dripped from her wrists as she inched toward him.

"You wish you didn't have to come," Zarieanna said. "How long has it been?"

"I visited you a year ago."

"Another year. It still feels like yesterday."

He sat on Jessica's bed, held up both of his palms. "Remember I told you about my daughter."

Zarieanna flung blood on the floor in front of them.

"She's on your side now," he said.

"Should I be sorry?"

"She can get you out."

Zarieanna said, "She's coming to free me?"

"She should be traveling along your way. She'll notice your energy."

"Why does she make things feel so bad?" Jessica asked, not ready to speak to the ghost directly. "Why does she have to be like this?"

One of his heads looked over his shoulder at Jessica before going back to its original position, focusing on the ghost. "Remember how I told you that who you are now still matters and that's why so many people vacate this home?"

Zarieanna sat back on the windowsill, wiped her arms down to get some of the blood off. "There's somebody with you. They want me to leave? Tell them, it's not my choice."

"She's moving. Her small family is being torn apart by you. She's suicidal and I suspect her dad is as well."

"There's nothing I can do," Zarieanna said, with a hint of sympathy.

"She's a little younger than you," he told Zarieanna. "You're important. You mean something to someone. People you don't know care about how you feel. Your life has meaning long after you passed. I think you can believe that."

This was him trying to make Zarieanna feel better. Whatever he said, she must have needed to hear because him saying it at least made Jessica feel lighter. If Zarieanna felt lighter, then so did she. He waved Jessica forward. She hesitated, needing to force herself the few feet to get next to him.

"She's to my side now," he said to Zarieanna.

"To the left or to the right?" Zarieanna pointed to either side of him.

"She's to my left, about your height."

Jessica gathered that the ghost couldn't see her. She could see the ghost, but she couldn't physically be touched by it. His ability was that he could see and touch it. He could exist in both her world and wherever Zarieanna was.

Zarieanna stared blankly at Jessica, the way a blind person stared at the stars. "I'm sorry I brought this on you. I'm sorry you're going through what you're going through." She shut her mouth, maybe stopping the truth from escaping. "I'm sorry."

Here is a woman who killed herself, apologizing for, what, slitting her own wrists?

"Tell her not to apologize and that, at the moment, I feel good enough to walk out of here," Jessica said. "Tell her to not apologize."

The two-headed man told Zarieanna she didn't need to apologize. He told her that Jessica understood and would be on her way out of the house.

"Before she leaves," Zarieanna said, with beads of blood dripping from her fingertips. "Before she leaves, give her a message."

"She can hear you."

"Person," Zarieanna said. "It feels better in my skin if I know there's somebody in the house with me. If I know somebody is in the house with me, it's better. It's the feeling alone. For so long. That's part of it. That's hard."

Jessica imagined herself in Zarieanna's place, forever alone and killing herself, feeling useless, guilty, and always sorry. The one thing Zarieanna looked forward to was once a year seeing this two-headed man who would tell her she wasn't useless, no matter her situation.

Jessica said, "I will try. Tell her I'll talk to my dad."

The grinning, two-headed man relayed Jessica's message.

Jessica added, "Tell her I feel better already. When my dad comes back, we'll figure it out."

The two-headed man told Zarieanna as much. She beamed at the news and continued bleeding.

Zarieanna searched the room, almost made eye contact with Jessica.

He rubbed his hand across his left head. "If you get a chance," he told Zarieanna, "look in your window, pay attention to the road. If my daughter passes, get her attention. You'll know it's her because she'll be someone you haven't seen before. Her name is Katy."

The two-headed man approached Zarieanna, embraced her. After he let her go, Zarieanna slouched on her windowsill and died, again.

Jessica followed the two-headed man down the stairs to her living room. "Did you know her when she was alive?"

"I met her by chance. I used to live in this house a long time ago. She was dead when I met her. How you're staring at me—"

"Not getting used to your…two…heads."

"You won't need to. You feel better, don't you? As long as she believes you're in the house, it'll be better. You can tell your father."

Although Jessica said, "Okay," she decided against asking her father to stay one more day.

Screw this house.

Hookers frequented the motel downtown. Jessica recalled several occasions when police raided it. The Boonies, it was called. The kind of place where the parking spaces were too small. Although the parking lot was full, all the units looked vacant, with their shadowy rooms behind closed curtains.

Jessica walked up, having received a ride from David. Normally she wouldn't have used him for a ride. This one time she'd let it happen. She felt hurried, desperate to get back to her dad who she felt confident around. The two-headed man was right. Zarieanna's good mood had finally rubbed off on her. That and David's company was nice.

Her father left her a key at the front desk. A skeptical-looking, front desk guy smirked when he handed her the key.

"Honestly, it's my dad." Jessica laughed, snatching the key from him.

"Just sayin. You can call *me* daddy."

She strolled all the way to the end of the walkway and made a left, not sure how to explain to her father that the man with two heads wound up being a pretty good guy.

At the end of the walkway, second room to the end, she slipped the key card into the door until it blinked green. She pushed the door open, took a step or so inside and turned on the lamp above the nearest bed. On the far bed, her father was stretched out on sheets splattered with blood. A firearm was on the floor between his bed and the one she leaned over. His hair had pushed to one side, his mouth agape in awe. He had fallen backward after shooting himself in the chest.

She sat on the clean bed, turned her gaze outside the wide-open door to see the small walkway running parallel to their room. The random woman in the parking lot in stockings and stilt-like heels, an over-sized purse. A man with a large bottle of wine followed her. The man with the large bottle said, "The night is what it should be if you sip on all of this. I ain't talking about the wine, neither."

Jessica watched them pass and heard the man's bottle of wine drop and explode into glitter. In the distance, the screams of sirens. She kicked the door shut with all the force she could gather. She cried into her pillow, smashed her fists into the mattress until she physically couldn't anymore.

The Attic Murders

Our past doesn't make a difference anymore, and there's no future. That's the kind of freedom me and Roger have.

He grabs my hand. I squeeze his in return. He might think us holding hands is romantic. It's more appreciating him being healthy, appreciating me feeling healthy. Sometimes you should just hold each other. Don't talk. I think it's why I like art so much. Sometimes words don't work the right way. Sometimes words mean too much. I don't want to say *everything*; I want to mean *one* thing.

Whomever we meet on this journey to who knows where, I doubt they'll be alive. I'm thinking about what my dad said about people being dead and suffering. People will be dead. I'm not exactly alive. Roger isn't alive. That guy I saw earlier, he wasn't alive. My mother? My dad said those like us come here—wherever this place is—when they've matured. You don't walk through a door; you *are* the door, is what I think he said.

My mother and others like myself have come through this world. I could find more of us on my way to Sunderland. I could find my mother. I tightly squeeze my eyelids shut. No matter how tightly I squeeze, no matter how much I shake my head, my mother's face doesn't come to mind. It wouldn't be there with a picture of her in hand.

I take my dad's advice and we go up Thirteenth. He said to keep going that way so that's that. I know nothing else. Explore on the way to Sunderland. Maybe he means I find my mom on this route. Follow Thirteenth as far as I can.

The sketchbook and pen are tucked in my waistband. There's power in these pages.

I point to the evening sky as we step into another time zone. We go from evening to afternoon. Up ahead the sun beams off the neighborhood rooftops. There's limited shade underneath trees along the street. Cars are parked on the side of the road. I look Roger up and down. The lack of a bullet in his head, the lack of blood.

"It's so quiet," he says. The worry in his eyes is a reminder that long before getting into drugs, he had anxiety issues. He was always fine when it was me and him. When he had to meet people he didn't know, that's when he became uncomfortable. Anxiety happened in class. Although he saw those people every day, it didn't mean he knew them.

"What year do you think it is?" I ask.

"We move through time?"

"Look at the cars. They're from when I was a kid. Nothing's new. I think it's a different time wherever we go. A different time of day and in another year."

"This is crazy." He intertwines his fingers with mine. "Early to mid-nineties?" he guesses.

We come up on the nicest house on the block, which isn't saying all that much. So, years ago, in this neighborhood, people didn't mow their lawns and they let their fences rust. In this area decades ago, the streets were cracked like a horrible earthquake came through. Around here years ago, the heat kept the grass yellow, weeds grew at the edges of everything, from under everything, except for at this one house. It has a manicured forest-green lawn. The squared bushes around the lawn give it a middle-class appearance. The walkway leading up the concrete porch is so clean, it's glowing beige. The porch steps must have been hosed off. Everything is edged, you can smell the fresh-cut lawn. What's odd is how the front door is wide open.

"You're thinking about going in?" Roger asks.

I lift the arm to the gate, push it open and step through. "Yeah, I am."

"I can't do what you do. I should stay out here. I don't want to be in the way."

The way he's observing this world, he's in awe, like a cartoon character stepping into reality, how amused he is. I have watched him run out of his death, watched him become safe. I can't forget that. It's free to help people like Roger. Anybody who could do it would do it. Maybe not Roger, himself. Most anybody else, though.

I tell him, "Let me see what's inside."

"You'll be right back?"

"Sure."

It's easy to say I'm thinking about helping people. Doing it is another thing. I take a deep breath while entering the house, kind of like preparing to go under water. I don't know what I'll see. I do know the door being open made me notice a possible bad situation. I do know people bringing bad things on themselves is one thing. That bad thing happening to them indefinitely, they didn't do that to themselves. I don't know if I can help. I'll sure as hell see about trying.

A clear rubber mat going through the living room to the hallway sits atop clean, beige carpet. The couches have plastic on them for protection. The homeowners were neat freaks. I follow the mat trail, hoping to not find anything. I know I will. There's no blood on the walls. There's no blood in a path on the hallway floor. There aren't drugs in the bathroom. There's nobody.

It's a two-story house. The stairs are back there where I came in across the living room near the front door. If anybody is home, they'll be upstairs. On my way back to the staircase, I cross the kitchen. Bright yellow, flowered wallpaper. The waxed tile floor completes the most disturbing kitchen ever. Pure drab and clean, like nobody has ever cooked in it.

I backtrack out of there and continue up the cream-colored, carpeted stairs. If these were at my place, there'd be stains going all the way up. The cleaning person deserves a Pulitzer for cleanliness.

The landing area has a stand and a clear, glass vase in front of the bathroom, which is pristine. Another vase—a glass one with flowers in it—is in front of the bedroom. I'm not surprised the flowers are real. I'm surprised they smell so good.

Two thumps, not directly above me. An attic, for sure. I follow the length of the landing area, tracking the gentle thumps. At the end of the landing area, right above me, is the attic's opening, which I see straight into.

"Hello," I call.

To my surprise a wooden ladder lowers, rattles against the sides of the square entrance hole. Small hands send it down inch by inch. Someone holds it from up there. I'm supposed to grab it, so I do.

"I'm coming up, I guess."

I pull the rest of the ladder down, hand over hand, and set the legs on the floor, lean the ladder against part of the opening, and climb. At the top, the smell of dirt and dust, of breath and wood. Not as tidy as anything below. Fully in, the person who delivered the ladder stands slumped in front of me. A little boy with shiny, brown hair. He's skinny, like he hasn't eaten in weeks.

"Who are you?" he asks in a babyish voice.

This is a huge question he's asked. Who am I? What am I doing here, is the other question floating in the air and yet to be asked?

"Who are *you*?"

"Bubby," he answers.

"Who? I'm Katy. I think I'm here to get you out."

"My mom said don't leave until dad comes back."

"Where's your mom?"

Bunny or Buddy, I think he said his name was, he steps to the side and gestures with a wave of his hand to the corner of the attic, in the direction of a set of dusty, opened cardboard boxes. There lies a woman in heeled boots and tight jeans that taper at her ankles. Her lipstick is almost as red as the blood splattered on the side of her face. The side of her skull has been destroyed. The whiteness of her teeth is right there at the top of her gums, her tongue frozen in time and flopped to the side.

Sunlight beams in from the window behind her, shines broken light between those boxes. It's a low ceiling, barely a few feet above if I extended my arms. The window, I guess it's been closed for years, from the time of their death. If I hadn't seen Roger die so many times I couldn't stand in front of this kid. I'm glad Roger shot himself in the head; I'm glad I'm a little better prepared to see this. A *little* better.

"It's okay to come with me," I tell the boy.

"I can't go anywhere. Have to wait for my daddy." He retreats to the corner and shrinks, brings his knees to his chest.

"We don't need to talk about it. Can we go? Come down with me. I have a friend waiting."

"She said no matter what," he mumbles, "wait for your father. I'm going to wait for my dad."

Does he know he's dead?

Once I get him out of the house, he'll be better. That was the case with Roger. I walk up to him, grab him by his collar and drag him, kicking and screaming, to the attic door. There's no rationale to asking. He needs to go.

"No! No! No!"

"I'm sorry. You can't stay."

I push him down the hole. When I look down, he's not there. There's rustling behind me. I turn and there's the kid. He's stuck in this attic. He's stuck enough that I can't help. I climb down the ladder, walk all the way back to the staircase.

He's on his own.

No, I need to go back up.

I'm down the stairs, through the living room. I'm down the porch steps, happy Roger is still here, because I'm not alone. The sketchbook is stiff in my waistband.

I point at Roger. "I have to go back up. No idea how long I'm going to be."

Roger looks around at this super nice day. "If you take too long, I'll come get you."

"You can come save me, if you feel you need to."

"Don't know anything about saving. I'll come get you."

With pen and sketchbook in hand I start back into the house. This is going to suck.

I climb back up the ladder. The boy's mother isn't shot yet. They sit cross-legged at the far end of this attic. I'm going to see her get murdered. If I pay attention to the room, I can sketch them out of it. That's what I did with Roger. It's the way of it. I've got to draw them out. You can help people escape their death. You just need to be super creative about it.

How did my dad put it? How does this make sense? How did it happen to work with Roger? So, everything around me, everything I'm seeing is a kind of recreated history, or a moment left behind in the DNA of the real world. It's a moment that is marked because of the trauma involved. You have to think you're part of the trauma in the world around you. If you ever see a ghost, you're seeing residue of violence and pain and suffering and all of that kind of stuff.

His mother jumps to her feet when she sees me. "Who are you?"

She's as thin as he is and she has the same kind of dark hair, only it's longer. Her jawbone, her elbows, the sides of her wrists, the edges of her are defined by rigid bone. She's not that much taller than he is, shorter and smaller than me. It's probably his mother, not in her twenties. More like thirties. He in like the fourth grade. In not too long, someone's going to climb the ladder and shoot her in the head or bludgeon her with something.

I say, "I was looking for your son."

"It's the lady I told you about," the little boy says to her.

"And..." She steps toward me, as if we're continuing a conversation.

I say, "I think someone's going to come up that ladder and—"

"I know that." She purses her lips. "You're, what, here to help? How? What can you do for us? How?"

I thrust my back against the wall, slide to the bottom and pull out my sketchbook. She knows they're dead. The look she gives me is like I'm the one who is going to kill them.

"What are you doing?" she says.

"Not sure."

The first line I draw is a reference point. It's hurried and not done well. With the line, I essentially split the room in two. The single line slightly bends across the page. The illusion of depth. I close my eyes, and everything that needs to go on the page is etched to the back of my eyelids. I can draw this room without opening my eyes. Boxes, gardening equipment and insulation lay against that one wall. The torn insulation stacked in places, it fell off the wall in strands. My hand keeps drawing: the four quadrants of each of the four windows, the painted shut latches. The wood beams in the ceiling are unevenly distributed, like a lazy railroad track. The patches of carpet, dingy and dusty, and stuck to the floor yet pulled up at its edges.

The ladder is somehow up. The cycle is going to begin again. I push myself away from the small, square attic entrance.

Someone below the attic claps three times. It's a heavy, hollow smack of the hands. The boy's eyes light up and he starts for the attic entrance. His mother tries to grab him, but he's too slippery for her, too aggressive. She's not surprised when he escapes her grasp. Gauging by her apathetic face, she's going through motions. "It's not your father. You know that," she says.

We all know there's nothing we can do.

I go the opposite direction of the boy. As he scurries to the ladder, I hurry to the other side of the room near the boxes. As he's lowering the ladder, his mother searches for a place to hide, thinks better of it. She stands there, accepting her fate.

"Chan, you're up here?" A man's voice at the attic entrance. He peeks his head in. His hair is thick with curls on the ends, slicked back otherwise. His opened collared shirt exposes curly chest hair, a thin gold chain around his neck. His well-worn slacks hang below his waistline. I'm surprised at his well-worn tennis shoes.

"Who's that?" He points to me.

The mother's body language says, oh, no, not again, but her eyes are happy to see this guy.

"What is this?" he says about me.

"Maybe a friend," she responds. "I don't know."

"Channy, baby, I need you to back up. Do that for me?"

Her face goes long. The boy stays where he is, confused. She backpedals next to me and these boxes. Expressionless, she stares inside the two boxes next to her, pulls her hair behind her ears, sticks her chin out, straightens up, stiffens, puffs out her chest.

"Baby, I told them there's no way you wouldn't tell me where it is. No way. Right? You've got to do it for us."

She shakes her head, mutters to herself. "I have nothing for you."

The guy removes a gun from the back of his waistband and aims it at her. Unlike Roger's weapon, this thing is intimidating.

Trembling, he squeezes the handle. "You've got to do it for us."

"I literally have nothing for you," she says.

"They're going to *kill me*."

She turns her palms up, like what do you want me to do?

He shoots her in the face. The bullet explodes in the side of her head. She flops over on the box where I saw her earlier. He points his weapon at my head, and I close my eyes. There's an explosion. A sharp burning at the back of my neck. I fall to a knee, knowing there's no way a bullet can go to the back of my neck without going through something. My thin sweater sticks to my back, my blood floods down it, hot and dramatic, and so much of it taps the floor upon landing. The burning in my neck is in such a way that my eyes stay shut. The weight of the man who shot me stomps across the room, each of his steps like someone dropped a bowling ball. He heads back down the ladder. You can tell by the brief creaking of each foot on each ladder step.

The boy's long-winded scream, like a bird being squeezed to death. The boy runs out of breath, takes in more air in gasps. Screams again.

The pain in my neck fizzles to near nothing and is gone. I'm looking at the boy's chest raging up and down as he touches his mother with the tips of his fingers, his head twisted to the side. This isn't the first, second or third time he's seen this happen to her; he'll never get used to it.

The pain I had is short-lived. That's the reality of it. There is pain in this world. For me, it's temporary, very short-lived. A good thing. I was shot barely underneath and to the side of my jaw. The bullet exited the back of my neck. Now I'm fine.

The boy runs to the ladder, his untied shoelaces repeatedly tap the floor, his ashy knees and legs are splattered with blood. He pulls up the ladder.

"What's your name?" I ask him. Bunny? Buddy? Barney?

He inches his way to the wall and walks along it. His version of staying the hell away from me.

"That your father who shot her?"

The boy shakes his head, wide-eyed.

"You know him?"

He stands there, in shock at seeing me get shot and turning out pretty well.

"I'm made of clay. That's why I'm not injured or anything," I tell him. "I know it doesn't seem right."

I'm not going to die here. I'm not dead. Roger is dead. These people are dead. I'm not. And I won't be.

For a while I gather myself and try to figure out what I want to draw to get them out. There's something missing. No rocks at my spine. No sunlight in my blood. No electricity. Something is missing.

There are the claps from downstairs. The boy goes to the opening of the attic.

"Stop," I tell him. "Why are you even over there?"

"My dad's going to come get me?"

"They need you to lower it so they can come up. Don't."

I know he's going to lower it. There's no way he's not. The way he stares at the ladder, the way he gazes at his mother's body with his hands flat to the floor, he knows it's the case. I thought it was the end of the cycle after she got shot. It's not. Something happens to him next.

I'm not going to keep watching this little boy get murdered while I draw things the right way so he can escape. Would you watch a child keep getting killed? Look how his mother is flopped over and stiff and dead and stuck. He's helpless and I can't stop it.

The three loud claps happen again. I point to the boy, place my index finger over my lips. I find a spot behind the boxes where his mother's body is.

The scraping and rattling of the ladder going down. A boisterous voice, and then two gunshots. I know it's safe to come out when it's silent. I lift my head. The boy is on his knees, his chest and face pressed against the wall. The blood is on the side of his face and skull as if someone splashed him with the inside of his head. Before their cycle begins again, I escape down to the house level, walk downstairs, and, finally, outside to Roger who is waiting for me.

"Are you okay?" he asks before I'm off the porch.

Every minute replays. All the different expressions on the boy's face, the look of diligence on the mother's face as she prepared to be murdered. She knows her son will keep getting killed.

I arrive at the gate near Roger.

I was shot in the face. For a second the sharp pain returns.

I open the gate.

"What happened?" he asks.

I guess I slid the sketchbook back into my waistband when I left because it's there. I pull it up and pat it. It might as well be a gun in a holster. A *misfired* gun in a holster. It didn't work when I needed it.

"I'm not dead." I close the gate behind me.

The boy's mother's face sits in my head. The boy is there too, chest and bloody face against the wall. In my mind, there's a gun to my head.

I sit on the curb.

Roger sits next to me as healthy as he's been in a while, better off dead as he put it. He wraps his arms around me. It's an embrace to help me stop trembling.

The farther up Thirteenth Street we go, the more confused I am. People on the fringes violently dying is what this place is. I already figured that, but now I feel it differently. Unlike the world where I know best, I can see more of my purpose here, as I try to walk straight with my flailing nerves, as I try to not be affected by seeing the mom and little boy killed.

I'm only now realizing Roger holding my hand. I shove it away.

"Calm down. Crazy stuff has happened to me, too," he says. "I didn't want to talk about it either."

I can help that boy. I knew it before, but I can feel it now. I can help them.

"What's wrong?" he asks.

No doubt he cares about what I'm going through. The problem is what I'm going through doesn't matter, if that boy keeps dying the way he's dying. It's like walking away in the middle of CPR. If it happens to them a thousand times, it means I ignored them being shot in the face a thousand times.

"I need to go back." I'm already headed in that direction. "Yeah. That's just how it is."

When I get back into that attic, I'm going to get shot through the face and it's going to hurt. I was born to be shot in the face.

I rub the slightly irritated spot on the back of my neck where the bullet exited. I speed up, trying to get to the people in the attic because they're getting shot right now, right *friggin'* now.

We jog the rest of the way. I demand Roger stay outside. Him going in won't speed things up and who knows what it means for him to be in there. Too many variables.

I run and leap up the porch steps, jog up the stairs. Underneath the attic doors, I clap. The little boy lowers the ladder. I climb up. He joins his mother again at the far end of the attic. I don't approach them. Instead, I go past them and to the corner, try to duck behind a few boxes. The mother, without a doubt, remembers me, though says nothing. Waiting for the gunman to come up the steps, my entire body is my heartbeat—my feet and head thump and I can't gather enough breath.

I'm going to get shot back here.

I'm going to get *shot*...back here.

The mother eyes me as if I'm some bastion of evil, like I've done something to them. I take out my sketchbook. This is the least creative anybody has ever felt. Fear does not hold a creative silver lining. Fear stunts you, paralyzes you.

Certain words come to mind. No, not words. Images. To myself, I say what those words for the images are. I don't say them aloud because I don't know what they mean. Elaborate hieroglyphs, I guess. Images of the boy and the woman moving toward escape.

I draw a line across the page. I need to start from scratch. For some reason, keep the artistic process I always have—you sort of finish part of something, don't complete it, you start over. I'm a scared artist trying to do a little less than bring the dead to life. I'll settle for giving them a chance.

Drawing this room, this time I think about it differently. There's so much wood, it might as well be a hollowed-out tree. I'm in a tree house.

The three claps from downstairs. The boy heads for the attic entrance. It's not his father. This time, his mother doesn't move. She stands and waits for it to happen to her. She slowly turns around and eyes me. It's not that she thinks I'm evil. This look, it's her asking for help.

The man is up here with them. He says his piece. Chan says her piece. There's nothing to talk about. She gets blasted in the face. I can't stop this from happening. The man sees me, but I remain focused, he approaches, shocked I'm here. He yells out, alludes to how I'm a reporter. I make my face available so he can shoot me where he did before, because I know what that's going to feel like. No need for something different.

I don't blackout but own this pain. For a moment. That's the key. I only own it for a moment. I'm not making a sacrifice. There are no consequences. Just get shot in the face and do your job.

The man leaves after shooting the kid in the head. Everybody is dead. We reset. Three. Two. One. My heart is my face and chest and back. My mouth is cardboard. I can bring up no saliva. I know what my drawing should look like. Chan needs to shove the gun guy to the side and grab her son, and then leap out of here.

No. That's all wrong.

This time he shoots me before Chan, which is crazy. These people aren't robots. They live these moments the best they can. I'm in it the best I can. I'm better than this moment. The pain is like getting stabbed in the back of your neck with an ice pick, multiple times. Made of wood. An ice pick made of wood. Things don't need to make sense.

"Chan," I yell-whisper, seated from behind my box.

She flings herself around.

"What's your son's name?" I ask.

"Bubby," he answers for her.

"Buddy?"

"Bubby," Chan corrects me.

"Bobby?"

"Bubby," he chimes in. "Hey, Bub. Bee."

"*Bubby?*"

Three claps. Bubby sends down the ladder. Everybody gets shot. Me, through the face.

This time, I have a lot more of the room already drawn to set the stage for their escape. Through the process of getting shot in the face, I also have drawn a still image of Bubby lowering the ladder and climbing down it. The plan is to draw him waving to his mother to follow him down.

"Chan," I yell-whisper from my same position behind the box, as rocks grind at my spine. How my stomach and back feels, it's like the engine on a spaceship igniting and spinning. The sensation, I know now, is that of me becoming inspired. Creative energy. You can feel yourself changing the world around you.

"This time let him go. It's going to be okay," I tell Chan.

"I don't believe you, I don't believe you."

"You have to."

As the claps happen, I'm sketching at the raw pace of madness. It's less of a drawing and more mutated, scribbled hope. What I put on the page is everything too fast, none of it how I was taught, none of it a skilled thing. Every stroke as perfect and imperfect as birth. If Chan looked at my picture, she wouldn't recognize it, wouldn't know the scene. I know the drawing. I know it's my vision of what will happen, roughly. I've never done scenes well. But I do hope well. That's what matters. That's the art of it. That's my skill. Creativity is hope.

I shout when the sunlight opens up my bloodstream. Chan is ready to tackle me. I point to Bubby who puts down the ladder, turns his back and scales down it.

Chan gazes at me and weeps at the sight of his success. She reaches out to hug me. I stay where she can't reach me, as I draw her freedom in a way only I can understand. She needs to go. When she does, she walks in the steps I roughly gave her in my drawing. Step one, step two, step three, just like I did for Roger. It's a scene of this small, broken family escaping. The picture I don't draw—because I don't know what it'll look like—is of them being whole again.

I get down the ladder and skip through the house. By the time I'm out the front door, I can't help but to laugh like I'm on a roller coaster. It might be a scary laugh. Roger tries not to make eye contact. He starts down the street a few feet ahead of me.

"Did you see them?" I ask him.

"Yeah, I did."

"They're alive because of me!"

Then I cackle like a hyena.

Ghosts

Greta had relayed the message through social media that she'd appreciate it if people wore formal black to Roger's funeral. She wanted shined shoes, ties, if possible. She wanted people to be on time, no matter how drunk they were, no matter how high they were. Bathe, she said. Show her son some respect, more respect than she showed him when he was alive.

Today, the day of the funeral, Tess had put on her black, ankle-high boots, the ones needing to be zipped up. She let her curly hair fall over her trimmed dark eyebrows. She didn't have black lipstick, but this burgundy made her lips look full. In the body-length mirror next to the dining room table, she patted down her form-fitting black dress. The only formal-like, black anything she had.

Not sure if she'd have a chance to speak to Greta at the funeral, she drove to Roger's hoping to meet her there. The funeral wasn't for hours, so Greta could be home. She parked on the main road and walked down that gravel alley that doubled as a street. Her feet pushed the gravel away the same way it did in middle school, long before heels and lipstick. Today could be the last time she saw Greta.

Rain clouds hurried in and the temperature dropped. As goose bumps raised on her arms, she wished she'd brought a jacket. Up ahead, Roger's house looked like the last place she wanted to be. For a split second, it made more sense to get in her car and drive the several hours back to school than to see Greta or attend the funeral.

Greta had been her friend, in a way. She shouldn't have been, not anymore. Roger and Sam and whomever, she didn't consider them friends anymore, realized it more with each heel that dug into the ground. Katy was a friend. Faceless Arcilla was more of a friend than Greta and the people Tess had known most of her life.

Classic rock blared from the house.

The door was open.

Greta slouched on the couch, alone, holding one of her favorite drinks, a glass of vodka or gin on the rocks. Her legs outstretched with slippers on the ends of them. Tess didn't bother announcing herself. Instead, she walked past Greta to the old-school entertainment system and dropped the volume of the music.

Greta stared at her through glassy eyes, her bottom lip curled over her upper lip. Her bathrobe shut and tied over her front. She swirled her vodka or gin, or whatever clear alcohol she gulped.

Tess checked her phone for the time. The funeral had been scheduled for three hours from now. Meanwhile, Greta epitomized how a person should look on the day they'd bury their son.

"Can I do anything for you?" Tess stood with her feet together. She leaned forward, ready to raise her voice and repeat the question.

"Do you know what happened the day he died? Do you know what really happened?"

"I'm sorry, Greta. I wanted to make sure to talk to you today. Not sure how many more times we'll be talking. Are you okay? How are you?"

"Do you *know* what *happened* that day? I thought I did. I didn't know—I don't think—until yesterday morning."

Tess tried to recall what Sam and Lollar had told her about finding Roger. "He shot himself. With your gun."

Greta scoffed, then took a gulp. "It's legally mine. We shared the damned thing. He shot it as often as I did. He's the one who cleaned it, not that it needed cleaning. He cleaned it anyway. I don't feel guilty about that."

"Can I ask, do we know if he was high?"

"Oh, yeah. I take some responsibility for that. I'll take it." She was drunk, slightly slurring her words. "A mother should keep their kids away from the drugs they themselves sometimes do. I'll have to eat that one. I'll bite the bullet. It's also not what I'm talking about. I'll tell you what I'm talking about. I'll tell you what." She tossed the glass of vodka to the carpet and spit. She pushed herself up, sat up like a real person. She swayed left to right, pointed toward the dining room.

"This is what happened," Greta said. "I know this now. I *know* this." Dragging her feet in her slippers, she pointed to the carpet. "He dragged himself on hands and knees from the kitchen, bled the whole way. You wouldn't know, since you hadn't been here for so long—this is a new rug, to make my house presentable to you judgmental, not-at-all-caring, rancid ingrates. Not you, of course."

"Course not."

"He dragged himself from the kitchen to the living room. Now why would he do that?" Hunched over to the side, Greta waited for a response.

"I-I wouldn't know."

"He didn't want to die. He still wanted to live, is what the truth is."

She must have been drunk to think that, Tess thought. Anybody who puts a gun to their head and pulls the trigger must have wanted to die.

"You look at me like I'm talking crazy. If I sound crazy it's 'cause..." Greta coughed and cracked her knuckles. "He shot himself in my room. Did you know that? He managed to drag himself over to the bathroom mirror. He stared in it for a little bit, probably didn't like what he saw. After that he went to the kitchen, right down that way to the kitchen. You know why he went to the kitchen? You want to know why?"

"Did Sam and Lollar tell you this?"

"He crawled from the kitchen—this is after shooting himself mind you—through the dining room and right there by the couch. *Right there*. You want to know why?"

"Why?"

"Because at some point he dropped his phone and was trying to call for help. Trying. To call. For. Help."

"Did you need a ride? I wouldn't think you could drive."

Greta said, "The other night after everyone left. I heard it. The whole thing. More than that. More than that."

"What's going on, Greta? What are you talking about?"

Greta gave a single nod. "Somebody was with him. I'm telling you, Ms. Tesla. His ghost opens that *door* and slips through. He slips through. He goes to the kitchen, sets his things down. I can hear it, he sets his things down, his backpack or something. You listen and he goes to his room. I know because his ghost opens his *muthafuckin door*, and it's in there. It's in there. It's talking to somebody, not always in his room. Somebody was here with my son."

"We're talking about ghosts?"

"Somebody watched. *They watched*. They might have told him to do it. Another ghost. I don't know."

After what Tess had seen and been told by Faceless, she couldn't discount there being ghosts. She wouldn't disregard it even if she could.

For a moment, she tried to connect ghosts with clay people. Why not there be a connection? However, she couldn't quite put them together.

Tess said, "If you were me, wouldn't you think you were sleep deprived and drunk? That comes off wrong, I know—"

"I'm one hundred percent sleep deprived. I'm drunk as all hell. Wouldn't you be if you saw the shit I saw? More than once! I don't see his ghost, but it's his ghost. He comes down the hall, goes into my room, slides my closet door open, digs through it, and while he's doing it, he's *talking* to someone. He's *talking* to someone."

"Okay, how do you know it's him doing everything rather than the other voice, if you don't see him?"

Greta presses her lips together. "It's how he shouts when the gun goes off."

"You hear him shoot himself?"

"I hear it!"

Things were becoming too weird for Tess to go to the funeral. She wiped hair from her eyes.

"Close the door for me," Greta said.

"I should go."

"Wait with me."

"I really should go."

"Weren't you offering a ride? How am I going to get a ride to his funeral with no ride? Too drunk to drive, as you can see. Way too drunk."

Tess walked over and closed the front door, locked the deadbolt, more to keep it shut than to lock it. Anyone who visited Roger knew the wind or anything could swing the door open if the deadbolt didn't get locked. "You going to shower or something to get ready?" Tess asked.

"I'm going to serve myself up another glass of that potato juice. Nothing happens till that happens."

Greta dragged herself to the kitchen to get more of that potato juice, that vodka or gin. Tess found it in her to be patient. If this were the last time she'd see Greta, then she'd ride it out, see about getting Greta to her son's funeral. Tess sat on the couch so she could be facing Greta when she returned.

In the kitchen, Greta made all the sounds of a drunk person pouring a glass of alcohol—the opening of a cabinet, the slamming of a glass on the counter. The opening of the freezer, the muted clanking of ice being juggled and dropped in the glass. The pouring of far too much potato juice. Meanwhile, Tess stared at the front door, thinking of abandoning Greta, because she might not be seeing this woman again, anyhow.

The deadbolt unlocked on the front door, somehow twisted to the left, like the hands of a clock going the wrong way. The latch pressed down with a click. The door flung partially open. Then to halfway open. No wind or breeze followed it, no wind or breeze would make it do that. Tess felt a presence pass her—the sensation of someone standing too close in an elevator, not touching but too close. The presence made an impression on the carpet on its way to the kitchen. She followed the sensation to the dining room, stopping when Greta reacted to it by pressing her body against the kitchen door jam.

"I know it's you, baby," Greta told the presence while sipping her potato juice. "Are you here?"

A clank on the kitchen floor. Tess leaned forward, trying to find something that might have dropped on the floor. She stepped back into the living room and took a seat on the couch. Greta dragged her feet into the living room, stared down at Tess.

"He's in my kitchen," Greta said in a low voice. She glanced at the front door. "He's in my kitchen." Holding her glass up near her head, Greta put her index and middle fingers to her lips, a gesture asking Tess to remain quiet.

Tess listened for movement in the kitchen. A distant voice came from directly next to her. It might as well have been her conscience.

"Listen," Greta said.

The distant voice was female. A presence moved past them and down the hall to Roger's room, its feet making small impressions in the carpet. The rattling of his bedroom door handle as it was pushed open. For a few seconds, his door remained ajar. Tess could see that in his room, clothes were all over the floor, his bed hadn't been made. Greta hadn't touched his room since he died. The door swung shut. Then the uneasy rustling of somebody navigating through the mess in the room. The distant voice on the couch shouted. Like a friend calling to another friend from across the park. Tess grabbed Greta's arm with an epiphany.

"What?" Greta said.

Tess thought about her epiphany, while still hearing a distinct female voice. She could almost make out words. All the while she focused on his room. Nope, she couldn't shake the idea that it was Katy's voice. No way she could tell Greta. Greta would think Tess was making fun of her. It didn't make sense for it to be Katy's voice, but it certainly sounded like Katy's voice.

"Sounds like it's Katy's," Tess said, bracing herself for repercussions of the statement.

Greta turned her head to the side and cupped her ear. "Katy, how?"

His bedroom door opened again. Greta twisted her way in front of the couch, collapsed onto it, spilled her glass of potato juice while holding it up at the side of her head.

Tess heard rummaging in Greta's closet. A muffled gunshot. A hollow sound seemingly from underneath a pillow in Greta's room. A guttural shout morphed into a scream that could have cut someone if they stood too close. So disturbing and clear, Tess trudged in that direction.

The violence in Greta's room gave the house new life. Violence opens doors, keeps the dead alive, creeps in on the breath of recognizable whispers, on the words of old friends who have disappeared and were most likely dead.

Tess stepped next to Greta's bedroom door, listened at it, and felt Roger's presence scoot past her. Blood, out of nowhere, drew itself fresh on the carpet in deep, meandering zigzags that arrived at the bathroom sink. Streaks of blood the width of fingers striped the mirror. Greta had seen this for the last few days. Her vodka made Absolut sense right about now.

"You promised me a ride," Greta said. "Don't you run off."

A single, deep breath blew in Tess's face. Everything in her body became icy and brittle. No matter how much she wanted to move, she couldn't. His breath was so right in front of her that she wiped her cheek to get his spittle off.

Greta sat on the couch and stared at the floor, so Tess gazed at the floor. Both watched half footprints leave bloody imprints on the way to the dining room, and then to the kitchen. Katy's voice, off in the distance, came to the forefront, Roger's voice, too.

An added streak of blood extended back towards the living room.

Tess jutted her head at Greta. "That's Katy."

"We know it's not."

"Have you talked to her since she left that night? *I* haven't."

Greta, with the expression like someone had been slapping her with a stick for hours, gulped the rest of her vodka.

The front door flung itself all the way open.

Then silence.

Greta stared at the front door as if somebody had thrown it at her. "I don't know if that happened before. Did you see that?"

"They left," Tess said under her breath.

The ghosts ripped the door open and ran away into the future. Could you walk through the door of your own death without dying?

"They left," Tess repeated. She kicked off her boots and wiped off her lipstick, first with her palm, then with the back of her hand. Much of it streaked to the sleeve of her dress. "I can come back if you need a ride."

"I'll be fine. Sit here and be in my skin, for better or worse. Most likely worse."

"Want me to help make some phone calls?" There might have been a way to call off the funeral or at the very least make it so that certain people didn't show up. Could they have a funeral if Greta didn't go?

"Nobody's calling anybody," Greta said. "I'll get there. Call a ride or something. You get on out of here." Greta looked her up and down. "I'll tell someone what happened, you'll back me up won't you? The ghost of my son was in my house, right before his funeral."

"Katy was with him. Will you back *me* up?"

"Katy wasn't with him when he died. She was out of town. You were with her."

"You heard her."

"She was out of town when he died. This haunting, and it's obviously a haunting, is about reliving that pain. Obviously about that. She wasn't with him."

Tess said, "What's true is that you're drunk, a drug addict, and should take responsibility for what happened to him."

Greta undid her robe and stepped out of her slippers. "You listen here. I'm taking full responsibility. *Full* responsibility. If they need to lock me up, they'll do that. I have no defense outside of the fact, outside the fact that I wasn't here, and I didn't pull the trigger. Let me tell you something else. If you knew a lick of anything, you'd know that if your only child kills themselves, you can get as drunk as you want, you can think anything you want."

"Katy was with him."

"What is your *problem?*"

"I'm going to ask this."

Greta slammed the front door shut.

For a second, Tess thought of not asking the ensuing question. Greta was already irate and might snap after hearing it. "Are you made of clay? Is Roger?"

Greta inhaled and held her breath for a few seconds. "I didn't realize my ears could be drunk. It sounded like you asked if my son was made of Play-Doh."

Tess tucked her heels under her arm, took those few steps to the door, pulled it open, and walked out.

"Play-Doh." Tess heard it from behind her as she walked down the steps. "You should have your ass kicked for asking such a *stupid* question, kicked up and down the street. A stupid, stupid joke. Do you know what I've been through to sit up here and listen to that crap? You know what I've seen. You seen it your damned self. Tesla, you come back here, and I'll beat your ass like Maxine is too old to."

Tess strolled down the alley-street feeling like something pulled off the bottom of someone's shoe. Such a dumb question. She should have done everything in her power not to insult Greta. None of what happened or what she said could be taken back. Other people in the area had to be made of clay. Why not Roger, since he and Katy were super close at some point? It was Katy with him, wasn't it? Wherever ghosts went is where people of clay can go, she surmised. Because Faceless was real.

Because Katy couldn't be dead.

Could she?

Tess yanked the wheel to turn down her cul-de-sac. She glanced at her phone that lay on the passenger seat, verbally asked it what's the place called where ghosts live? Her phone referred to that place as haunted. According to her phone, ghosts were spirits stuck on Earth in a place they found familiar. It's also what films suggested. It must have been true. Roger was in that house, for whatever reason, not ready to move on.

Maxine was awake and downstairs when she entered her home.

"Are you back already?" Maxine asked, staring at the television.

"I'm not going."

"What happened?"

"I don't know."

Maxine raised an eyebrow. "Something happened."

Tess sat on the back of the couch and dropped her heeled boot on the floor. "I'm going to tell you something that's going to sound crazy."

"I'm certain I've heard crazier."

How Maxine focused on her, it didn't matter what she said, Maxine would understand. That's the deal they made with each other, not that they ever talked about it. Maxine would be there for her, no matter what.

"I think Katy's gone missing," Tess began.

"Oh. That's disconcerting. Have you talked to anyone? Her father? Have you called her phone?"

"Obviously, I called her phone. Forget I brought it up."

"Well, I didn't realize you were so upset."

"I swear, I swear, I swear me and Greta saw Roger's ghost. Less than ten minutes ago."

Maxine cupped her chin. "Didn't expect to hear that."

"I didn't expect to say it."

"Well, then. Does it bother you?" Maxine said.

"Shouldn't it?"

"It might bother me. I suppose it's something that *might*."

A distant, confusing answer from someone clearly not taking her seriously, despite trying hard—for some reason—to seem like it. She couldn't think of a time when Maxine had not been truthful or forthcoming with her. This is what Maxine placating her looked like.

Tess straightened her dress. "I, um, it's more than that."

"What's 'it'?"

"Things are happening. It's crazy stuff."

"I'm sure I've heard crazier."

There's no way she heard crazier. But there was no one else to talk to. "I, um… The things that are happening, it feels like they go together, if that makes sense."

"Tell me all the crazy stuff that's happening. I'll tell you if they make sense."

"I ran into a woman the other day who had no face." She paused to give Maxine a chance to respond. "I think I thought she was drunk, at first. I went to help her. It wound up being Katy's mom. I know how it sounds. It's true. It was Katy's mom. And, yeah, I know I said I thought Katy was missing, when really, I came from Greta's and I heard Katy there, like not in the house but *in* the house."

Maxine turned off the television. "Go on. Continue."

"That's weird, huh."

"Quite awkward. Is that all it is you're going to tell me?"

"I don't know. Now that I'm saying it aloud it might not be worth saying. Me and Greta got into it. Lately, it's been nothing but super-weird stuff smacked together."

"That's fine."

Saying it aloud helped. Now she needed to brush off the impending awkward looks and the probable lecture about the dangers of drug use.

"I don't know if it's worth it for you to say everything you said." Maxine scrunched her lips. "It's certainly worth it for me to hear it."

"Katy's mom, the faceless lady, told me all this crazy stuff. I don't know. Seeing ghosts. It's, uh, it's maybe stressful. It happened. I'm not making it up—"

"If you've seen Arcilla, well, I have to tell you," Maxine cleared her throat, presumably searching for the right words, "I was hoping one day you'd be ready for this conversation. You're not losing it or saying anything crazy. I'll help your mental and tell you this: Don't worry about Katy. She'll be fine."

That she claimed to know about more than she had let on kept Tess quiet.

"I'm sorry I lied to you," Maxine said. "Your impression is I was your nanny who took you on as my own after your parents left you.

You're going to have to knuckle it through this truth I'm about to give you. You've seen Arcilla, so—"

"She came to me the other night, right to the front door."

"Is that who that was? Should have let her in. She can tell you what I'm about to tell you if you ask, I'm sure. Better for me to pull my own weight as an elder. It didn't happen in any simple way."

"What didn't happen?" Katy asked.

Ms. Maxine scrunched her lips. "Let me tell you about your parents. This is an old house built in 1934. The first owners were a young man and his wife. Your parents. I think he was thirty or so when they moved in, in 1935. That sounds about right. She was a little younger than him. That was your mother and father."

"So, you're saying my dad and mom were in their thirties in 1935?"

"Haven't said anything yet." Maxine glowed with anticipation. "Listen to this, ma'am. Your father, not quite able to pay all the bills and having a little debt, or a lot of debt, was in trouble with a certain type of people. See, the bank wouldn't give him a loan. He got into the house by going into debt under somebody else's name. He owed them with interest. Well, he couldn't keep his end of the bargain. Guess what."

"What?" Maxine never told these types of far out stories. It felt regurgitated. Tess's mind wandered back to Greta's where she had seen Roger's ghost and heard Katy speaking with him. "I saw Roger's blood all over the floor."

Maxine tapped her fingers on her knee. "I'm sorry. It's a horrible thing." She stopped tapping. "Katy will be okay. I'm telling you about your parents because it actually relates to Katy. It relates to how you treat yourself going forward. Now listen, they burned part of it down. With your parents in it. They meant to make an example to anyone else who didn't pay their debts. The men who lit it on fire stood outside with the doors barricaded so your parents couldn't get out. That's the story that was told to me."

"Maxine, stop it. My parents weren't that old."

"I found out about their story after I moved in, in 1958 or so. I'm a woman, and nobody wanted to touch the house, so it was hard to fix it, all the way around. People said it would be too hard to finish fixing up. For me, it was too cheap to turn down. The realtor came right on out and said it: The place is expensive to fix and really, really haunted. He explained the whole story to me, nice and straightforward. I bought it anyway. At the time I didn't believe in ghosts. It was quite a project. I'm talking about a new roof, the new bathroom and basement, all the new floors. Even the facade has been uplifted. All new pipes and reinforced windows since all that happened. I made sure of it myself."

"Haunted? Stop it."

"By. Your. Parents."

Mostly not engaged in the questionable and mostly insane story Maxine was telling, Tess's mind wandered again to the idea of Katy being with Roger's ghost. Arcilla made of clay. Tess's ears rang when thinking of the gunshot and Roger's ghost screaming. She thought back Faceless writing all the notes, because she didn't have a mouth. All of it make it hard to not be frustrated with the story Maxine was telling—a clear attempt to make her feel better somehow, a tone-deaf attempt at it. Tess thought back to Greta in the dining room with her glass of potato juice while a long streak of blood drew itself across the floor. *The scream gave his suicide a special place in her history. The dead bleed long after they die.*

"Today, I saw and heard a friend of mine's ghost scream out in *pain*," Tess blurted.

For a moment they sat in silence, showing respect to Roger or what Tess had said about him.

Tess said, "His mother—"

"Greta—"

"Is all broke up about it."

Maxine stared at her, patted her on the leg. "Twice a month I could sit right over there—that's where the couch was—and listen to your parents burn to death. It's why the house came cheap."

"Oh my god, why are you doing this? You can't possibly be believing this."

"No less true than what Greta is going through. That poor lady, despite her shortcomings. It's how it was," Maxine said. "Previous owners couldn't handle the screaming, like a torture chamber, louder upstairs than down. Owners didn't stay long, and this beautiful home lost its value.

"One day, a man showed up, all done up in a suit and nice shoes. Real respectable looking. He said he was acquainted to the people who previously lived in the house, the ones burned to death. You believe that? You better believe that. He walked right up the stairs and announced himself to them. Yes, he knew them. You believe that?

"While they screamed and cursed and pounded on the walls and cried out, they also acknowledged him. I see I have your attention. A few weeks later that man came back with several heavy crates that I helped him drag to the corner of the living room. Right over there." She gestured like a museum guide to the far end of the room where the dining room table sat.

On the table, a large, empty bowl, and some ripped open envelopes.

Maxine folded her arms. "He opened the crate and inside of it was a pasty, mud, dirt-rock kind of thing. He and I talked for a while and he said the wildest thing to me. He said he's going to make figures out of what he had in the crates, to get the ghosts out of my house. Since he had already talked to them before, I believed him. If the chef says he can cook it, you believe it.

"For hours he shaped the clay into what looked like grown folk, and the size of grown folk, too. Never seen anything like it. An artist showing me magic. He molded those figures in one try, and snap, just like that, considering the quality. Gosh, I think it took hours and hours. It should have been longer. He came over, I want to say, in the afternoon, didn't get done until that night.

"He told me to leave the sculptures there, to not touch them, so I didn't. The next day, in the early, early morning, I thought I could hear the sculptures breathing. Can you believe that? I think about it now and it sounds almost unbelievable, doesn't it? The whole thing sounds fantastical."

"It does sound crazy," Tess said, tugging on her dress, not believing it, but remembering the stiff body of Faceless in Katy's basement.

"That afternoon, the man came back and got his thumbs underneath the surface of those human-esque clay figures, pulled it right off your mother and father. They were now alive and healthy. Reminded me of peeling boiled eggs. The most amazing thing I'd ever seen. Amazing enough, I let them, the miracle they were live in the house. Suggested it, even."

"*What?*"

"When you witness magic, you want to stay near it, always. You don't need to believe what I'm telling you, though it's as true as your friend committing suicide. I'm certainly sorry to hear about him, by the way. Not my favorite. A good kid anyway. I am sorry."

Tess folded her arms, pondering what sounded like, quite possibly, the wildest thing she could hear at the moment. This might have been what Greta felt like. "My parents jump out of clay and he disappears?"

"Not at all." Maxine laughed as if she had told some classic joke. "He wanted to keep track of them. Since he liked the neighborhood so much, he moved in next door. Katy's *father* pulled the dead right out of their suffering and straight into this world. When I die, he said he'd do it for me if he had to."

Tess stood. Paced across the room. Like a child she touched things, contemplating everything. She couldn't believe it. Just couldn't. Wouldn't.

Maxine patted the couch. "If you want to continue with this, come sit, baby. You're pacing."

"My parents weren't *fucking* ghosts."

Ashamed of not being able to hold it together, she stomped off to her room.

New World Problems

Roger points to the window of a family sitting at their dining room table. "They're all dead," he says.

"I think so."

"Craziness."

That's also how I think of it. This is craziness.

We continue up Thirteenth, heading to Sunderland. There must be a place along the way where my mom could be.

"You seem okay," he says, not making eye contact.

"That's who I am. I'm okay."

"Those people are fine. It's not all violent and lame in this place."

He's coming to terms with who or what I am, with what he is, with what this place is. I'm coming to terms that I don't know him too much. We'll figure it out or we won't. Who knows what this all means?

It's hot underneath this clear, blue sky. We might have arrived in hell, it's so hot.

Roger waves across the street at a dude about our age standing in a driveway. Since Roger waves, I wave. The dude waves back with his thin frame and over-sized clothing. The creased shirt and pants, the bright-red ball cap to the side of his head. This is a gang member. He waves to us, like how are you guys, what a nice day. He takes off his cap and wipes his forehead. Why in the world isn't he wearing shorts?

A car that can only be bad news cruises down the street—a new sedan, four doors, going too slow. As it gets closer, it's clearly full of young men. I've heard about drive-by shootings. Never seen one. This is in the middle of the day. I wouldn't make any of these assumptions if I didn't know the guy was already dead.

The car accelerates. Our guy across the street flees up the driveway. The car slows, and they shoot at the entire area across the street. Explosion after explosion sending bullets bouncing off the chain-link fencing and skidding off the concrete. Bullets get our guy in the back. The car peels off having shot through his living room windows, having shot through the neighbor's house. They skid to stop at the end of the block, screech around the corner and speed off with the roar of their engine.

"I don't know what to say," Roger says, losing his breath and staring at the guy who got shot.

Although death is natural, how the guy collapsed, isn't. When you see it, your creativity, your energy, it freezes, like a deer hiding in plain sight.

"You weren't in that attic," I tell Roger. "Way worse."

"Are you going to help him?"

"I'd rather keep moving." I don't have the energy to do what might need to happen.

Roger jogs across the street. Before too long he's standing next to our shot guy. The guy stands. Roger says something to him. The guy looks around like somebody's playing a joke on him. Wow. It's like Roger's a ghost to the ghost. The dude barely knows Roger's there. He had been waving to me not Roger.

The shot guy, who is no longer bloody, he steps down to the end of the driveway, and stops. He needs to stop there so he can get shot again. Roger stands at the top of the driveway. I wave to Roger to come back. Our soon to be shot guy thinks I'm waving to him.

"Nah, my lady, you find your way to this side," he says.

Roger steps in front of him, waves his hands. The guy shoos him as if he's a fly. Roger shouts and hits him. The guy rubs his shoulder where Roger hit him.

Dejected, Roger jogs back across the street. "I don't like this."

"I guess I'm coming over," I tell the guy. There's something to say about the gangster not realizing he's dead. To him this moment is happening for the first time. His situation is different than Roger's, who when I found him in his cycle, was confused if he was alive or not. The soon-to-be-shot guy's situation is different from the people in the attic, as well. They knew they had died.

Roger has a certain look on his face. Years ago, I would have thought this was a look of jealousy, how he'd go quiet. Now, I'm sure he's thinking of peeling my clothes off and biting into me.

I pull Roger forward.

"You're not going to say hi to your new friend?" he asks.

"He's about to get shot again."

Roger's eyebrows lift.

At the end of the block, the temperature significantly drops. We both look back, see the drive-by car turn down the block. It's that drive-by repeating. I don't need to see the guy in the driveway murdered again. Roger, on the other hand, he can't look away. I bet he looks like this while checking out porn.

A few steps and we're all the way in a different person's death sequence, their cycle. If we're lucky, we don't need to see the death occur. That's all we're doing—moving from one cycle to another.

Roger tugs on my fingertips.

I stop.

He shakes his head. "Thank you for not leaving me to shoot myself."

They like to say we've seen so much violence on television and movies that we're desensitized to it. Nothing I've seen on TV or in movies makes it easier to watch what we saw. None of it makes it so I can sit in a room and watch and hear that boy in the attic get shot in the face.

I tell Roger, "I didn't want to get shot either."

"You got shot?" He looks at me like he's going to peel my clothes off and chew me. "You're not like me."

"I told you that."

"Other ghosts don't see me. Did you know that? Why are you pretending to be like me?"

"I wouldn't do anything to confuse you."

"What are you?"

I wipe the remaining sweat off my forehead onto my leggings, pull my hair back and tie it into a horrible bun-thing.

He taps the sketchbook on my hip. "How do you do that?"

"I haven't figured out the rules."

"Alien?"

"That's stupid. Whatever ability I have, it's channeled through this good ol' sketchbook. I feel a certain way when it's ready to happen. I don't know for sure when it's going to happen. I haven't figured out all the rules."

We keep going. He has no idea where he's following me. I'm more or less headed to Sunderland, more or less hoping to run into my mother along the way. I bet she knows more about me than I do. We keep up Thirteenth Street.

"Did I have a funeral?" he asks.

"I got here too soon for that. Your mom had a get-together."

"How was it? A lot of tears?"

"Not a drop."

"Who came?"

"Sam. Tess. Lollar. I didn't know everybody." I prompt him to keep moving. There's still a chance to see someone die, and I'd rather miss that. "Your mom was getting loaded."

"Close as I'll get." He flings his hands in the air. "How are you here, if you're alive?"

"I'm not the only one."

He walks ahead, his head on a swivel. "For sure? Being dead isn't what we thought it would be, is it."

I catch up to him on this cool evening, in yet someone else's cycle. A slight breeze. Patches of clouds travel fast overhead and hide the moon. Imagine someone has died. In a short while, we'll hear the sounds of their cycle begin. Maybe there'll be gunshots. Maybe a drive-by. It could be, I don't know, a hammer to someone's face right in the middle of the road. Someone could jump off their roof with a rope around their neck. Who knows? When it happens, all the noise will kick-in and then just like that it'll all be over. It'll go quiet again, just like that.

In this world's odd quietness, we travel side-by-side through several more cycles, managing to avoid death. Each cycle has different weather and is in a different year—the 50's we passed through, I think the 1980's, the early 2000's. Without seeing the deaths in the cycles, it's like going through a living museum, the most elaborate sets anybody will ever witness, yet you get used to it. Roger gets used to it.

Being around him, as if we're normal, gets me missing how we were before he became an addict. He paid attention to everyone and was affected by them, yet now that I think of it, I don't know in what way. He's healthy now, though I'm not sure what that means. Seeing him healthy and not needing me, it feels as if something has been taken from me.

Not everything makes sense on our journey. The sidewalks don't always match up. The smells don't always go together. On this surreal landscape, we cross plains of concrete and rolling hills of apartments. I don't recognize this park we've arrived at, somewhere that might not exist anymore. Crossing through this park, over in the distance near a large, full tree, a man is on top of someone, stabbing them. It's a series of yelps and cries. Me and Roger pretend to not see or hear anything. Aloud, I tell myself to not look, to stop looking.

Roger picks up the pace. I keep up with him despite stiffness that feels like stress. Part of me wants to run over to the stabbing and make it stop. The other part of me knows I'm not going to sit there and watch until I get some drawing correct and make that situation better. This is a representation of the world that happens when people like me have the tools to help yet do nothing.

I look back at the stabbing, at the man circling his victim, leaping, diving, landing head-first onto a defenseless, motionless body. He lies there, writhing, like a pig in mud.

"Go, go, go," I whisper-shout to Roger.

Fat raindrops dot my head. The park, the stabbing, it's suddenly a memory replaced by rundown duplexes; we move from the park and it's neighborhood to these dingy, tract homes. These inner neighborhood streets aren't quite dark yet, aren't quite wide enough, don't feel quite safe. Nothing feels safe.

Roger meanders to the middle of the road. "When do we stop?"

"Are you tired?"

"Do I *get* tired?"

We're on the back side of town, almost to the border. I don't ever come over this way. "We should be making a map."

"I shot myself in the head," he says. "Drug addict and all that."

He's losing it. Slipping back to the emotionally gimpy Roger who shot himself.

We stop in front of an old, craftsman-style home because it's time to stop. He stays in the middle of the street, gawking at the very normal home in front of us. He looks disgusted. I'm disgusted that he's disgusted. We're both going through the same big thing, yet it feels much larger than that.

Roger makes a fist and punches his hand. "You ever want to strangle the hell out of yourself. I know why I put a bullet in my head."

The house in front of us is more than a normal home. It has the aura of a castle. The closer I get to it, the more I feel it buzzing with negativity.

"Stay where you are." I point my finger at Roger. The closer we get to this house, the more frustrated he gets.

"I know this feeling," he says, mouth agape. He creeps past me, opens the chain-link fence, and stops part way up the walkway. "Like at home." He backtracks to the short gate, slips back through the exit, and keeps backing away. "Yeah, this is that feeling. It's like a crappy day made into a house."

I drop to my ass and sit cross-legged on the sidewalk, pat the ground—an invitation for him to join me. He squats, leans his elbows on his knees for balance, a sneer on his face.

"I know I should be trying to help whoever is in there," I say.

"You're going to try and talk yourself out of going in?"

"I don't know."

He rocks. "If you're going to recover from any injuries that you might get, I would."

"Whatever's in there's going to be horrific."

"You have to use your talent at some point. Really use them. That could be me in there. It kind of looks like my place."

It looks nothing like his place.

I say, "What do you think happens to people if I remove them from their cycle? What's going to happen to you?"

"I don't care. Nothing is worse than what you pulled me from." He stops rocking. "I have things going on in my head from when I was an addict. I feel like an addict on a bad day right now."

The vibe near this house is making him relapse and become sick. "You're fine, though?"

"I always told myself I understood why you left. Why don't you explain it to me? Why would you leave somebody if you knew you were all they had?"

I stand, dust off my shorts. "I had no future if I stayed with you."

"You ever think I had no future without *you*?"

"I was going off to school in a while anyway."

He says, "The only rational person in my life wouldn't even take my damned phone calls. What do you think I'd do next? What did you *think* I'd do next?"

"When Tess told me, I wasn't surprised. I love you, would never hurt you. It doesn't mean I need to stand next to you and let you hurt me."

"I was hurting you? I thought about hurting you. I really did. I'm going to let you know, I could have ripped your skin off, you pissed me off so much—not taking my calls, talking to all my friends except me."

"I'm sorry 'bout that."

"Whatever. I was so pissed." His voice raises, eyes wander. "You had me so messed up in the head, I thought you were trying to piss me off. I thought you wanted me to break into your house at night, sneak into your room while you were sleeping and—"

"I don't want to hear it."

"No, you don't. Maybe smother you with a pillow and—"

"Stop it!"

"You thought you were killing me."

I've got nothing for him. I didn't try to kill him.

He focuses on the house. "I'm going in there."

"I can't stop you."

"What are the chances a lot of people in their cycle are like me, and their friends couldn't come around to showing up for them? Probably the case, huh."

"Trying to convince me to go in?"

"The privileged can't afford to act privileged."

I get back to being comfy and crossing my legs. My sketchbook turned to a blank page. The house, a shitty turquoise, maybe a story and a half. The chipped handrails are painted that color as well. So many dead leaves in the yard, I can't find the grass. At the back of the front porch sits an autumn-brown door, a square window at the top center of it. A side yard on either side of the home, and all the lights are off.

"Katy."

"Huh?"

There's something in his eyes that's always been there that I can see better now. He alluded to thoughts of raping me. At one point he wanted to murder me. That's what I gather.

"I'll go in," I tell him. "You stay right here. Like before."

The look he gives me, it's like I wronged him. There's fear and disappointment in his crossed arms, in his flat-footed stance. I know being near this house has a negative effect on my thoughts. That doesn't mean I need to trust him inside. The reason why he won't come in with me is because he's scared of what me and my notebook might be able to do to him. He thinks I'm a liar. The person who, at one point, contemplated raping and killing me, he thinks I'm a liar.

I find myself stepping up the walkway, knowing I'm not going to get killed. Stabbed or shot or poisoned isn't off the table.

Promises

Tess couldn't imagine her parents burning to death as ghosts. Even from what she had seen and witnessed in the last few days, what Maxine said about her parents was impenetrable.

As she sat in the porch chair and rocked back and forth with her eyes closed this morning, she stared hard at Katy's house, tried to take everything she discovered and make it bite-sized.

She rocked, alone, simplifying matters.

If she saw things in the easiest way to look at them, then Roger simply died, Katy simply ran away; her parents were simply dead. She wiped that imaginary hanging hair from in front of her face, again and again, mumbling that Roger simply died, Katy simply ran away; her parents were simply dead.

It'd be best to take everything day by day, go back to school. Whatever.

She pictured Arcilla's blank, empty face. Despite it, faceless Arcilla had merely died. The hair wouldn't stay off her forehead. Roger simply died, Katy simply ran away; her parents were simply dead, Arcilla had gone nuts and died. That's all anybody would know or believe, anyway. If she said it louder and clearer, she might believe the simplicity herself.

The screen door creaked open. Maxine appeared. Her baggy sweater was meant to keep her a warm, although the weather was damn near perfect this morning.

"You're depressed," Maxine said.

"Thinking about everything."

"Oh, don't do that. If you need to figure out more, we can talk about it. It's not for you to do by yourself."

"I don't want to stress you out."

"I'm not the one who's stressed."

Her guardian stared across the cul-de-sac like the captain of a ship gazing at the horizon. How would she guide the youth through this new discovery?

"Your problem is you have a future," Maxine said.

Tess stopped rocking, awaiting the rest of the statement.

"You heard me," Maxine said. "The problem is you have a future. You think as you were told to think. Reach for the stars, use your imagination, is what they told you."

"All the time."

"Gotta make those goals, am I wrong? After you complete your goals, what do you do? Make more goals. That's fine. Now, if you're like me and have listened, for example, to your parents burn to death, your only goals become to not burn to death. After that you don't see things the same way. From that situation forward, I've been observing the world more than living in it."

She stiffened at the continued assertion of her parents having been ghosts rescued by Katy's father. Then she pictured Arcilla in Katy's basement. She would still be there.

"Observe more than live?" Tess asked.

"Imagine being in one of those stories you write. You observe things, see what I'm saying? You don't live your characters' lives. You walk in their shoes when they're not paying attention. I observe people, have sympathy and empathy and I feel sad for folks. I don't think of things like they do. You won't anymore either. That's what your run-in with Arcilla did, whether you understand it or not."

Tess said, "People seem like nothing more than characters to you?"

"In too many ways to count, everyone is part of an arc in their own story I'm looking at from a certain distance. You're an artist. You know what I mean."

In fact, Tess did recognize what she had said. The only surprise was that the observation came from Maxine.

Tess asked, "How does the information you know make what you do every day any different? How are your conversations different? How are your days any different than anybody else's? How does any of it matter? Does it matter?"

"How has witnessing our neighbor pluck your parents from their state of suffering changed how I think of things?"

"Yeah." Tess still couldn't ingest it, so Roger simply died, Katy simply ran away, and her parents were simply dead.

"I'll tell you what. It makes me feel in control. Unlike other people I know, I don't need to be here. I can make any day be my last. Any moment. He already said he'll come back for me. I don't have a nice little future and a list of goals. I can't achieve anything more than your parents did. I don't have a set future."

"I don't think he's coming back."

"He keeps his word, yes, he does. There's a girl he visits every so often—a dead girl, a ghost, if we want to make this conversation worth it. He said she's got it so bad that he won't pull her out of her haunting. She's in such a bad way he can't help her, not in the way he helped your parents. Doesn't mean he doesn't visit her, if for no other reason than that he promised to. If I deem it time to go, he'll be back for me as well."

"Deeming it time to go means taking your own life?"

"I wouldn't but if I did, he'd be there for me."

"He'd do for you what you said he did for my parents?"

Maxine responded, "He keeps his promises."

"Why not stay alive?"

"I'm not doing the unimaginable to myself. I'm just letting you know that because of what I know, I'm in control. It makes things different from my perspective. When you know truth about the other side, a pinch of fear disappears once you come to terms with it."

"Simplify it."

"Keep it simple if you can."

Tess rocked. "How would you do it?"

"How would I do what?"

"What way would you, you know, do it?" She didn't think Maxine would actually kill herself, though she had to know how far Ms. Maxine would take her story. All to show sympathy?

Maxine scrunched her face and smacked her hands together inches from Tess's head. "Snap out of it. You don't have any promises owed to you. We can't be out here on the porch talking about killing ourselves. It's a nice day. Let's live it. Do you want eggs?"

"Scrambled."

"Syrup on the side?"

"Please."

Ms. Maxine pushed the door open. "No more talk of death."

Tess went back to staring at Katy's abandoned house. Katy's father would surely be back. No way to know when. She pictured Faceless Arcilla wandering up the island right there not too long ago. Then it struck her. The story. Katy's father creating people, and Faceless, had been part of a story, in some way. Hearing Katy with Roger. The two ideas together seemed part of the same story, and it didn't matter if she knew how to connect them precisely. What if Maxine had been telling the truth? She still couldn't imagine her parents as ghosts. But she didn't need to believe the story for it to be true. Somehow, she knew it to be true. The problem was that Tess wasn't ready to see things so differently, as Maxine had said would happen to her. She wanted things simple—Katy simply ran away, Roger had simply died, Katy's father was merely a deadbeat dad, and Arcilla had simply died.

However, being simple didn't make the situation sit in her the right way. She could more easily ingest it, but it didn't sit right in her. Maxine was telling the truth and told the truth because Tess had seen Roger's ghost, heard Katy with his ghost, and seen Faceless. It was time for her to know it all. Education was validation; Maxine did nothing but tell Tess what she had already seen and heard. She didn't need to believe it; she had witnessed it. What she *needed* was to be able to tell the story on her own terms. She needed to find a way to put Katy's father into the story and hear from Katy. She had to talk about all of this with the people who were living it, so she could live it with them. To confirm the story, everybody needed to be in it, not just Maxine.

"Maxine!"

"Yes," came the reply from the living room. Her guardian arrived at the threshold. "Yes?"

"The ghost he visits. Where is that?"

According to Maxine, the haunted house frequented by Katy's father was in the Belmont community about seven miles away. Maxine didn't have the address. She did know it was near a large park close to the center of the neighborhood. Katy's father had talked about going up the stairs, so she knew the house had two stories. The house would often be unoccupied.

According to Maxine, Katy's father could never find it in him to extract the girl from her haunting. He feared what she would become if freed. He couldn't take responsibility for her.

Tess pulled into a gas station in the Belmont area, paid for a few gallons of gas. In front of the skinny, acne-riddled boy of a cashier, she facetiously asked if he knew where to find the nearest haunted house.

"I guess you're not from around here," he said.

"Nah, uh uh. I'm not."

"You do know what happened there or you wouldn't go. Do you know what happened, what, a few weeks ago?"

"Nah, uh uh, what happened?" she asked.

"It's weird how groomed you are despite living in a deep hole somewhere."

"What?"

"The dad offed himself. You didn't hear about that?"

"Nah, uh uh."

"I don't know if it's for real haunted. A shitty situation, for sure. Did you want a receipt?"

"You know where it is?"

"There's no *way* you're from around here."

"Not the immediate area."

"Everybody knows where it is. You're making a video or something like that?"

She said, "Doing something more important than social media."

"For sure, for sure."

He didn't believe her. However, to her surprise, he gave directions as if he were a conductor on a theme park ride.

Using the cashier's directions, she drove past the large park, went up a few blocks and made the left. There were three, two-story houses on the block. One of them had been painted a disturbing off-green and had chipped paint. The yard, albeit trimmed and dim from the quickly disappearing light of day, it had all yellow grass and rather tall weeds outside the yard near the curb. Of the two-story houses on the block, this one looked the most haunted.

Tess parked, exited her car across the street and stared at the house. Could it be she lived a life with options most other people didn't have? If she could confirm Maxine's story, then the answer was, yes, she could make a deal to get to the other side. But suicide wasn't the answer. There had to be another way to get there. Of *course.* Because Katy could be alive.

She slogged across the street, pondered what needed to happen. She'd need to confirm Katy's father was acquainted with a ghost that haunted the house.

Tess opened the gate, cruised up the wooden porch steps. For a second, she felt stupid. How would she go about this? What would she say? She stood several feet away from the door, not ready to knock, not ready to speak to somebody inside whom, according to the skinny dude at the gas station, would be mourning her recently deceased father. Damn, this was a bad idea.

Jessica answered the door. "Something I can help you with?"

Jessica stood a few inches shorter than Tess and had one bare foot sticking out of the house, her leg draped in a sweat pant legging. To Tess, this girl might have represented the reemergence of latchkey kids—a bushel of knotted hair, a hint of marijuana wafted her direction. This girl had become a mess with old makeup around her eyes. This girl, who was a few years younger than her, which meant she was far too young to be on her own, didn't care about a whole lot right now. Judging by her eyes she was high. Judging by her demeanor she had no patience. Judging by what Maxine had said, this girl might have seen things the rest of the community had not.

"I'm Tess."

"I don't even have time."

This really might have been a bad idea, only hadn't she heard Katy at Greta's with Roger's ghost? She heard her. *She heard her.* "Fuck it. I'm looking for a man who might have come to speak with a ghost. Call me crazy."

Jessica dragged herself outside and shut the door behind her. "Are you like him?"

"Am I like him? Well, I'm Tess."

Jessica bit her bottom lip. "I'm Jessica. You talk to ghosts? You can talk to her?"

"Can I?"

"Please. Yes, please. Did you want to come in? Or were you going to be back later?"

"I can come in?"

Jessica's fingers straightened and a sad look of disgust fell over her face. "Is it that you need to change inside?"

"I don't need to change. *At all.*"

"I have weed."

"Oh my god, I hope you do."

She passed the joint back to Jessica. After a few small drags, Tess appreciated the head-change. She leaned back. The stiff loveseat facing Jessica did horrible things to a person's back. She could hardly see the coffee table between them, it was so full of loose marijuana leaves and ash, not only from the current session, but from many in Jessica's recent past. The whole place seemed ripe for depression. It couldn't have been lit any worse. The lamp next to Jessica had a dim, yellow bulb that produced more shadow than light. All the curtains and shades were shut. The kitchen lights were dim and yellow. The dining room lacked an option to be well-lit.

"How were you going to try and see if you could talk to her?" Jessica asked.

"I really have no idea. I don't know jack about haunted anything."

Their nervousness burst towards the ceiling in the form of laughter.

Tess squirmed in her seat, repositioned herself as a pillar of knowledge compared to the person in front of her. Tess had gotten further along in her education and in life experience than Jessica, and it showed. Jessica, a pothead, mostly empty and slow, was a good person, though she did not have much going on, in general.

"You're in college?" Jessica crossed her legs underneath herself on the couch. "Is it worth it to go?"

"Haven't tried to get a job yet."

"Was it hard to get in?"

"Kind of a lot of hoops and all that."

"You're pretty," Jessica said, through pursed lips.

"Thank you." Tess couldn't return the compliment. The girl looked like a fleshy mop. It's possible she hadn't been eating. There wasn't a lot of nutrition in weed.

They conversed for a while. Tess found herself predicting question after question, letting the idea of the ghost and suicide sit at the back of her mind for the time being.

"Does college make you smarter?" Jessica asked.

"God, no. Outside of few extracurricular things, it's a whole bunch of time to practice and tons of reading."

"I'm screwed."

"It's stuff you do or don't do. Not much else."

Those streaks of sunlight that shone through the windows earlier, they didn't anymore. The dim lighting lit the room enough to let Tess know she couldn't stay much longer and not pay attention to time. Her idea of the house changed since arriving. It was a well-lived-in, cozy home. It's a shame what had happened. Jessica could have had a happy future. That couldn't be the case now, could it?

Since they started talking, Jessica's posture had changed. She gazed at Tess through glassy eyes, as if Tess were a commercial on late night television. Jessica sat there, debris from the ash lingering on and around her. Didn't Jessica have relatives or friends to call?

"You shouldn't be by yourself."

Jessica wiped her face. "I'm working it out."

"Are you okay?"

Jessica's bottom lip quivered. "She's come back."

Sorrow, like Tess had never experienced, made her belly heavy.

"Yeah, she's here." Jessica turned toward the stairwell. She wiped tears from both of her cheeks. "Did you still want to try?"

Tess peered ahead to try and see the ghost, certain that if she saw anything it would only be a hint of it.

Right there.

If she focused her eyes, Tess could see it. With muddy, bare feet, and in a dress or a kind of nightgown, the ghost walked up the steps, weeping. Disappearing and reappearing, the image, frizzy hair, and all, headed up the stairs.

"Grandma Poe, Grandma," Jessica whispered.

Tess's stomach strained like she had been working out for the past hour.

"She's worse this time." Jessica patted the couch, kicked her legs out in front of her. "She's a lot worse."

The ghost got to the top of the stairs and stepped out of sight. The click from it twisting the doorknob, the creak of a door being pushed open. Tess's mouth went dry.

"She's in my room." Jessica stood. "Let's go."

"Why the hell…?"

"We're feeling what she's feeling. If she senses people, it makes her feel better."

Tess shooed her. "*You* go."

"Come on, you have to try. How you feel right now, it doesn't *all* go away."

"What do you mean?"

"If she leaves while feeling like this, we might feel this way until she comes back. The house is contagious. My dad carried what he felt from this house to the motel where he shot himself. Didn't even know he owned a gun. Please. Try."

Tess lifted her foot and set it down, the first step to helping Jessica. A few steps later she found herself leaning on the wall as she made her way up the stairwell. Jessica followed, head down, hands clasped.

Upstairs, at the threshold of the bedroom, Tess stopped.

Jessica went around her, crossed into the bedroom first.

Tess, not even a foot behind her, peeked over Jessica's shoulder. The ghost, around Tess's age, sat on a rather long windowsill, arms cut to shreds and bleeding. A scream started from Tess's heart, and then up to her esophagus, but stopped right there. The reactionary part of herself had been cut off. The distance between her and the moment, at first it was noticeable, but now it seemed as if she had been reinserted with a different skin, from a different place in the spectrum of anger and sadness and anxiousness.

The ghost screamed.

Tess's hands tightened into fists, as a rage like she had never had draped over her. The ghost wept. Tess felt the weight of the sadness and anger it carried, that she herself now carried.

Ghosts were real.

Ghosts had control.

"What's her name, again?" Tess asked Jessica.

"Zarieanna."

Tess gathered all the courage she thought she should have and raised her voice. "Zarieanna."

Zarieanna backed against the windowsill, looked out the window.

"She can't hear me," Tess said, smacking her hands together. She had become so upset that she felt a fever wash over her. She trembled.

For a moment they watched the weeping ghost bleed onto the wide windowsill. It's as if she was in the room, until Tess moved, causing Zarieanna to disappear. Zarieanna seemed to sit between slats in the blinds of reality.

"Quick." Jessica tapped Tess on the arm. "Come with me, come with me." Jessica pulled Tess by the wrist. "Hurry up, come on."

Not ready to hurry, Tess yanked her arm away.

Jessica planted her feet on the carpet. "Outside, so she can see us."

Jessica bolted from the room.

Tess ran behind her.

So many thoughts and impulses shot through Tess's head, it was as if her body did things on its own. At the bottom of the stairs, she had an impulse to find a knife in the drawer closest to the sink and stab herself in the chest with it. An urge to shove Jessica, to hit her across the face. A character in her head shouted her real name. *Tesla. Tesla.*

That's me, she thought.

Outside, she stopped next to Jessica. The streetlight across the street shined on the upstairs window. The bedroom light was on, obscured by the ghost. Although Tess saw the ghost flickering when they were inside and going up the stairs, she could see it clearly right now. Jessica pointed at it, making certain she and Tess were both seeing it. Perhaps anyone could see it.

Zarieanna stared down from the bedroom, not focused on them, just gazing downward.

"Come on," Jessica pleaded to it. "See us. Come on. Please feel safe, please feel safe, please feel safe."

Zarieanna tilted her head to the side, acknowledging their presence. She waved them up with a head nod.

If going back up those stairs and standing in front of Zarieanna made Zarieanna feel better than that's what had to happen. Knowing that didn't stop a narrative voice from being the skeptic. *More than the sum of her parts, she stood for the only thing to stand for: herself. In the face of fear, she'd stand for herself. The enemy is a ghost from the past. The enemy is a ghost. The enemy is the past.*

The tension in Tess's stomach wouldn't let up. The thought to grab a knife became more detailed. She pictured herself on one knee, plunging a steak knife half into her chest. They needed to make sure the ghost felt better.

"I'm coming up with you," Tess said.

"You're not like the guy you're looking for?"

Tess shook her head, caught herself biting her bottom lip. "I'm nothing like him. Basically, nothing."

The Murderer

The first time I drove a car by myself, I almost hit a little boy on a bike. I screamed with my eyes closed as I mashed on the brakes trying to avoid him. I stopped but hit something. Going as fast as I was in that residential neighborhood, I thought I had killed him. Massive worry and guilt smacked me before I made it out of the car. Come to find out, he had ghosted his bike in front of me, in an attempt to not get hit. His bike, all I had hit, was mangled under my right tire. This house has gifted me the same kind of burst of guilt and worry from that moment. My gut knows the house is causing it. I should have told Roger to go across the street where it's much safer. Instead, he's right outside the fence, probably contemplating eating me.

In the middle of the living room, the negativity is something physical. You look for it, like it's going to leap out from somewhere. For me, it ebbs, goes away as I hold my breath. It goes away. It's like I was sick and got better.

I scan the area for what I'm going to draw. They have individual photos of their faces lined up horizontally on the wall leading into the house. Father, mother, daughter, younger daughter, all of them so gorgeous, you'd think they'd taken this picture in heaven after they died, they all look so damned happy and dream-like. At the wooden dining room table, the chairs are pushed in, plates, knives, forks, and spoons in the correct places. It's not a large home. It's average and cozy.

Something is *so* wrong. A wave of negativity climbs into me. I take several breaths to wait it out. It's not long before I'm well again. It leaves residue behind. For that brief moment, for no reason, I thought of harming myself, cutting myself specifically. That's what was in me seconds ago? Shit. I'm going to run into someone who's going to need me. Roger is right. I need to push through at some point. It doesn't matter what I think or feel about it.

Sketching starts off pretty rough, despite the subject matter being clear. There's smeared blood on the tile floor of the kitchen. Do I need to draw that? I didn't in Roger's place. The kitchen is all smooth corners on the counter and cabinets. Droplets of blood are splashed in the sink. I pause. Someone washed their bloody hands in it. I exit the kitchen, step into the living room, and enter the hallway. Someone will be in one of these rooms, dead or alive.

The first door is on the right, ajar. I push it open, then feel myself leap with my heart. Two people are in here. A naked, middle aged man lies on the floor next to the bed with his neck slashed. Probably the father. It's most likely his wife face-down on the far side of the bed in a T-shirt and panties. I walk in a few steps, see her hanging off. I'm not looking for proof her neck is slashed, as well. I have faith it is.

It's best to wait, to see if they wake up, to see if one of them is the ghost I'm looking for.

Should I be drawing this? At least one of the two kids must be wandering around; somebody needs to be the main character in this scene. With Roger, and with the attic people, there was a buffer period, a transition between cycles. Either somebody is at rest right now or it's the middle of the cycle. I don't need to go down the hall and see any more violence than I need to. Whomever I can get out of here, they'll come to me.

A door slams shut somewhere beyond the dining and living room. Not an angry slam. Someone let the screen door close behind them. I focus my sights across the dining and living room and wait for whomever to step from around the corner near the staircase. Can't see them yet, though I hear them dragging their feet across the carpet.

When they're in front of me, I'll say hello. I'll ask if they know they're dead.

A young woman about my age appears in a cream-shaded nightgown with short sleeves. She's my height, kind of athletic, looking angry as hell. The dirt on her feet makes me nervous. The closer she gets, the angrier I feel. She gets closer and I'm more anxious, so anxious and upset I tremble. It's not the house influencing me. It's her. She's the sickness.

She sees me and stops.

"Hello," I say as calm as I can.

"Are you…Katy?"

"I, well, I am her. Who are *you*?" Do I recognize this person? I scan the room again. Nothing is familiar.

"Zarieanna," she says.

The light pulsing through me is the cure, brings the aftermath of levity. I can do this. I can help this person.

"He said you'd come for me," she says.

"Who is *he*?"

She straightens herself. "Your dad."

"Really?" I scan her up and down. How is she mentioning my dad? "Who do you think is my dad?"

Keeping her eyes on me, she stomps to the kitchen sink, her hands curl into fists, she's so ticked off. She tosses things, screams like a baby being pinched. She throws a few pieces of silverware from the dish rack against the far wall. She reaches into the drawer and pulls out a small knife. She glances at it. Her body goes quiet. "I first thought I'd stab myself in front of him and his family," she says.

She flips the knife the opposite way, so the point is upside down. With that point is how she slices herself, starting from her wrists. It's not trying to kill herself. It's self-mutilation. I close my eyes. Why watch? Not watching doesn't stop my ears from hearing her hiss through her teeth. The hissing morphs into near breathless squeals.

"Stop it!" I shout and open my eyes.

"He said you'd rescue me." She scrapes her arms like she's whittling wood. It makes no sense, makes zero sense.

She screams and stomps, turns in circles, shocked at the blood.

I turn my back on her, as to not be a witness to the cuts and bleeding. She stomps to the kitchen sink and turns the faucet on full blast.

If you heard what she's doing, you'd need to step away from it. I do that and find myself again close to the heavenly family graduation headshots. She's not in any of the photos. No matter how I try to twist my mind into believing it's her face on the wall, none of them are her. It's not only that she's older than the girls in the picture, she has a different nose and forehead, too.

What was she doing outside, barefoot?

It means, there are still two daughters to find.

I backpedal a few steps toward the front door.

She pushes a scream through gnashed teeth. Rocks grind at my spine. My pen doesn't move. The water runs over her arms. Steam lifts from the sink, as she continues to angrily slice herself, not because of me. She's no different than Roger in his cycle before I freed him. It's not my job to rescue her, because did she kill these people? I could have it wrong. I head outside, the way she entered. What was she doing out there? I do need to see more violence. I have to know, not assume, but know this person is a piece of shit.

Did Roger deserve rescuing?

Did the dude in the driveway deserve it?

Could the woman in the attic have saved her child by giving the men what they wanted?

Did any of them deserve rescuing?

I open the screen door, step out into the last of the evening. The older girl from the wall photo, she's out here naked. Her throat is cut like her father's. Near the fence are discarded jeans and another clothing item, along with tennis shoes. The woman inside is wearing this naked girl's clothing. I laugh because light inside of me shines on my brain right now, like sunlight on the idea of this moment.

I back into the house in enough time to see the murderer start up the stairs. If I follow her, she might have something to say about my dad. That's the thing, she knows my dad.

I lose sight of her upstairs as she enters the first room on the left.

This murderer sits on the windowsill across the room, looking relaxed, content with what she's done, as well as her death. "How long are you going to not help?" she asks. Her words are snide and rude, and she knows it.

"Did you kill the family?"

"I murdered the *entire* family. Your father promised you'd help."

She bleeds all over her feet, all over the floor, down her arms, all over the bottom of her nightgown. She looks out the closed window and kind of hangs her head. She nods to somebody or something.

"I never promised," I tell her.

"It's not as if I don't have a story."

What kind of story justifies killing a family?"

"He promised."

"And?"

She scoffs. "I was fifteen when I met this man. I didn't know he had a family. Twice my age. More than that. I had sent a silly love letter out to the world. Through the post office. In no way expecting it to get to anybody. Unless it was my true love. Didn't even use an address. Destiny would bring us together. I stamped it. Perfumed it. He said he knew someone who worked at the post office. That's how he got it."

She rolls her head. A far calmer person when she has far less blood. "He mailed a letter back to me. Can you imagine that? I'm looking for the love of my life and get a response, at fifteen. I had to have an abortion. My mom didn't know anything about it, friends didn't know, and then in not too long I didn't have friends. Too embarrassed to stay in school. Stopped going."

The weight of her anger presses down from the ceiling.

"Six, seven years later, I was pregnant again and keeping it. Because *fuck* him and it's my child. *Fuck. Him.* It's my child."

A wave of anger departs and is replaced by a wave of paralyzing sadness and confusion.

She says, "We met for lunch on a Saturday. He poisoned my drink. I know he did. It made me vomit. He killed my child."

This can't be all true.

Her words slur. "I got a key to his house. I didn't intend to do any of this." Her eyes close. "When I saw his daughter, I got so livid I put a hammer to her head, and then I—"

"*Shut* up." I turn my back on her, head down the stairs, and hurry to go find Roger outside.

Tess and Jessica briskly made their way up the stairs in the hopes that Zarieanna would feel their presence and release them from her emotional disposition. They crossed into Jessica's room to see Zarieanna on the edge of the windowsill dripping blood from her arms, off her fingers and onto the floor near her feet. She spoke to herself aloud, as if in front of an open mic audience.

"She's never done this before," Jessica said. "She doesn't talk like this."

Zarieanna spoke about sending a letter despite not attaching an address. That letter not only reached someone special to her, but it was someone who she had never met. The person who responded had discovered it because of his friend who worked at the post office. A bizarre story to tell, because of how sincerely she told it. "Six, seven years later," Zarieanna continued, "I was pregnant again and keeping it. Because *fuck* him and it's my child. *Fuck. Him.* It's my child." She sat there for a second, idling. "We met for lunch on a Saturday. He poisoned my drink. I know he did. It made me vomit. He killed my child."

"Who's she talking to?" Tess asked.

"Us, I think. There's nobody else to listen to her. Nobody except us."

"I got a key to his house..." Zarieanna appeared diminished, while slouching and fading. "I didn't intend to do any of this. When I saw his daughter, I got so livid, I put a hammer to her head. I—"

"*Shut* up!" came a distant shout.

"Did you hear that?" Tess slapped Jessica on the arm.

"Oh my god, I did."

"Was it there before?"

"Never heard it."

It might have been that she wanted the voice to be Katy, but didn't it sound like her? Katy was alive on the other side? She was alive.

When Tess stepped to the side, Zarieanna dissipated into oblivion. Tess shuffled back to her original position and from this slight change of view it was revealed that Zarieanna hadn't gone anywhere. Tess thought she could walk over and touch her.

Zarieanna eyeballed the room. "I smashed the younger girl in the head with a hammer in her sleep. She was awake. I meant to knock her out. She would have been the same age as my first child, the one I didn't have. It was the second blow that did it." Her eyes lifted, as she searched the room again. "Are you guys there? I believe you're there."

"She disappears in a minute," Jessica said, backing to the door.

"After that…"

"Sh— Sh— She comes back another day, tomorrow," Jessica said, "the day after, whenever, like this. She comes back like this."

The despair hanging in the air had not subsided. Tess waited for what the relief would feel like. She had convincing thoughts of going to the kitchen drawer, opening it, getting a knife, and harming herself.

Zarieanna straightened herself, patted herself down, barefoot in the small puddle of blood. "You're there. Thank you. I didn't mean to kill them. I'm no murderer. That's how it happened. I left his kid's room, walked down the hall, and sneaked into his room, saw the blade on his dresser, stabbed him in the throat with it. Slashed his neck right where he slept. His ugly wife opened her eyes, so I had to cut her throat. I had to. You can't kill a family and keep yours. I'm not a murderer. The rest of his family didn't have anything to do with his actions. I think that's why I can't leave. I should have only killed him. That's my regret."

Zarieanna faded, a fast fade like the bulb to a hologram blew out.

Jessica stomped down the stairs, as if trying to kick through each step.

Tess lingered in the room, shuffled to the left trying to get a different view of where Zarieanna had been, making sure the ghost had left. Zarieanna's emotions had become deeper and more negative than before. If Zarieanna believed what had happened to her was true, nothing else mattered. Speaking about it hadn't helped. In fact, Tess knew for certain she would hurt herself once she got down to the kitchen; she suffered from the thoughts of someone angry enough to murder a family and then kill herself.

Tess stomped down those stairs.

She found Jessica in the kitchen already sawing herself open at her wrists with a steak knife she found in that kitchen drawer—her eyes wide, tears streaming, small spurts of sounds escaping through her grinding teeth. Jessica must have been like her, in control, but with almost no choice. It made more sense to reach into the drawer and get a knife than to escape the moment, for some reason. She joined Jessica in the kitchen, grabbed a knife from that same drawer and followed Jessica's lead.

Wordless, yet deep inside Tess's gut, Zarieanna's thoughts let her know that nobody had ever loved her. The tax of needing to earn absolutely everything you deserve from people who have nothing to offer, is useless and helpless, until you give up and send the last of whatever remains of the love you have into the universe, in the form of a love letter. You write down the way to express that love, fold it and place it in a sealed envelope.

What if someone finds the letter and they discover you? a character in her head said. *Love has no eyes or ears; it can't see or hear me, but it can seek and find me.*

Disappointed she would never leave the house, Tess screamed, as she scraped away at her flesh.

Road to Mother

Roger waits for me outside Zarieanna's gate, his body language like I owe him a hit of meth. "What happened? In there forever."

"She murdered the family," I say.

"Who did?"

"Whoever is in there." I swipe at the air, demanding him to get the hell out of my way.

"Are you okay?"

Examining him, he doesn't actually care if I'm doing well. "What are you talking about?"

"Come on, is she like me? She's all messed up in the head? You going to leave her in there?"

"It's different." Why can't he shut up after I told him I saw a family had been killed? How did this become about him?

He moves out of the way, while backpedaling in my path. "You get to pick and choose who suffers?"

"I'm not picking or choosing anything."

"You're going to help them?"

"She slashed everyone's throat. She earned that shithole she's in, might as well have built it herself."

"Screwed up," he says.

"I'm screwed up? Roger, she's already dead."

"So was I."

"You didn't murder a family."

"I sold some toxic shit to a lot of people, kids younger than me."

His nobody-is-innocent talk, I don't want to hear it, even if I agree. "You're not thinking straight. We'll pick this up away from this house. It messes with our heads."

He stops and steps to the side. "I think clearer closer to it. The anger clears my head."

A few feet in front of him and it already feels weird to not have him following me. "Are you coming?"

"You have nothing better to do but help out people like me and whoever is in there."

I could do what he suggests or find my dad in Sunderland. My dad will have answers. We used to go there for their anniversary, right there near the docks at Rowe Park. "I know where I'm going."

He purses his lips, hangs his head to the side. "You might think it's horrible. The house calms me down."

"What are you suggesting?"

He takes a few long strides toward Zarieanna's home. "Me and you can kick out the ghost, do for it like you did for me, send it on her way, and then me and you can be like before I died. Maybe like before you left to school."

"Oh, Roger. Roger, that's not worth a thought right now. No."

He grabs his side as if somebody punched him in the kidney.

"What do you want me to say?" I say, finding myself tapping my chest with my index finger. "What the hell do you want? From this point forward, before you say something lame, remember I don't owe you anything."

He rubs the stubs of hair on his chin. He measures his glare while scanning me up and down. Finally, eye to eye, I hear mental echoes of him implying how he wanted to murder me. It's me and him on the sidewalk less than an arm's length apart. He threatened to want to murder me. I take a large step backward. Maybe it's leftover negative thoughts from the house, but Roger is dangerous. I don't know what I am, but I'm having a harder time recognizing what kind of creature is standing in front of me. He wants me to free someone who is more like him. He likes the clarity of his anger, of her anger.

"I'm not trying to get her out of there," I say. "You can try."

His brows scrunch together. "Will that work?"

"I don't think so. Go ahead and try." He has no idea what it feels like in Zarieanna's house. Outside is one thing. Inside is a sort of internal beast. I'm almost certain I had an easier time in there because—I need to accept this—I'm not like other people who have died. I have the privilege of being made from clay. In this world, I quickly heal, physically and mentally.

"I'd never want to hurt you," he says.

What he said doesn't match his facial expression or body language. He didn't say he *wouldn't* hurt me. He said he wouldn't *want* to. He's lying to himself or to me.

I clutch my notebook, feel the bulk of the pen near its spine. "What if I come back for you?"

"You said a woman in that house killed the whole family?"

"I don't think she'll hurt you." I might have lied right now. She could indirectly hurt him, like she might be doing as we speak.

"No, it's fine." He inches toward Zarieanna's house. "How old is she?"

"Not much older than us."

"She's probably pretty strong, yeah? In shape?"

"I don't…" He's doing everything except asking if she's got a boyfriend.

"She's already dead. You're not freeing her, so you don't care what I do to her. I'll figure it out."

The guy in the drive-by didn't do as much as notice Roger's existence. "She might not know you're there."

"As if you care." His tongue hangs at the side of his mouth. There's something inside of him he's hiding below the surface.

"This is it? This is what you're doing?"

"It's time I explored some stuff."

"Just because there aren't any consequences, it doesn't mean you can do whatever you want," I say.

"I'm pretty sure that after you've died, you can do whatever the hell you want. There are some things I want to do that you won't like."

He winks, an awkward signal on some foreign frequency I don't understand.

There's no point in keeping him around. I step in the direction of Sunderland.

He offers a hug. As awkward as it is, I give him one. My face rubs against his. It's like saying farewell to a big brother or a cousin, or an illegitimate uncle who molested other family members. There's something sinister about Roger. I'm leaving him behind again when he's at his lowest, at his worst, when I'm the one who can help him. I'll be back. That's the point, I'll be back.

"How are you going to do it?" I say, releasing him. He can't draw, which is how you do things around these parts.

"If she recognizes me or sees me, notices me at all, I guess I'll introduce myself. If she gets aggressive, I don't have a problem getting aggressive back."

"That doesn't sound like a rescue."

Roger bats his eyelids. "When you come back, you'll find out."

It's horrible how snide he is about it.

"I'll be back," I tell him.

He turns his head to the side and backs away. "You do whatever you're going to do."

I wipe my hands off on my shorts. Dad said stay on Thirteenth as long as I can. If I'm lucky, it's my mom who he means for me to run into on my way to Sunderland. It makes sense. We were all there for all those vacations.

Roger turns his back on me, eager to be in that house. Too eager.

I see him walk into Zarieanna's yard.

I'll be back.

Up ahead, there's a pack of people. No way I'm trying to go around them. Whatever horror that's about to happen up ahead, they can do it without me. Long before getting to the end of the street where the crowd is starting to yell, I slip through someone's side yard gate, stroll across their brittle grass on my way past their brick home. Looking back the way I came—the concrete patio and the yellowing of the lawn in this backyard reminds me of my old backyard. My dad tried to play catch with me one day in our backyard. I didn't know how to wear a baseball glove and neither did he. Neither of us could throw very well. I got frustrated, he got frustrated. Mom came out and she got frustrated. Nobody could throw a ball. That life feels so long ago.

It wasn't.

I cross the yard and struggle to scale an awkwardly bent chest-high, chain-link fence. Flopping over it, I roll my ankle. It means I'm staggering to the middle of a gravel and dirt-covered alley. At either end of the alley is a quiet neighborhood street.

I reach over and unlatch the wooden gate to the backyard at the right of me. Inside, the lawn isn't mowed. Strands of grass rise above my ankles. Overalls drape over a rusty clothesline. It's the 21st century. Who is still using clotheslines? Seriously, who is wearing overalls?

The back door is open. Not only unlocked, but open.

I stop. Chances are I find somebody dead inside or about to be killed. If I'm lucky they're not hidden somewhere in this messy kitchen. Egg shells sit in the sink. A pot of water sits on the stove. Smells like bacon. A plate with a few strips of the bacon I smell, and a good amount of grease, sits to the left of the sink. I snag a strip, not because I'm hungry. From what I can tell, I don't do hunger on this side. I don't do sleep. I don't do being injured. I have a piece of bacon because I like bacon fat. Whenever I want bacon, I can come here to get it. If I want it to be hot outside, I can go to where it's hot outside. Could be a block away. If I want it to be raining, I'm sure I can find some rain. It's not all bad.

As quiet as possible, I head out the back door, out the back gate. I jog to the end of the alley and exit onto a sidewalk. Images of my old yard and my family drift by attached to the wind. I don't remember my parents arguing, until she got sick. Only, she didn't get sick. Her clay hardened, is what the truth is. Her clay matured. This life I'm in, I should say past life I'm in, has no guidelines or directions, zero structure. There's no government or group of friends to lean on. There're no opinions to maintain. The challenge is to just be.

On the corner, a woman closer to ancient than old exits the house behind me and sits on the porch swing. She waves. I wave back.

"Beautiful evening," she says. Her curly, gray hair contrasts the gray paint of the swing. The brown splotches on her face are easy to see even from where I stand.

"Do you even know if you're dead or not?" I ask.

"Come again."

"Nothing."

The area doesn't look familiar. I've never stepped foot on this street.

"Are you lost?" She sounds concerned. "Where are you from?"

"Am I in the same state? What state am I in?"

"I'd say the state of confusion. Where'd you come from?"

I wave goodbye to the old lady. The last thing I need is to answer a list of questions.

She waves back, the concern still on her face. She stands, pudgy like a pear in running shoes, although she probably never ran in that faded, green, knitted sweater. With each step towards me, she gets a little taller, a little thinner. A few steps away, her wrinkles are gone, she's a full head taller than I am and not old anymore.

Before I can run, she grabs my arm and squeezes. "Why're you doing this?"

"Let go!"

Something bulges from underneath her sweater. What caused the bulge grows from underneath the throat area of her sweater. A chunk of something soft yet firm, pinkish and blue with creases like scales, only much deeper. That chunk of something thins and stretches, widens around my face, now mere inches from it. The chunk becomes the shape of a hand, a palm that squeezes my face, slender fingers at my temples. Darkness and the smell of dirt press against my nose and cheeks, presses against my mouth. She squeezes with this third hand, shoves my head back and tosses it away from her.

She says, "Do you know what she's going through? You announce yourself like that? How'd you get out?"

"I…"

She shoves me away by my shoulders, makes me stumble backward off the curb. This woman's layered curls are unprecedentedly large and round, like stacked hoop earrings. A wide nose and three arms, one of them grown out of her chest. Her chest hand rests on her stomach, like the hands resting on her hips.

"You're like me." I gasp. How can she not be made from clay? Can I manipulate my body like she does?

"I'm not like you." She dips her head and glares. "They manage to pull you out. They don't tell you what happens next. They don't know or care. This isn't a second chance or something new. I'm nothing like you."

"I don't—"

The hand at the end of that third arm folds into a fist that might hit me. She's athletic. I've never been in a fight. Know nothing about it, though if she hits me first, I don't know what's going to happen to me.

So, I swing at her.

With an open palm.

She steps to the side.

I graze the bottom of her jaw.

She lifts me straight up with that chest arm, and then releases me into her two normal ones, before slamming me to the concrete. She stands overhead like she might spit on me, like she might kick me. There's no respect lost.

"I'm sorry," she says. "I don't give a rip what you've been through. You swing on me and I can destroy you."

The thing is you don't get over the arm that's grown out of her chest. She's not old anymore, only wearing old people clothes that are too small.

"You're a ghost," she says. "Respect other ghosts."

"I'm not a ghost."

She wanders off the curb, giving me a chance to stand, to explain myself. I'm not sure what to say. She circles me, sizes me up. She's waiting. She's taller than I am, stronger than I am, has an extra arm, and is probably going to beat my ass with it. To defend myself, all I have is a sketchbook in my waistband with a pen. Coming full circle, she steps up the curb.

She examines my face, my body language. "You're not a ghost?"

"I'm not dead." I pull my hair into a tighter ponytail, for no other reason than to keep moving all this nervous energy.

"How did you come to be here?"

"My clay hardened. This is where I wound up, looking for my mom."

She flicks all three wrists at me and turns her head to the side, like get this shit out of my face. She swings her head back my direction, letting her eyes bear down on me. "Your clay hardened?" she says. "Looking for your mommy. Looking for…your *mommy*?"

One of the most intimidating things you will ever see is an angry, shapeshifting, clay woman with a third arm who thinks you're lying.

"I think I am," I tell her.

"You *think*."

"I don't know what she looks like."

She throws her hands in the air. "You're not trying to be rude. You're actually stupid."

"My mother is Arcilla. I'm like her. I'm like you."

She winces, closes her eyes, and holds one hand in the air, like, wait. "Arcilla? Your mother is Arcilla?"

"Oh, my god, yes."

That's not shock draped all over her. It's recognition.

"I can't think of any reason to lie," I say.

She nods. "You can't remember her."

"Like, it's a thing."

She grimaces and cups her face. She stands there for a second, pondering. More importantly, it's clear she's not going to kick my ass.

"I'm sorry," she says. "Ghosts come in all types and can be horrible. Truly horrible."

"I'm not a ghost."

The clay person steps right next to me. "Your name is…"

"Katy." Then I wait for a verdict.

She places her chin hand on my shoulder. "They can be hateful. And rude. Ms. Katy, of course you don't remember her face." She laughs, placing all three hands on her hips. "Damn, of course you don't remember."

If someone offered me twenty dollars to tell them who is on a twenty-dollar bill, they'd owe me twenty dollars. To this day, I can identify the dog my dad brought home for me over a decade ago. We only had it for a few weeks. Too aggressive. I can name lists of people from my senior year high school yearbook by their black-and-white photos. I cannot remember what my mom looks like. I can recite the pledge of allegiance upon request. Most songs on the radio, I can remember their hooks and the bands that perform those songs. But I can't remember my mom's face.

"Wait here." The woman disappears inside the house. Moments later, she's back swinging car keys on the end of her third index finger. She drags her feet past me. "Come on."

The woman stops and stands at the driver's side door, fondling the keys. She unlocks the door, opens it, leans over the passenger seat, and unlocks the passenger door. "You were shaped on the other side," she says sitting upright in her seat. "You seem lost on this side. I've only met one other person like you. You say you're that person's daughter.

If you'll let me, I think I can introduce you to her and others. We'd all love to hear from you."

"You're not going to beat my ass?"

"Katy, I'm Bernadette. It's nice to meet you. I mean that from the bottom of my heart. The *bottom* of my heart."

"Okay."

"You're suddenly shy?"

"I don't know what's going on."

"If you're who you say you are, we're going to treat you that way. We're going to pretend as if we're showing you the way home. Arcilla's daughter. She still talks about you."

You don't know how lost you've been until you've been found. Going home is both concrete and relative, especially when you don't know or remember where it is. Where am I going?

After all of this is done, if Bernadette gets me to my mom—because I've been found—then me, my dad, and my mom can be together again in Sunderland. I don't remember it being that great when we were together. Still, we were together. The fact is that when we do come together, we'll have a lot to think and talk about. Surely, my dad wants me to find my mom. That has to be the case. Although I went off course, he means for me to find my mother, doesn't he?

Doesn't he?

I can grow now, with people who really know me. Isn't that the case? Up to this point I've always been, at best, a student or in a role to be told what to do. Bernadette said they'd appreciate me because of who I am, not because of what they could plant in my head. When was the last time you walked into a room and you knew, for sure knew, people would cherish what you'd say? When was the last time that what you said held more weight for others than it did for yourself?

This time, I'm the satellite moving around her. I'm on the far side of the vehicle, and into the passenger door. It's unlocked. I get in and buckle my belt.

Bernadette is like a cop, how she's focused on the road. I can't stop staring. She can become somebody else entirely. What she is, that's what I can be, minus the chest arm.

"Where is this?" I ask, staring out the window in this indistinct time of day and year. Evening, I'm sure. "What year is it?"

"We came from the 1990's. I believe we're coming up on the 1920's. I know that much."

"You were on my case about being a ghost."

"I was on your case about being rude to other ghosts. They're already in enough pain, you don't need to be rude as well. That's what that was about. You find someone who has been through more pain than they can handle, and you want to talk down. If there is no other reason to judge a person, that would be it."

"So, expectations. Am I supposed to learn how to change the shape of my body?"

"You're talking about me changing from Patricia to myself."

"I'm not sure if I—"

"When I'm not in her world, I'm Bernadette. I'm as you see me now. In the area we left—"

"Her cycle—"

"I'm Patricia. Every three days the body I share—Patricia's— realizes how much she misses her daughter who killed herself. Decades after her daughter's death, she still hadn't come to terms, and then her husband died. That's the idea that got the best of me. Without explaining too much, I do the hard part for her."

I can only guess what the hard part is.

"Everyone I run into has been killed. Or it's suicide," I say. "Or they were murdered."

"This is true. Patricia hung herself."

"Shit. Why is it like that? Why can't I be allowed to come across normal deaths. Ones that aren't from crazy situations. Shoot yourself in the head and do it forever? Why is it like that?"

She taps the wheel with two of her hands. "Don't act like this place is the problem. In your world cancer takes lives. Car accidents take lives. Stabbings kill people. They make food in a way that if you eat enough of it, it kills you. Where you're from, there are places where breathing shortens your life span. Don't blame here on what happens there. You see my world as the afterlife. I've always been here. The only negative things here come from there."

I straighten my back, lift my chin. "If where I'm from isn't more important, then why is it that everything here is based on where I'm from?"

"Am I based on where you're from? Are *you* based on where you're from? You were shaped by someone who came from this side. Nobody from your side does what we do."

Although Bernadette sounds negative about where I came from, she's going out of her way to help me. In her way, she's doing for Patricia what I did for Roger. She won't admit it, but we're alike, for sure.

We pass several antique cars, like Model-T's, parked in the dirt near rundown shacks that might be used as homes. Cracking the window, the scent of pine and morning dew. It's crisp outside. What happened in this beautiful place, this simple place? What tragedy? It's wild that so much of the full moment is missing. Cars should be on the road. I imagine middle-aged men, even back then, working on a few of the cars. It would make the open hood on that vehicle make sense. I can almost see it, kids in that rundown house right there, running around in the living room, brothers chasing each other.

A giggle slips through my teeth.

She does a double take. "What's the deal with you?"

"The light and electricity. You know what I mean?"

My symptoms are available when I'm being creative. It's my creative energy. I can use let this energy move through me when I draw. My dad gave me a notebook to help me practice. When I think of it, my sketchbook is like a wand to a wizard. Or, in my world, a pen to an artist. It's all magic, the same feeling. A symptom over there, a tool over here. It's only now that I can see an opportunity to accept it. My skull is hot with light, makes me stronger, more powerful. Confident. I take out my sketchbook, examine the page, stare at it. By the time I lift my head, the sky is dark, and the windshield is berated by rain. Where we came from stays fresh in my head and immovable, so I'm drawing it, the old cars, the trees. My fingers race each other down the page, pen in hand, scratching out the inspired recent past in a little sketch, a detailed little sketch.

Bernadette glances at what I've done. "You did that?"

I part my lips to say something. A cackle slips out.

She looks at me with a question pulling her face down.

I ask, "Are you more an older lady or younger, tall and athletic?"

"Why can't I be all of them?"

Damn. Okay. She can be all of them. Can I be human and from Clay? Why can't I be both?

The rocks that are my spine, they grind. The light in my blood, it shines.

"Do you have sunshine in your blood?" I ask.

"What?"

Up ahead, a car is flipped upside down off on the side of the road. Not an antique car, a contemporary one.

I flip the page and begin to draw what I see. It's clear we're looking at half the scene. We don't see everything that's happened, merely the results. The cars that passed them and left them on the road, we're not experiencing. If folks parked and made video for social media, they're not part of it.

"You've seen this before?" I ask her. You can see the crooked streaks of tire across the highway, and then it's clear where their wheels left the highway. They landed upside down, their forward motion stopped by that tree down off the side of the road.

I laugh because the light tickles me from the inside. It's raining sideways.

She slows our vehicle so it's like driving through a zoo.

She points across me with her third arm. "A boy will climb from the passenger seat. He'll stumble into the road, trip, and not get up. Dies before he hits the ground."

"What does he look like?"

Before I'm done saying it, the boy climbs from out of the upside-down passenger side. We can't be more than a few thousand feet away. He stumbles into the road, gathers his footing, and waits for the oncoming vehicle, us, to pass.

"Oh, my shit, stop," I yell. "Slow down, stop, stop, stop!"

Bernadette, you know what she does? She gives me a questioning look, takes her foot off the gas. As I do the roughest drawing of a boy at the side of the road that any paper has ever seen, the real boy takes a step back and waits for us to stop. We pull up to him like we're going to give him money for sex. I roll down my window. The kid is soaked from the rain, and crying, and shaking. He's got nothing to say, standing at my window. He might as well be melting into the puddle he's in, it's raining so much.

"You have to get in." I chuckle, reach into the back to make sure it's unlocked. I draw the backseat he's getting into. I know it's the backseat, although the page might not realize it. The reason he didn't fall and die this time is because I drew him to wait for us. He doesn't know this, Bernadette doesn't know it, and I'm only now really figuring it out.

"Don't go anywhere yet," I tell Bernadette. "We'll get him in. Finishing touches." I don't finish drawing the backseat or him in it. I do finish the door and window back there. I'm drawing him into the vehicle. "Okay, do you mind if we go out and get him?"

The boy says, "My mom is stuck."

"She probably is," I say. The lightning in my brain makes me grin. "She's going to stay stuck, is my guess."

"She's stuck!"

"Get in. We'll go get help."

He steps away from my window. "I better wait here." Bernadette flings her door open, exits the car, slamming her door shut. The whole time, I'm drawing him sitting in the backseat.

"Bernadette, wait!" I hurry out 'cause the boy can't be ready to talk to Bernadette.

He sees her third arm and her awkward, deeply creased skin, and he loses his shit. At first, he jumps back, then he flings his wrists like he's trying to keep his own hand from biting him. Bernadette shouts for him to get in the car. The whole time she has her eyes on the flipped over vehicle.

"No one is alive," I tell him. "And if you stay here, chances are you'll never leave."

Bernadette stomps back around and gets back in, already soaked from the constant rain.

I get back in on the passenger side, hoping the boy will find his way into the backseat.

She lays eyes on what I've drawn. "Can you get the driver out?"

"No."

"Why not?"

"I don't know, not exactly."

She pounds the wheel, seemingly disappointed. Pounds it again.

The boy, he opens the back door and stands there. He yells, all maybe fifteen, soggy years of him. He doesn't sit. He collapses on his side, pulls himself all the way into our car as if he's paraplegic. I get out to shut his door. The drops of rain are brilliant. This is *his* rain. *His* moment. *His* death. With my foot I kick his door shut. When I get into the vehicle, Bernadette rests the sketchbook on the steering wheel.

The boy shakes in the backseat.

She says to me, "No, I'm not like you."

The boy won't stop weeping.

Here's what you don't say to someone coming to terms with their mother being dead: "At least you know what she looks like." They freak out if you say that, I found out.

I guess Bernadette will decide what needs to be said, and what will be done with him. She's the veteran in this thing, been in what I'm going to call his afterlife the longest. Despite her not being the quiet type, we sit in silence, with the ominous, gentle hum of the engine and the distant sound of the tires grinding against the road.

I reach for the radio. Bernadette smacks my hand away.

"Explain it to me," she says.

I have no full explanation for any of this.

We leave the darkened sky behind. All the trees disappear, and the sky is oxygen-blue forever. The plain of yellow grass is forever. I crack my window to let in elements of this new day, the new crisp morning. Chances are we've again traveled to a different place, a different time.

"Can you pull over?" I ask Bernadette.

"Why?"

"Is it fine if I'm tired of moving?" Despite the unknown horror that happened somewhere near us in this new place, I feel more present than in any moment in my world; I—get this—feel more alive. Have you ever taken in so much that you need to stop? You ever been eating a plate of food and decide to stop and taste it? Ever do that? Ever put a book down in the middle of a chapter to think about what you read? No different here. If for not only a minute, I'd like to do nothing else besides sit here. Feel this, see this, and touch this.

"What you did…" She shakes her head, not unlike how people do after being impressed by a magic trick.

She guides us to the shoulder and stops the car. The side of the road is dirt and yellow grass. The boy sits up in the backseat, exits the vehicle. I do what he does. Both of us swish around on the loose dirt and strands of dead grass. All indications are that he has something to say.

"You can't say anything wrong," I let him know. "You can talk to me."

"What is this place?"

"Not sure how to say it. I bet Bernadette has all the words and things."

Bernadette hears her name. She exits the vehicle, strides around to the front, slides her third hand across the hood before continuing around to where we are. "What're we talking about?"

"Are we in another dimension? He wants to know."

"Claudio," he says, patting himself down, my guess, feeling how wet he still is. "My name is Claudio."

"I suppose nobody knows how to explain it." She glances at me. "I'll tell you what's going on, don't mean to sound cruel by any means. You died with your mother on the side of the road years ago. Claudio. That's what happened. Can't explain it. I'm sure you have questions about my appearance. I can't explain myself or my appearance any more than you can explain *yourself*. The difference? Folks like me are from the Earth. Ghosts like you merely spent your whole life dying there. I'm sorry if I can't make myself more clear."

He responds, "I'm a ghost?"

She says, "I'm sure that eventually someone would come across your flipped vehicle and swear they'd heard the screeching of your car tires, maybe heard you scream." She backtracked the way she came. "You don't think somebody has seen a boy stumble into the road and disappear? That's what you are." She stops at the driver's side door, gazes over it. "You're a glimpse." She gets back in the car.

He looks out at the countryside or whatever he thinks that vast amount of space is out there. "I don't know where we are," he says.

"Neither do I," I tell him. "Hey, you knew you were already dead, right? This isn't complete news?"

He glances over his shoulder, probably looking back for his mother. If he was much older, he might be happy it had all ended. If he were much older, maybe with an illness—he'd have already been thinking about dying for a long time. Claudio lost everything in the blink of an eye. His stringy, jet-black hair falls over his ears, tumbles down his back like strips of oil.

"Listen." I glance in the car and Bernadette is relaxing, at least for the time being. I turn to him, reach over, and nudge his elbow. "Do you mind if I ask what happened?"

It could be different for him, if he said aloud how he lost his life, if he kind of recapped it and made sure he believed it. That's the key to everything. Believe it and move on. There's no reason to defend whatever happened, no reason to understand it. Believe it and go forward. It's the one thing I had going for me when I arrived.

I believe in my life.

He rubs his arms. "We take an annual trip."

"Claudio. Tell the truth." Inside the vehicle, Bernadette's brows dip in a V, she's so ready to go. "Go ahead."

"We take this annual trip. I didn't want to go," he says, beginning to hyperventilate. "I climbed in the backseat. I didn't want to be in the front with her. I didn't need that shit!" he blurts. "I kicked her seat."

"Did you kick it, or did you keep kicking it?" I ask.

"She yanked the wheel really hard. Couldn't control it. The car flipped. I killed us. I guess, I killed us."

He kicks the ground, exhales through his nose. His knees knock together. His hands clasped, hair wet, and the rest of him much soggier than I am.

"It's not like you're alone," I tell him. "Listen. Real quick. I'm new here, too. There's a learning curve. I'm learning that what you need to pay attention to are things you'd normally not pay so close attention to. Like this sky. Like how quiet it is. Like how you haven't lost that much."

For a minute we look up at the sky. If I had the ability to draw a sky into existence, I'd draw *this* sky. *This* one.

He faces where we came from. "If I go back will she be there?"

"It's up to you if you want to go find out."

"How far is it?"

"You got in the car at the same place where we picked you up."

Bernadette honks.

I slap my leg. "Time to go."

"Does it keep happening?" he asks.

"Does what keep happening?"

"My mom crashing the car with us in it. Is it happening right now?"

"I bet it is."

"I need to go back."

"Not going to stop you," I say. "You want to try to stop her from crashing? Let's say you do. You're already dead. That's not going to change."

"I'm here. You're here."

Claudio says something else to me with his eyes, something sad and over the top. It's misplaced. I don't owe him anything.

He turns on his heel, starts that direction, hands in pockets, head down.

I open the passenger door, sit, close the door. "What happens to ghosts who wander?"

Bernadette peeks in the rear-view mirror, sets her third hand on my shoulder. "They move on." She flicks her twelve fingers and three thumbs in the air, as if to say, poof.

"You think he's okay?"

Claudio drags his feet down the road. If he finds his way back to his mother, he'll find her dead. At best, he can slide into that moment and stay like that, I suppose.

She starts the car and accelerates onto the highway. "The worst that can happen to him already has."

Thinking of what Roger might be doing, I doubt what she says is true.

Déjà vu

T hinking this moment had happened before, Tess passed the joint back to Jessica. After a few small drags, she appreciated the head-change. She leaned back, hardly able to see the coffee table between them, it was so full of loose marijuana leaves and ash, not from the current session as much as many recent smoking sessions.

"Have we met before today?" Tess asked.

The place seemed geared to wallow in. It couldn't have been lit any worse.

"How were you going to try and see if you could talk to her?" Jessica's eyes were bloodshot.

"I have no idea. Something doesn't make sense."

Jessica leaned back. "There's no point in always making sense anymore."

Tess didn't know how to go forward. She perceived her upcoming actions as more prophetic than anything. Deja Vu was the most accurate way to think of it.

You're going to die in this house, a narrative voice said inside her ear.

"I don't know jack about haunted anything," Tess said. "Seriously, have we met before?"

"I know we haven't. I think I know what you're talking about though. Are you having something like Deja Vu?"

"Maybe. Or stoned."

Tess's nervousness burst toward the ceiling in the form of laughter. Jessica laughed right along with her.

Tess squirmed in her seat, repositioned herself as a pillar of knowledge compared to the person in front of her. Tess had gotten further along in her education and in life experience than Jessica. It showed. Jessica, a pothead, mostly empty and slow. A good person. Not much going on, anyhow.

"You're in college?" Jessica crossed her legs underneath herself on the couch. "Is it worth it to go?"

"Not if you die in your sophomore year in someone's living room."

"That's not what you said before." Jessica pursed her lips. "You're pretty."

"Thank you." Tess couldn't return the compliment. The girl looked like a fleshy mop. "Before any of this happened to you, I bet you were very pretty. Something definitely happened. I know that much."

They spoke back and forth on simple terms for a while. Tess found herself correctly predicting question after question, letting the idea of the ghost and suicide sit at the back of her mind for the time being. Talking about nothing was doing a lot of good.

"Does college make you smarter?" Jessica asked.

"God, no. It's a whole lot of time to practice and tons of reading."

"I'm not going to make it there anyway." Jessica teared up. "I'm sorry. I feel out of control." Then she whispered, "I might really hurt myself."

Tess knew she was going to do worse than harm herself. Tess would kill herself. She visualized it, had an impulse, a craving. "Is there a steak knife in that drawer?" she asked Jessica.

Jessica gazed at Tess through glassy eyes, as if Tess were a commercial on late night television. "I'm not sure how I know this. We're going to kill ourselves. It's what's going to happen. God *this sucks*. She's back. She's come back." Her bottom lip shook.

Sorrow, like Tess had never experienced, announced itself to her. Regret that made her belly heavy.

"Yeah, she's here." Jessica faced the stairwell, wiped tears from both her cheeks. "She's going up the... Did you still want to try?"

If Tess focused her eyes just right, she could see it. With muddy, bare feet and in a dress, the ghost walked up the steps, weeping. Disappearing and reappearing, the image, frizzy hair, and all, headed up the stairs.

You're going to die in this house.

"We both realize why you know about the knives in the kitchen drawer, right?" Jessica said.

"I don't want to kill myself again."

They made their way up the stairs, found themselves in the bedroom and in front of Zarieanna's bloody self. The ghost screamed and then calmed into a pitiful cry.

A rage came over Tess like she had never had. She felt feverish. This is how the ghost felt.

"What's her name, again?" Tess asked.

"Zarieanna."

"Zarieanna," Tess shouted to the ghost. "Help us! Can you hear me? Help us!"

Zarieanna backed against the ledge of the windowsill, gave all of her attention to whatever was present outside. "I don't make the rules," Zarieanna said.

Tess and Jessica went through the pains of scurrying down the stairs and then going outside to get Zarieanna's attention. The entire time, Tess did nothing but brace herself to take actions beyond her control. Whose rules were these? This is all she had left, all there would be. This is what her parents had gone through, only they did it on fire.

Tesla. Tesla. You're going to die in this house.

"I know," she mumbled a response to her author voice. "I know."

Arcilla

If you use your imagination, you can tell that years and years ago, all along this highway had been nothing but roots and life, stuff from the Earth. You can tell ecosystems had been here, and so much had opportunity to grow. You can tell a great plan took place. You can tell that as a society we started pulling up those roots and had a process to dismantle all this life that was in our way. To do so—I mean look at it—we made permanent marks on the land. Like unpracticed alchemists we twisted the world into something only a few could understand, made a road only a few could build. We haven't been only destroying our world, we've been making something most of us can't imagine. We've been making it unimaginable.

Claudio, in hindsight, he knew he'd rather repeatedly die with his mother than wander along this path into oblivion. It's how myself and Claudio differ. One of us is privileged to at least know what his mother looks like. I wouldn't recognize mine if she stood next to me.

I might know her voice.

My dad counted down the days until he recognized my symptoms. From there he tried to tell me about myself. What he did to me is what older people do to young people all the time. After us young people acknowledge our skills or traits that make us worth something, older adults tell us what to do with our skills, as if we don't already know.

From there, they give us some vague direction of where to go find ourselves. For me, that place was college. Look, you have a skill. Go to this location and draw. Come back and tell us what you drew. My father acknowledged part of my skill. He told me nothing. My mother told me nothing. My destination is Sunderland?

Bernadette has one arm hanging out the window, the other one holding the wheel. Her third hand in her lap.

"Is he still wandering?"

"You're thinking of that boy," she answers.

"His name is Claudio."

"For *Claudio*, it would have been a better decision for you to extract both he and his mother. You said you couldn't do that. Is that still true?"

"I can't. I can't control when I can do it."

"Did you try?"

"It's a feeling I get. It's an energy, like rocks grinding up and down my spine, like sunlight in my blood. The creative energy. I thought we all could do what I did with him."

"No, no. It's not something most of us can do. When he waited for us to pull up, I knew it was your doing. You can't teach that."

"I'm sorry."

"Don't be."

The far-off trees to the side of the road creep closer and the modern road is now smaller with its one lane. We slow and come to a stop. It's dark enough in this night that without the headlights on we wouldn't be able to see anything in front of us. The sky is nothing but flecks of glitter.

She exits the vehicle. "Stay close."

Closing my door, it's so silent out here, air seems to swallow sound. Our headlights pierce the darkness and spread streaks of color in front of us through a thick, woodsy area that's cut the road off. Trees as tall as buildings. Behind us looms the vast highway we've been traveling. The land in front of me didn't merely change time zones, we've advanced through geographies.

"How does this work?" I step closer to the woodsy area. "Can we go around?"

"I'll get you across to where you should go. I've got to head back soon, no real choice in the matter."

"I don't get it."

"I can go wherever I want to go. Doesn't change the fact I hang myself at the same time every third day."

She can skip most of her cycle because she's taken over Patricia. The important stuff still needs to happen. Bernadette hangs for her. She *hangs* for her.

"Maybe I can help. Patricia could wander and disappear like Claudio."

"Maybe if you could learn how to do what you do on call. Come on."

I follow her into the woods. My arms wet from being in the middle of all this cold air. The ground has mini hills to trip on, weeds and bushes pushed up against trees twice as wide as my arms if I stretched my arms out.

How she confidently steps, I can tell she's done this before. "Let's keep moving," she says. "We're not in a hurry. Doesn't mean we should waste time."

The farther in we get, the thinner the streaks of light from the headlights become. So many branches and leaves over us, if it rained, I don't know if we'd get wet.

I trip on one of the largest roots mankind has ever seen. "You can't stop Patricia from hanging herself?" I ask.

"I don't have that ability. Nobody does. It's crazy you do what you do."

The farther we get, the harder my lungs work. "If nobody can do it, how do you know about it?"

"Individuals like your dad free them from the other side. The best we can do for those who aren't freed is sit in their place for a time. Well, that's what I do." She extends her third hand. "Here. Hold my hand. I'll go slow."

I nearly slip but she catches me.

"Then there's you," she says, letting me go.

The darkness is so thick, it's a reminder a part of us is always that child scared of the dark. The headlights are no longer with us, because those lights happened in another day, in another time. For all I know, we're stepping over bodies, walking across graves.

"What happened here?" I expect for her to tell me about a mass murder or to find out animals have partially eaten dozens of people and took days to pick them apart in the dark. Something messed up like that.

"Katy, we're walking through the beginning of a place that's barely been touched."

We smack into a wall of sunlight.

I shield my eyes. "Is this Sunderland?"

"It's not. Come on. I need to introduce you and get back."

"What you're doing for Patricia is as unique as what I do."

"I don't want her to have to do it alone." She jogs ahead. "We're wasting time. Let's jog."

We're still on the road. It no longer has the lines dividing the left and right sides. It's far dirtier, less respectful. I labor to catch up. A few hundred yards in front of us people sit hundreds of feet from each other in this green desert underneath rays of sunlight that extends across a transparent sky; it's all glorious-blue. Layered atop the sky is a perfect, jaw-dropping view of the blackness of space. It's an amazing and obvious layer that stays in your peripheral. To see space sitting on top of daylight makes you jog slower. Hundreds of these people, my people, sit and imitate rocks or other objects and natural things. They look like they're part of the landscape. They're in meditation, in no particular position. A few of them roll around as if leaves in the wind.

The closer we get, the more you can feel a presence. These are the people who want to hear from me.

These are the ones allowed to point to my talent.

They don't know I'm coming, yet want to hear from me, having never met me.

This is where my education begins.

Bernadette stops and sets her third hand on my chest. "Wait here. Don't go anywhere. Wait. Here."

She vigorously claps her hands while walking away from me. She claps with all three hands above her head. At first, I think she's trying to get their attention, which she is, but if you look at how she's doing it, I want to say, joyfully, she's applauding. She applauds them to get their attention. They approach her on this flat land full of crumbling rocks and vast stretches of never-touched sand and dirt. Far behind them, in the way off distance, rests a snow-capped volcano with that never-breathed air of its own atmosphere. See the glorious-blue sky below the perfect blackness of space. As they gather near her, she points in my direction. A few look over. I want to start over to them, which I'm sure is why she told me to wait.

The crowd becomes deep enough—in the dozens—that Bernadette disappears amongst them. Many of them now have their eyes on me. Remember, it's not people I'm looking at. From what I know, none of them have real mothers, none of them have real fathers. They're not educated. They've done no formal schooling, and yet they know everything about this world. I've only known school, and of my world, I know basically nothing.

I hear one loud clap.

Another clap.

The claps multiply until it's an applause. Who knows what to say or do, so I rest one hand on my waist, and I wave. Bernadette said they'd want to speak to me. They also want to applaud me.

Thank you.

Thank you.

As the applause settles, Bernadette, and someone else, heads my direction. The third arm lets me know it's Bernadette. The person to the left of her has a familiar gait. Bernadette said to wait. Whatever, I need to get a closer look. This person calls out to me in my mother's voice. She shouts my name. "Katy!"

I run to her.

She shouts again. It's a voice from the past telling me grades don't matter. It's the voice that shouted for me to not cross the street alone. "Katy!"

"Mom?"

My mother comes for me, guides Bernadette back this direction, back toward Patricia's cycle.

We stop a few feet from one another. My mother is made from clay. I'm learning those who are made of clay have something extra to them. It's no different with my mother. Bernadette, although I thought her third arm was a nice touch, I also thought it equated to a tattoo. It's extra, something to make her stand out clay-person style. My mother has something similar. She looks at me and her face morphs into another face.

"You change your face?"

"I do." She opens her arms. "We'll get to that."

I embrace her. I bet this is why Bernadette believed me. My mother's face is always changing.

My mom smells like something forgotten, like something on the tip of my tongue. I squeeze her, hoping to remember what she looks like. Nothing about her makes me go ah-ha. I still can't picture her face. Her memory is beyond faded.

"I have to get back," Bernadette says. "I'm sorry I didn't know Arcilla was your mother. I'm sorry I didn't treat Katy like your daughter. I have to go."

"I'm sorry you have to go do what you have to do," my mother says to her.

Bernadette jogs back the way we came. I can't imagine not seeing her again.

"You're my mom?"

She has thick eyebrows and a wide nose. Thin lips. Her eyes are beady and black like pellets.

"Is this your face? Where's *your* face?" I plead.

"I decided against that face an awfully long time ago. I don't serve that face anymore."

Sometimes you want to ask the most obvious question, although it'd be insulting. If you're like me, you wait a second and stare at this face. The voice and the face don't match. How does she have the right to take her history from me? Show me your true face!

"Why don't you serve that face?" I ask.

She turns her back on me, and heads off the road, into the desert. "Follow me."

What she had obstructed that I can now see, is almost a hundred clay souls, about fifty yards in front of me. They pay close attention to our conversation. Not willing to turn my back on everyone Bernadette had gathered to applaud me, I stare back.

One of them yells, "Follow your mom, girl!"

I take the advice. By the time I catch up, she's sitting in the grass and weeds and dirt. She tucks her hemp dress underneath her. Her hair is like mine, only shorter, much shorter. It's even more kinky, solid and glistens in the daylight.

Sitting in front of her, again I ask, "Why don't you serve that face?"

She taps her hands on her knees. "It's the face your father helped shape. I'll keep the voice and the body. I've earned the right to not have that face."

"So crazy."

"Isn't it? I see you've happened perfectly. You're wonderful. You're beautiful. You're keen." She smiles and smacks my leg like we're old friends. "You're clever aren't you."

She's always been fun, but at the same time, serious. It's not only her face I've forgotten.

"I don't want to go around telling you things," she says, through an awkward smile. "It must have been a frightening journey to find me. I'll let you talk."

"It's not that I was trying to find you. I mean, I wanted to find you and thought I could. My dad said to go to Sunderland."

"We'll get to your dad."

"Why is Sunderland such a big deal?"

"We'll get to that, too. Right now, I want to hear your voice. I want to hear your stories." She grabs my arm. "I'm so glad you're here."

I don't know what she means by stories. Does she mean experiences? What experiences? Experiences from this side of living? It's weird for her to ask. She must know more about me than I do. She should be giving me context for my experiences, even the ones she doesn't know I had. She was before me. She saw it all happen. She knows what this world is. What is she asking? "I don't know what you mean."

The features of her face dive back into it, like debris sinking into mud. New features rise from it. This new nose is thin with small nostrils. Her brows are thin and arched. Her cheeks are high on her face. "Whatever you want to tell me is fine," she says. "There's nothing I want to do. I'm all about listening."

It's like she's changing her face to try and get certain results from me. What face might I respond to best? What is she trying to get me to say? What am I getting out of this? What if this isn't my mother? Her face is a lie, why can't her voice be a lie? What if I only wanted her gait to look like that of my mother. Do I really remember how she walks? What if I'm lying to myself?

I say, "Can you point me in the direction of Sunderland?"

"We'll get to that."

"We need to get to that soon or right *friggin* now. It would help if you could show me your face. It's your face."

She folds her arms. "I told you—"

"Not to even to prove it's you? I can't remember what you look like. Why can't you show me?"

Her legs are crossed as well as her arms. If I saw her from a distance, I'd think she was meditating. This is not my mother.

"I know we sent you to an elementary school where everyone there had money and we didn't. You didn't complain. You fit right in. When you were small, we straightened your hair. You hated it."

"That's anybody."

"Your favorite flavor of ice cream is chocolate. You loved to run when you were younger."

"That's anybody." I take out my sketchbook. It's bent to the shape of my waist.

Her face sinks into itself so it's a bit concave. An alien before me. Its facial features reemerge into somebody I've never seen.

She says, "When it was time for me to venture off to this world, when the time came, your father, when he could have kept me going, he didn't. I was thrown away. He didn't only help sculpt us. It's love he put into us. He still let us go. I don't need the face that represents his second one." A different face came forward, one full of slits across a wide forehead, a long chin. "I'll use any other face. I don't know if I remember the one you're looking for."

"Why can't I remember the one from when I was a kid? I remember you taking me to school in the morning. Not your face. I remember you laughing. In the basement. All night. You were sick. Don't remember your face. Why is that? It doesn't make sense."

She straightens. "I don't know. When you get to Sunderland, ask him."

"You have to be lying."

"I'm not lying, and I wasn't sick."

"You were sick. You didn't come out of the basement. If you did, sometimes you wandered. You can't pretend like you don't remember. The heart attack."

"Oh, yeah? There was all that."

"It wasn't an easy time."

"I'm glad you see I'm your mother." She pats her chest. "I was never sick. I didn't have a heart attack. You wouldn't believe those things unless you wanted to. You wouldn't forget me unless you wanted to."

"You were *sick*."

"My time was up. It's what it's like when you're about to leave from one side to the other. I often stayed up all night, sometimes standing between these two worlds. In ways, straddling both sides. I was creating, doing things with my hands that I couldn't ignore. No heart attack. I felt amazing. I felt so overwhelmed with joy that your father couldn't handle it, so he kept me in the basement. I moved on as I should have. My clay matured, like yours, and I moved on. Didn't abandon you. When you finally arrived, it was worthy of an ovation."

Okay, the applause was nice. Okay, she had the symptoms like I have. Okay, nobody knows why I can't remember her face. Maybe it doesn't matter.

"I'm not lying to you. I'm not conveniently forgetting things. Some things I don't know. Some things I do. Can't we get to relearn each other? Your little book looks important."

I guess it makes sense she doesn't know everything. Not everyone you need answers from has them, I suppose. Plenty of my teachers have a limited scope and have ways of teaching that reflect it. My mom refuses to have her real face.

I don't have words to explain the sketchbook or myself and its journey to her. I hand it over.

She opens it. "You're good. You've always been good."

"On that page, it's a picture of a friend of mine, Roger. That's him escaping from his cycle."

"What's a cycle, if you don't mind me asking?"

"He's a ghost."

"You freed a ghost?" she says. "You drew about it? That's wonderful."

"Drawing him freed him."

The face she puts on is a long, man's face. Ingrown hairs, a thin mustache.

She cups her man-chin, hunches over. "Katy, do you understand why you don't have early childhood memories? Do you have early childhood memories?"

"I remember Tess. Plenty of people don't have those memories. I guess it's because I was never an infant."

"I was never an infant either. I was never twelve. I was never a teenager. I was never in my early twenties. I'm sorry you don't remember my face. I'm sorry. There are things you don't know, and without some of those things, you can't mature." She holds up my book. "I don't think you're what he thinks you are. Follow me."

I follow her deeper into the desert, farther into the future, into a place I can see but still have a hard time imagining. I follow her farther away from the road, from Thirteenth Street, from all the murders and deaths waiting out there. I follower her farther away from Roger, which can't be that bad.

At the same time, each step is a step farther away from everything I've ever known, from who or what I've always been. I'm a lifetime away from home, and maybe farther away from Tess than I'd ever hope.

Devil and Us

Tess found herself, once again, on a couch facing Jessica, looking to reenact that repetitive moment where she ventured upstairs, spoke with Zarieanna, came back downstairs, and murdered herself.

Tess passed the joint back to Jessica. "We, one hundred percent, need something stronger."

Jessica slumped in her place. "You think people can see us?"

Tess rubbed her eyes. There must have been a way to escape. They couldn't have been stuck here forever. If it's true they had died, it still didn't need to mean they were stuck there. *Screaming won't work. Hope won't work. Patience won't work. Your actions don't work. You don't work.* Tess screamed. The frustration of living in Zarieanna's thoughts and actions and having no choice scratched its way through her and out of her.

She and Jessica stared at each other.

Jessica took a drag off the joint.

"We're added to the damned story," Tess said. "People will say they heard how two girls committed suicide in the kitchen at the same house Zarieanna killed that family."

"I don't think people know her name. I don't think they even know the family member names. They'll forget our names. They won't care."

Jessica was right, Tess figured. They hadn't been in the world long enough to leave a mark. The people who cared about them most would be dead soon.

A heavy, sharp sensation pressed into Tess's shoulder, like something pierced her. "*Shit*. What's that?" She grabbed her shoulder and lunged over in her seat.

"What happened?"

"Seriously sharp pain in my shoulder for no reason."

Clutching her shoulder, she bounced away from the spot where she had been sitting. The sharp pain came again, this time on her other arm, as if a heavy piece of broken glass fell on it from the ceiling. Blood from both arms soaked her shirt.

"It's me, Tess. Stay still and let me do this, this one time." She recognized Roger's voice. "You can't do shit to stop me anyway," he said.

She howled when something sharp plunged into the right side of her shoulder. He was stabbing her. She dived on the floor and rolled to avoid him. On her back, she saw Jessica's face twist in horror.

"*Hell* no." Tess grunted and blew air from between her teeth, seething. "Roger!" She thought back to him escaping his house with someone who sounded like Katy.

She waited for him to say something, anything, if for no other reason, to find out where he stood in the room.

"You feel that, Tess?" Roger said.

She imagined him above her, looking into her eyes, yet she couldn't see him, couldn't touch him. Fear like she had never had, made her stiff. Simultaneously, depression from the house punched her. *Why is this happening?*

Tess screamed, as blows to the body continued, stab after stab after stab. The pain was such that she felt nauseous. A subtle, cold breeze pushed through her. "Stop it!"

"What's happening?" Jessica said to her dead grandmother, though looking at Tess, who was frantic and cowering.

Before Jessica could hide or brace herself, something stabbed her in the chest.

She stumbled, reached for whatever had stabbed her. She fell to the floor and pushed herself to hands and knees. Despite having been stabbed and bleeding, despite barely being able to breathe, she crawled to her spot on the couch. Jessica knew that no matter what, the moment would call for her to go sit in her spot and witness Zarieanna head up the stairs to her room. And that's what she did. She crawled, pulled herself fist by fist in the direction this moment pushed her toward. Tess writhed in front of her, looking more pissed off than in pain.

Something or someone jammed what felt like a knife into Jessica's back. And again. The pain would not and could not stop her, because nothing would or could stop this moment from fulfilling itself. She pulled herself up to sit on the couch, turned her head in enough time to see Zarieanna dragging her feet up the stairs, weeping with those heavy steps. Jessica pointed to the young woman ghost, the same thing she had always done at this moment. This is everything she could expect from now on. She heard herself whisper a plea for help to Grandma Poe, and this time also to her father and even to Tess.

A hand grabbed her breast, groped her. She flung her hands about, felt painful repercussions in her movements. Whomever or whatever was in the room with them thankfully stopped.

"Please," she whispered. Her quiet plea didn't stop the ceiling from dropping that foreign sadness that made this house what it was. She saw that Tess had pushed herself to her feet. Time to follow Zarieanna up the stairs. Maybe the person assaulting her saw the ghost, maybe they saw Zarieanna and her bloody feet and hands and arms clomping up the stairs like a bride who recently murdered the groom.

"I'll be okay, I'll be okay." Jessica didn't quite say the words, didn't quite believe them.

Still near the bottom of the staircase, Zarieanna's eyes went wide. She turned around and came back down the stairs, reached out and grabbed the two-headed man's hand at the bottom of the staircase. He maneuvered past Zarieanna. When he arrived in front of Jessica and Tess, he batted his eyes and clapped his hands together. His clean suit buttoned in the front. His slacks, a little too long, didn't stop him from showing off his black, shiny shoes. He had the power to change everything.

For the moment, Jessica could no longer sense Zarieanna's despair. This was their chance at moving on. Of course, she could move on from this. Jessica closed her eyes and hoped this two-headed man would do what he should and could do.

"Your daughter didn't want to take me," Zarieanna shouted to him.

"I know." One of his faces contemplated. The other focused on a spot to the right of Jessica. The two-headed man noticed her bleeding, recognized her pain. She remembered him being oddly respectful and nice and bewildering.

"Oh my god," Tess said.

"Tesla," he responded, "I'm so sorry to find you here. But I'm glad that I *did* find you."

He focused on the spot next to Jessica. "Roger, I'm looking at you because I can see you. If you need consequences for what it looks like you've been doing, I can give them to you."

They all waited for a response.

Tess cupped her mouth, "What's going on?

"Zarieanna, I apologize," the two-headed man said. "I thought something was wrong when she didn't make it to Sunderland. I imagine she's lost."

"She was here," Zarieanna said.

"What'd she say?" the two-headed man responded.

Zarieanna took a few steps forward. "She doesn't like how I killed the family."

"She doesn't like how, or is it that you did?"

"That I did."

"I'm sorry. I didn't count on her knowing. I don't know everything." He took a deep breath. "Roger, you can leave now, or I can take you back to your haunting where you belong. You're too destructive and horrible to let go, aren't you?"

"I'm not going back there," is what Jessica heard from an invisible voice.

"You're sure about that?" the two-headed man said.

"What the hell are you?" the invisible voice said. "Not human."

"*You're* not human," the two-headed man said. The two-headed man looked too old to be strong or quick or violent, but he lunged forward with both hands and gripped the air like his claws had sunk into something. One of his faces strained. The other smirked. Then a crack, and the invisible voice yelped like a dog being kicked. The two-headed man made a violent action with both arms, as if spiking a medicine ball. He stomped on the something. Jessica heard another crack.

The two-headed man backed away. "You can go have your last moments. You'll have to have them while broken."

Dragging of feet to the front door, the moaning, the punching of the wall. The front door flung open, smashed into the wall.

The two-headed man ignored the whole thing. "Tess, Ms. Maxine thinks she killed you by telling you where to go." He set his hands on his hips. "It's not too late to come back."

Jessica underestimated how much joy she got from seeing Tess smile. If Tess could be free, it meant he might extend her the same offer.

One of his heads flipped around to look at Zarieanna. "You couldn't have done anything to keep him honest?"

"Nothing I could do," she said.

"I'm going to offer you two a way back." One head looked at Tess, the other focused on Jessica.

"What do you mean a way back?" Jessica asked. "We're dead. Aren't we dead?"

Ignoring Jessica, he found his way back to the staircase, both heads bobbing as he went. "I'll be right back," he said.

"Me, too?" Zarieanna asked in a suddenly small voice.

"I'll be back," Jessica heard him say from down the walkway.

Jessica stood there as unsure as she could be, choking on suspicion and doubt. She closed her eyes to let everything happen. She had to remain an individual, minus choices.

Zarieanna's clunky footsteps stomped up the stairs, almost like the director of this scene shouted, action. "Nothing I could do," Zarieanna repeated, taking her bloody self into the room.

Jessica followed Tess up the stairs and inside her room. They did the whole ritual where they headed back outside and saw Zarieanna in the window. She gestured for them to come back upstairs. The two-headed man would return soon, hopefully, with a cure for this moment.

When they returned to the kitchen, Jessica grabbed the same knife she always grabbed, because Zarieanna's depressing and suicidal impulses floated around the room like an airborne virus. In no way was it fair that she had to kill herself but the guy who stabbed her for fun walked free. She braced for the pain and humiliation of slicing her wrists. Then she did the chore of harming herself.

Across the Divide

The screen door slammed shut. Who else could it be besides Katy's father? Too early for Zarieanna.

"You're not scared of him?" Tess whispered to Jessica, while they smoked weed in their respective seats.

"At the very beginning. Not anymore. He's super nice and has done nothing but try to help."

He peeked one of his heads from around the corner, grinned when Tess acknowledged his presence. It was as if he strategically arrived while they were in this moment between their deaths, almost as if he didn't take it seriously.

He approached, tugging a wagon around the corner. Tess caught herself involuntarily backing away near her seat. His necks were too thin, his heads too perfect. Tess said hello, as if he didn't have a second head, as if he was only Katy's old father who always kept his shoes shined, who almost never left the house, who always wore the same lame suits. The same man who saved her from someone who she considered a friend till the day she died.

One head bowed to Jessica, the other to her, each with a different take on an apologetic expression.

"If you agree, I'm going to pull you two back to where you came from," he said. "In this wheelie is something rare as life. I will apply it to you no different than mud if you want to think about it that way. This is how you get home. You'll need to be naked. Only if you agree."

He had offered for her to live again. "Like my parents?" Tess added.

"I'm happy you know about them. I was close to them. I consider this a worthwhile favor. You know your parents are the reason I stayed so close."

"Next door."

"Very close." He stared at her with both heads as if he had more to say. "I felt guilty when Ms. Maxine told me you had come. I'm going to fix all this."

Jessica said, "Don't people know we died?"

"We'll see what happens. You're young. Take a few moments and come up with the best lie you can come up with. Or tell the truth. I don't mind if you stay. Up to you, assuming you can accept it."

Tess stripped off her clothes. Not an option to stay. She'd find a lie, a perfect lie.

"My father is out there?" Jessica pointed to the door. Her feet shuffled, possibly thinking of going out and finding him.

"I don't know him," he answered.

"Zarieanna made him shoot himself in the chest, at some motel."

"That'd be a favor, to find him," he said. "Am I someone you don't mind owing something to?"

Jessica took off her socks and shoes. "Does that mean he's still out there shooting himself in the chest?"

"There is an entire world conjured from the trauma of people murdering themselves or being murdered. It's an entire land of actions so violent that it can't go forward. Your father could be there, right outside those doors. He could have moved on."

Jessica took off the rest of her clothes. "I can owe you."

"Thank you," Tess said to him. The thought of people murdering themselves again and again didn't sit well with her. "I can't tell you how grateful I am." She could easily be like any of those less fortunate. In fact, she had been.

"I'm asking to find my father, please," Jessica said, tossing her clothes to the side.

"I'll see what I can do," he replied.

By this time Tess was naked and ready for whatever came next. In the near future she'd go back to school, make tons of fearless love to whomever, do a bunch of second chance things, many of which she hadn't thought about yet.

He asked them both to go into the kitchen. Naked, they did precisely that, crossing their arms over their breasts, crossing their legs as to not be seen by him. He pulled the wagon behind him all the way up to the edge of the kitchen tile.

"Don't worry about going through your death again," he said. "That's over."

Jessica grabbed Tess's hand. Tess agreed with the gesture. They shouldn't pretend like they weren't in this situation together. They'd be leaning on one another in the future. Jessica squeezed her hand as Katy's father approached.

The tile felt sticky on Tess's feet. A small breeze from the kitchen window split the hairs on her neck. She'd tell everyone and anyone that dying was fine, though you must treat yourself like a shrine. It's the worst of things that last after you're gone.

Tess watched Katy's father pull the wagon up to the side of the refrigerator next to Jessica. With one head focused on the handling of the clay, the other head gazed at Jessica. Tess cringed at the awkward duology of Katy's father's face and body language. Part of him leaned toward Jessica and pet her arms, as if to soothe her, to get a sense of her, though somehow it looked animalistic, like a dog sniffing another dog. The other side of him had a handful of whatever sat in the wagon, mud looking stuff. It reminded her of Arcilla.

"It's going to be okay," she told Jessica. "He's going to cover you in magic."

Jessica trembled. Tess felt the sting of guilt from not being able to console her.

He leaned down and grabbed two large handfuls of the stuff. Then he took a step forward and smothered it on Jessica's thigh, her inner thigh, her knee. He let it sit. "Don't touch it. Only I should touch it." He dug back in the wagon and continued to slather it on her. He insisted they unlock their fingers.

Once Jessica was completely covered, the room felt emptier, as if Jessica had gone. Tess said her name, but somehow knew Jessica couldn't hear her, couldn't see her.

"Don't be down on yourself," one of his mouths said. "You're going home."

As he placed the clay on her, its thickness and wetness gave Tess the impression she was being buried standing up. She wiped the hair from in front of her eyes, closed them.

Katy's father rubbed the clay on her breasts, under them, on her neck, in her ears, around the back of her ears, and on her face. She had a sense like her doctor had violated her. His heavy hands touched her as if she were a thing, and maybe to him she *was* a thing.

"Do me a favor and squeeze your eyes shut," he said.

He slathered the stuff over her face.

A few minutes later, things became as dark and quiet as ever. She might as well have been underground, unsure if she was still upright or lying flat or suspended above or under anything. She couldn't move, though she didn't have the will to do so anyhow. The darkness expanded inside and outside of her; she had become the darkness, lathered in space and time.

In the distance, a single star shone. How far did they say stars were? Millions of miles or billions? A small pinhead peeking through blackness. The star expanded, and the light from it scattered all over her direct sight and peripheral, bright lines slashing into a meaningless, colorless, infinite fabric.

"I'm with you," she heard.

Enough light got inside that once it settled, she could now see a backyard. Zarieanna's backyard. The weeds sprouted from a retaining wall where a garden might have stood at one time. The rather small yard, a haven for dirt and holes. Tess's feet had found their way underneath her. Katy's father pulled away chunks of the mud he had placed on her.

Beside Tess, Jessica wept, naked, either happy or shocked. Katy's father took a few steps back.

The world around them sounded fantastic and, not alive, but something else. Not enough words for what she heard. Birds sang, though that was the wrong description of it. Cars rumbled through the streets. She couldn't see them, but knew the action, the hurried to and fro. Shifting in a circle, she found the houses represented something she couldn't quite word. An overwhelming sense of words having no meaning. Perhaps the feeling would go away soon, a side-effect of her other-than-life experience. This is why Jessica wept. This is why Katy's father stepped away. Her unusual thoughts and emotions following her arrival from the other side was part of the process.

"What's the word for the process of people dying?" she heard her literary, authorial mouth ask. She continued turning in a circle, taking in everything with all her senses.

"It's only called dying," he said. "It tends to end in trauma that lasts."

So, the world around them sounded like it was dying. The birds were communicating, hunting for food, every action to stave off death. Vehicles transported people back and forth in the process to comfort themselves on the way to their graves. When the comforts worked, people thought, damn, we're alive. You had to find the comfort in everything, or the trauma would last.

"Thank you," Tess told him. The words needed to express her gratitude came easy enough. "Thank you so much. I can't thank you enough for bringing me back to this, this, this, this horrible place."

"It's not horrible," he said. "It *is* dying. You two go inside, shower, get clean. Think of what you're going to tell the people who may have missed you. You need to do that."

Each of his heads bowed at different times. One smiled, the other pursed its lips. This part, she could tell he had done it before. What he said had been canned. He knew how they felt in this situation. He had seen people like them, most likely, a ton of times.

Tess led the way inside the empty house. No furniture, although the blinds remained. The carpet had been cleaned. The pictures no longer hung on the walls. Jessica endlessly cried, wouldn't stop, as they crossed a spotless kitchen that Tess knew, at one time, had been covered in their blood and surrounded by their screams. It's the screams that bonded them more than anything.

Fresh clothes were on the sink in the bathroom and on the toilet seat. They were expected to choose from these items. Now that they had come from the dead, simple decisions as what to wear became a darker gray area. She needed to pick something that enhanced her day. Her life depended on it.

While Tess prepared the shower, Jessica stood in the doorway, a rejuvenating vat of tears. She suffered from bursts of limited breaths and no words, not that Tess didn't understand.

Tess showered first. Chose her clothing, certain Jessica wouldn't die from the choices she had left her. Outside, she found herself in the sunshine kicking the dirt with brand-new, white running shoes, tube socks, baggy jeans, a T-shirt covered by a bright, orange sweater. Her hair had fallen to the side, and she let it. *Screw it.*

Katy's dad, returning, entered through the backyard gate. To Tess's surprise, he only had one head.

"You can go." He waved, as if she should pass.

"Your head."

"I can't necessarily walk around like that in the middle of the day." He chuckled. "Nobody should be in the house. It's why we use the back door. Are you waiting for something?" he asked, deep concern sprinkled on his bald head.

"Where? Where are our bodies that originally died here?"

"I know how to take care of things," he answered. "What else are you waiting for?"

"Jessica."

"No, you're not waiting for her. Or don't. Do you have time to waste?"

On the way passed, she thought of touching him in some way, like a hug or a handshake.

"Hurry," he said. "Life is something you run to."

From here, she'd hurry to find a voice she could trust, Katy's, most likely. Only, Tess was nearly certain Katy had made a place for herself on the other side. So, where would she run toward? For a split second, she pictured Katy physically struggling on the other side, fighting men with multiple heads, dead creatures she couldn't imagine. Tess entered this old world made new, pondering having left Katy behind.

Creating Clay

My mom drags her feet to a halt, faces where we came from. From here, it looks like everyone is scattered in a design I can't quite make out. Beyond them, it's beautiful. The volcano with the snow on top, the hint of the sun rising or setting. I can't tell which one.

I look at my mother the same way, basically in wonderment, and at the same time trying to decipher what it is about her I would remember. Yet it's my features pushing up through her skin and settling on her blank face. It's perfectly me looking back at me. It's my eyes. The acne blemishes. It's my lingering hint of anger I've never actually seen.

"Help me understand drawing people from their haunting," she says, squinting.

If you stare at somebody with your face, you'd hesitate exactly like I am now. "You mean their cycle?" I finally say.

She opens my little book, as she called it.

From the spine she withdraws my pen, starts sketching something. "I don't draw well at all. You're like me. A visual learner."

"Uh huh."

She raises the page so I can see it. She's drawn a Venn diagram that fills the whole page. "All three sections together represent what would happen if we saw everything in our lives as a whole. Okay?" With my pen she taps on the middle slice of the Venn diagram. Taps again. "This is where you started, where your father took decades thinking up me and you. I can tell you haven't thought about what an amazing thing he did in deciding the process of us." She taps the middle slice of the Venn diagram, taps again. "This is where it happened. You met all your friends, decided on a future and this is where your history is." She taps it. "You can't shed this no matter what you do. Look at it any way you'd like. Okay? Respect all the memories." She folds the pen inside her fist. "You're not going back to that story, okay?"

"Okay."

"You're with us now." She waves her hand at our people in the distance. "We're made from the original dirt of the Earth. The clay. You're my daughter, despite the crudeness of the story."

"Is this Sunderland?" Bernadette said we weren't in Sunderland, but when trying to understand something, you might ask the same question numerous times. "Maybe an old version of it?"

She laughs. "We're not in Sunderland."

No matter what, if you look at yourself long enough, like I'm looking at my mother using mine, you close your eyes. If this face I'm looking at were in a mirror, I'd control its expressions, make small judgments. My eyebrows are too thick, it's why I trim them. My eyes sit too deep in my skull. When I was younger, people liked to always touch my nose. They liked to remind me of how soft it is. It made me question my features. The expression on her face is smug, not something I think I do. I'm not overly confident like she portrays me. It's like she's patronizing me, trying to make me think a certain way about myself. What does she know, smiling, waving to the clay people meditating in the distance under an orange-red sky?

"If you're so determined to go there, I should ask why?" she says. "You're here with me. I thought I'd never see you again."

"To meet my dad."

"You're going to meet him and then what?"

"I think coming through here, finding you and all of them out there, he can start to teach me who I am. Or what I am."

"Stay and I'll do all of that. We can do all of that."

What I'm looking at, this world around me, it's beautiful and amazing, and stunning. I couldn't make it any better, only worse, if I think about it. Like she said, my story isn't here.

"I don't see why I can't do both," I say. "I'll come back."

"You should worry at least a tiny bit about your father."

"Why do you say that?"

The smugness returns on the face she's borrowed from me. "He's willing to get rid of the people he loves."

"He didn't think he was getting rid of us."

"I'm not trying to stop you from making your own decisions." She turns her face, my face to the folks in the distance once more. "He had no intention of seeing me again. He failed himself before he loved me."

She feels rejected. It doesn't mean things aren't kind of amazing for her. She can have any face she wants. Look how beautiful this place is. She's rejected, but there's nothing wrong, not that I can tell.

She lifts my sketchbook, looks at the Venn diagram. She closes it. Drops it. Her hands raise to the sky, so outstretched, it's the happiest yawn you've ever seen. "It should worry you that he understands none of this."

She's on her tiptoes facing the beauty of the volcano. Albeit it's my face, she looks so happy. I can't see what she's complaining about. If you're happy where you are, why complain about who put you there?

Why can't it be that instead of getting rid of her, he let her go? My father hasn't hurt anybody. Has he? She dislikes him, yet appreciates what he's done, and she's happy. I don't see how it's not confusing.

Standing flat-footed, she points to the ground and waves at the people in front of her way out there. "All of us, we created almost everything you see in front of you. The volcano, the grass and weeds, the cracks in the ground. Look at it. The grass right there. We made it. All of it. In much of what's in front of us, nobody has ever taken a step, not even me. Nobody. No ghost. Your dad doesn't think any of this matters."

"If you like this place so much, why are you mad at him?"

"Ah." She lifts my sketchbook, opens it, flips to the page of the Venn diagram. She taps the Venn diagram. "This is why."

Oh, it's never crossed my mind that she's not mad about being here. She's upset he's not here with her. Correction. She's bitter he chooses to not be here with her. If I had all my history with someone, and they sent me away without notice or didn't care, I'd sure as hell be pissed.

She tosses my book to me. "Do you mind me using your face?"

"It's fine."

"You're sure? It'd freak me out."

"Okay, it *is* kind of disturbing. Any other face is better."

She thinks about it for a second. It's Bernadette's face that she adds. "What do you think?"

Rocks grind at my spine.

She bends over and picks up the sketchbook. "Let's take these steps."

My mother has the sketchbook open with one hand, arm outstretched as if she's about to read her poetry to an audience. It's Bernadette's face scowling into the spine of my little book. "Do you understand how this works?" she says.

Sunlight races through my blood, has me giggling.

She laughs with me. "I used to save your art. You received this tool from your father?"

"Yeah. He was like, draw on this notepad to save space."

"You think he bought it for you or made it for you?"

How she stares at me through Bernadette's eyes, she's looking for a straight answer. I never had the impression he made it. People don't make spiral bound sketchbooks. They buy them. "I know he made it. I don't understand fully."

She chuckles with her ultra-super, organic Bernadette mask. "It's made from the same clay as us. It's important you know and believe that."

"I'm not special; the sketchbook is?"

She hands it to me. "Let's see."

What I had been registering as kind of a headache is lightning at the top of my skull. You can't be out here as an artist and not try to draw the sunset, even in black pen you need to give it a shot. I'll add color and what not later. This isn't something I'm going to forget.

Something is wrong, I don't know what. What I'm creating, for the most part, so far, it's accurate. Doesn't mean something isn't wrong. I know this feeling. You're working, working, working, trying your best, nothing is going wrong, yet nothing is right. It's more than frustrating. It's demeaning, makes you question yourself like I am now. Like, I'm not good at what I do, but the sketchbook is good at being a sketchbook. Like, I didn't create the drawing, the people who made the pen are good at creating the drawing. When you feel the need to impress, it's like being a passenger in your own life rather than a person with agency. It doesn't matter that you're creating something nobody else can create. That's my sunset. It's beautiful despite me.

I remove the pen from the page. It's a relief to stop. I'm so excited, my mouth goes dry.

"What I have, to this point, it's not right," I say.

"It's not right?" The question on her face, her expression shines through the Bernadette mask. "I don't agree. It's very special."

The deep creases in her cheeks are Bernadette's. How they move, the slight curl near the lips, that's my mom. That's Arcilla. She wears Bernadette's eyes. Behind them, how they sink and hide, that's all my mother.

I flip to a blank page. The ground is much like in a desert. I dropped tabs of acid out in the desert, will always have that memory of the colors and that anarchist thought process, accepting everything that came to mind as truth with a capital T. With my pen, it's difficult to imitate the grass, not the entire bunches of them—the strands. I purposely draw them too long because I need space to draw every crease in the blades. It would be too much to draw the sunset. Give me a single small thing instead.

My mom doesn't bother me, doesn't comment. She was created, invented at the age my father wanted her, and she doesn't comment. The rocks grinding my spine could be anger. On the ends of the drawn blades of grass are small incisions, like a bug came through and violently kicked through it. Although I draw it in black and white, the picture comes out with color.

I must catch my breath.

"This isn't right," I tell her.

"You have to hate yourself to not like this. This is perfect." She rips the page out of the sketchbook, raises it above her head with pride. Her contagious grin makes me imitate the smile. The picture is hers now. She's done nothing to not accept one hell of a blade of grass. She loves it so much, it's plagiarism. She sets it on the ground and my sketch no longer resembles a sketch. It fits into the landscape as if it had grown from it. I did that. The blade I drew, it's green with holes where bugs have chewed through it. When she said they created everything in front of us, she meant they invented the world I'm seeing. They're not out there squatting and doing a whole lot of nothing in a land full of nothing. Our people concentrate, bring the world into being, blade of grass by blade of grass.

And I tilt my head back and laugh. Look! Look! I can tear out page after page, toss it in the air like it's confetti, and there aren't any fewer pages. What is this?

I yell, "I don't want to understand it."

"It's not just myself and you who are made of the world. It's this sketchbook."

Of course. Roger never knew he had it. What other childhood objects did my dad make? "Did I make the pictures you guys saved? Or were they magic clay ones?"

"The magic you're talking about is you. Effort creates things, not the lack of in."

"I'm talking about the paper, the pens, the colors."

"How much assistance did you receive? I wouldn't be asking that. Can you learn to ride a bike without the bike? It's rare for somebody to be able to remove a ghost from their haunt. In every way you're special and amazing. You shouldn't be leaving."

"I'm coming back."

"Nobody you see out there has the ability to up and leave. Nobody out there is thinking about it. It's impossible for them. You've done all of this before understanding what you're doing."

It hadn't occurred to me she couldn't come with me. I was thinking she *wouldn't,* not that she *couldn't.* He banished her. I presume I can get back. I understand why they applauded my arrival, why Bernadette thought all these people would want to hear from me. My mom thinks I can leave and come back, something none of them can do. Walk back and forth between death and life. No doubt, the person who can grant someone this type of ability is, like she said, on some level, dangerous.

"I can't imagine what he wants for you," she says. "I feel how special you are. He knows how special you are. Your decision."

"Can I see your real face?"

"I already told you—"

"I'm not going anywhere until I see your real face."

The face that takes shape is that of a high school, preppy cheerleader. "Accept it. I don't use that face. And I won't. Don't ask again."

I shift my footing and start in the direction of the others. It's confusing to both want to believe every word coming out of my mom's mouth and at the same time wonder why she doesn't want me to see her.

It's easy to stumble on the uneven ground. So many holes and twisted cracks. The grass in many places grows in elongated patches. It's flat and soft and green, like a grassy beach. Do I slip my shoes off and drag my feet through it?

I don't look back, don't want to make my mother think she should follow. Her many faces won't confuse me. I glance over my shoulder. She's on her knees a few yards back, hands at her sides, fake face forward.

The three clay people I've met so far have something awkward and deliberate about them. Bernadette with the arm protruding from her chest, something she did to herself, and my mother, my supposed mother with the often-changing faces. My supposed mother who isn't that much older than I am. She never saw her teens.

Seeing I'm truly discovering myself, I'm the third person I've met. I have a thing, too. Unlike anybody else, I can produce real things with this sketchbook that's tucked in my waistband. As my mother implied, the clay is the bike. We're all pedaling, learning, and discovering these tricks.

The first person I come across is a skinny old man, no shirt, nothing but wrinkles, no shoes or socks or sandals, no hair, no eyelashes. He's a whole lot of nothing, looks stuck in the lotus position, his legs so long and tangled.

He stays expressionless with his eyes closed, a dried-out poker face. "You're the one."

"Hello. I'm—"

"I hope you take to what and how this place is, quickly."

His voice is scratchy, not bothering to look at me or even say hello. This is the first person in a largely separated cluster of people like him. The landscape is exaggerated by dense silence. The mountains give the illusion of being so large that they block out any noise that might come from the far side of it. The ground works as insulation, somehow. Nothing vibrates from it. The blackness of the sky, a canopy of crisp air so dense, nothing can get in, not even ideas, because my mind is quiet, as well. Those out here are as motionless as the world they're sitting on.

"You're part of what's in front of us," he says, with his eyes closed. "You're part of anything you see all around us."

"I'm me, first and foremost."

In his first movement, he looks up at me with his eyes closed, a grin, a smirk, and a sneer all combined around his mouth, eyes, and pursed lips. "It's not a question if you're part of us. There's no question in that." Annoyed, he adjusts back to his original posture.

This talk about a home I'm part of, well, a home has a roof, as in a home in California, in Washington, a home in Sunderland, in Rowe Park, on Thirteenth Street, that's where a roof is, for example. You can live outside, but nobody's shelter is under the stars.

"Sit," he says.

His words are firm enough that I do as he suggests without argument.

Scanning the landscape, everyone is sitting in some way, though that's not right. I want to say they're praying. It might be closer to meditating or concentrating. I want to say it makes me happy to see. It doesn't, though. I don't want to learn how to be calm. I want to create in my own way. I'd rather reinvent the sun's rays and the nature of shadows. I want to fish from the clear, pristine lakes I draw. I want to make a tree the scent of pine and make roses the scent of lemons. I don't want to just create life. I want to invent it. I suppose, as awkward as he is, I want to be a little like my dad.

"I'm glad to meet you," I say.

He stiffens, except for his head that leans toward me. His fingers dip into the soil, brace him as he leans further forward, his grin straightening his wrinkled face. The creepiest thing ever is when you notice someone staring at you from behind their closed eyelids.

Ever so slightly, he shifts away from me. "Close your eyes," he says.

His eyes have not opened once. Closing my eyes would be counterintuitive. I get creative from what I see, not from what I don't see.

He kind of sings, "Close your eyes."

Behind me, my mother is in her own way doing what everyone else is doing. I'd bet all their eyes are shut.

"Close your eyes." The skinny, wrinkled, old man sniffs, as if the whole world around us is a mere giant rose. "Close your eyes and join us."

On cue, the giggles are with me. On cue, the electricity is there for me. On cue, I close my eyes.

He says, "See how there's nothing there?"

It's darkness.

"Feel the soil underneath you."

What should be weeds and grass and dirt, it doesn't feel like that. It's soft and kind of damp.

"Don't you feel that? Stay with us."

Running my hands through the new ground, it's the scent of a vegetable garden. My eyes are closed, but there, in front of me, are vegetables stacked like dominoes. Dozens of feet away the garden spreads rapidly outward. I'm a seed. Everything rapidly sprouts from my extremities. Everything is new and alive and, on the surface, different colors and scents.

I stand.

"Do you feel it?" he asks.

"I see it."

I open my eyes. There're some carrots near us. Carrots, of all things. Of everything that went on in my head right now, all we produce are these carrots. The withered old man, there's an ulterior motive in his grin. There's a secret.

"Sit, sit, sit," he says.

I sit, lean back on my palms, close my eyes. The quiet allows me to listen. Not sure for how long, I listen. Uncertain of time, I listen.

As an artist, I listen. With my eyes closed, it's easier to recognize roots snapping and the skin of food crackling away as it expands and grows. The rocks at my spine, they spin and grind, massage the idea of me, as a reminder, into my DNA. The electricity fires off at my skull. Sunlight starts from my toes, as I squeeze my eyes shut, bite down to keep from shouting.

He wipes a tear from my face with a calloused finger. Pets my hair with a steady stroke. Although my eyes are closed, I find myself gazing around at this new world. I am like them, smiling, and on the inside, so happy that I'm in tears. The electricity, my skulltricity bounces from his head to that person's head to my mother's head to somebody else's head, to everybody's head. I didn't need to learn about this connection. I've landed in a place to realize it.

The sunshine is *my* blood.

The sunlight is in *our* blood.

My fingers in the soil.

Energy from my hands, shaping and recreating clay.

Mother's Creator is Me

I arrive in front of my mother and basically tower over her, since she's on her knees. From a distance, I might look like her executioner.

My sketchbook lies next to her.

The tips of her nose and eyebrows rise and sink into her face like a small creature peeking from its home. A face comes into full shape—first the tip of the nose, then the nostrils. Eyebrows come forward, sliver of hair by sliver of hair. Her tongue licks her protruding dry and pink lips.

As electricity zaps me from the inside, I laugh and laugh that high-on-nitrous oxide laugh.

"Do you understand?" she asks with a fully formed face staring back at me. "You can see, that, Katy, you're one of us."

I flip to a new page in the sketchbook. There will always be a new page. With little to go on, I begin to try and draw her face. Once I start drawing, the eyes that had pierced the surface of her current fake face, retreat. Her tongue sinks back into it like the tail of a snake. Her lips fold in on themselves. All of it shifting to what I have in my sketchbook. She hurries to her feet, stumbles, confused and shocked by what I'm doing to her.

"Mom, you should sit. Sit. *Sit.*"

Since she's between faces, she only has one eyeball staring at me. Her hands wrap into fists. I leave her with no mouth to speak with.

"I'm going to find your real face," I tell her. I tell her knowing that if my sketchbook is a wand that I channel powerful creative energy through to scatter traumatic energy so it can dissipate into whatever. I don't know. But I can do that. What she's learning, as I'm learning, is that it's not merely traumatic energy I can move.

My mother smacks her hands together. A nonverbal threat because she can't talk.

"All your fake faces don't make me trust you," I tell her. "Go ahead and be mad. Stay mad. Let me see your face."

She smacks her hands together, and then juts a finger at me.

"I'll draw your face right here for you. Does that make sense?"

She flips me off, kicks dirt in my face. She stomps away, pissed, throwing her arms and hands around. She kicks rocks and dirt away from her.

I sit, sketchbook in my lap, and wait. In a second, she'll understand her face is nothing less than my canvas to have my way with. And I laugh and laugh the sunshine-in-my-blood laugh. She knows what this laugh is. She used to do it in our basement all night on some nights, all the way into the early morning. She gets so far away before she freezes, one hand in the air, the other in front of her so I can't see it. My mom resembles a small, dead tree. She swings around, begins to drag her feet back my direction.

The creativity that dominated this area moments ago, it has stopped. The clay people who were meditating, they use their own eyes to stare at us from way over there. They're staring because I don't think they can be creative like I can be creative, not on their own. They need each other to do it. They need their process, while I don't.

There's shame in her soft steps toward me. Imagine somebody tells you they own a part of your body, then you need to, in front of people you respect, admit that person owns you. That's what she thinks she's doing while heading to me, small step by small step, being owned. I hope she's like me and can see both sides. I'm actually trying to impress her by remembering her face. I need to know it's my mom with me if I'm going to trust her. You need to see the person you trust, the whole time, the entire time. I want to *see* her, not Bernadette or some weird guy. I want *her*.

She arrives in front of me, kicks dirt in my face and takes a few steps back, arms folded, legs spread. The dust I slap off the book doesn't matter, the pen I dig into the sketchbook doesn't matter. It's that she's still and ready to let this happen, which *is* what matters.

Looking up at her half-emerged face, it's not much different than the look of the project I've been working on at school. I could never finish it, I giggle.

My mother's eyes must be beautiful, like a cat's, in how they're soft and meaningful. I draw them in the book, kind of feather around them. Her lashes aren't long. I highly doubt my mother wears makeup. I'd ask her about these features if I thought she'd answer my questions. She'd rather lie to me than be honest to herself, so here we are.

Her body language shifts. She taps her fingers on her thighs. She knows I can be here for a while doing this. At the same time, yeah, she knows she's a subject of an art piece. That's her body language, *get this over with I'm bored.* An improvement from kicking dirt in my face.

"It's coming to me," I tell her. "Hang in there."

It's a shame I have no other colors besides this black pen. With some of the lines around her eyes in the sketchbook, I do a firm trace, you know, to get the contrast.

My mother stands before me with her hands flat to her sides, with her beautiful brown eyes I've remembered for her. In the years of screwing with this picture, it's never been a problem to get this far. Getting it right is the problem. How about I don't try to add myself to the picture this time.

She taps her foot, taps her foot. You can tell the tapping of her foot is on the sarcastic side. She appreciates the results I'm getting. She sees me as an artist, recognizes my damned vision. Creativity is like rocks up and down my spine, and sudden electrical bursts at my skull keep me focused.

It's stupid, like you'll never understand, to forget your mother's face. How do you describe your mother's face so that it's nobody else's but hers? I remember the absence of her more than her actions. I know her by my father's body language, by my father's words. Her sayings and phrases always meant less without a face. They disappear into a nearly impossible to recall daydream.

I know she had amazing lips, thick lips that look great with red lipstick. That's not what I'm going to draw, though. Deep down, shit, she never had that feature. That's something I've always wanted for myself. That's usually where it all stops. Her actual mouth, it's implied on other faces she uses. She has dry lips, colorless lips. She has thin eyebrows. They must be thin. Those deep furrowed ones I've given her before, they're intimidating. She's never intimidated me, so that can't be right. I picture her with dimples, with creases in her cheeks from smiling so often. This must be true, I mean, she has sunshine in her blood as well.

I take my eyes off the sketchbook, gaze up at a woman in her late forties with sagging and creased cheeks, deep eyes, yet the thinnest of manicured eyebrows, like she stole them from some pretty little girl.

Her eyes are so damned sweet, they're so humble that they hint at being ashamed.

"Did you get it right?" she asks, sucking her bottom lip. "It all feels familiar. Do you think you got it right?"

"I've got work to do."

I look down at the sketchbook, up at her face, the sketchbook, then up at her face. Yeah, work to do. I feel close, and, sure, she thinks I'm close, too. She pretends to be difficult. *Pretends.* She's with me now. This is the mom who danced with me and Tess and helped us put on plays.

I've never been good at ears, haven't met anyone who is. At this point, it's not a choice, rather, it's a duty. I sketch them too small, thinking I'll trace over them before filling them in. But are they her ears? They need to be hers. Fuck it, they are.

"You're doing so well," she says.

"Is it you?"

"Keep going, keep going," she says.

"I wish you looked like me."

She mouths what I say as I say it. It's like she knew the words were coming.

I finish the ears, make her chin longer, give her lines for flatter cheekbones.

Needing to do more, I drop the sketchbook, more like spike it, and I place each of my hands on each of her cheeks. "It needs to be smoother." She mouths it as I say it, in my moment of Deja vu. I'm nothing but an amateur artist working with clay. I'm also clay working with clay, closing my eyes, and I can feel this. I started with the sketchpad, finishing with my hands. The sketchpad, kind of like my artistic wand, I don't need it anymore. The creative energy is in my fingertips. It's always been in my fingertips. With my fingernail, I make a few age lines on her forehead. I make certain her nose is firmer than mine, because she doesn't have that feature, not in the same way.

I search around for my father. Wasn't he next to me when I helped him put the finishing touches on her? Geez, isn't that how it happened? What seems like learning is me remembering. "You're done," we say at the same time.

I know we're done. I know what her face should look like, in part, because I've helped create it before.

For a second, I'm stuck.

My thumb marks are left underneath her chin, behind her ears. Impressions from my fingers along her forehead. No wonder I could never finish this project. I needed her in front of me to recreate the moment when I helped create her face.

Closing my sketchbook, I look up at my mother, Arcilla, a name that roughly means altar of heaven. I rise, brush myself off, give her some space.

Her smile is so human, you'd think my father couldn't have created such a fantastic woman.

"I didn't know you remembered," she says.

"I didn't. I don't all the way."

She stares at me. "I love you *so* much."

What she said doesn't manifest in her body language. It's not like she's that distant Jesus hippy from a few hours ago, rocking those sandals and all. If I didn't know better, I'd say she has a hard time expressing things she considers personal. We're alike in that way. From her point of view, she sees my hands at my sides, sees whatever is on my face and thinks I'm still a little girl who isn't ready to express herself.

I stick both hands out in front of me and leap into her chest. I'm not used to doing it, so it feels less like an attempted hug and more like an attempted tackle. She understands, wraps one arm over my shoulder and the other around my waist. Our breaths are the same. My teeth chatter, there's so much to filter. She squeezes and squeezes. She does a wobble thing where she switches from leg to leg. I kiss this beautiful woman on the cheek, and she reciprocates.

We need to figure out how to do this, again. We need to relearn us.

We've hugged many times, I can vaguely remember, from mother to daughter. But we've never embraced to celebrate ourselves as equals, as flawed people, as individuals who have molded each other, even when years and worlds have separated us. She's my mother, she raised me. It doesn't mean we weren't thought about and conceived differently. My dad did it to perfection. A true, skilled, and practiced artist. A wizard in his craft, really, and kind of an anomaly.

We leave the embrace, speechless. Both of us turn to our community of clay people and head that way, the same direction as the road.

She holds me by the wrist. I yank it away, grab her hand instead.

I need to relearn how to do be her daughter, despite needing to be ready to move-on from this lesson.

Sunderland

The meaning of my life is Tesla and my mother and father. The meaning of my life is in the artistic skills I learned at school. It's the combined weight of it all that sits on my heart, while tapping my feet down this two-way highway with my mother. I can't keep my eyes off her.

My mom thinks it would be wonderful for me to not meet up with Dad, for me to not find out why he wanted me to take such a trip. Considering the experience I've had, I think I do need to find out what he can show me. That said, I'm not sure if he thinks I'll make it there.

"It's rare to be able to leave," she says, using her real face. "Rarer to come back."

"You're walking with me, hoping I can't make it out."

"I don't want you to fail. I want you to succeed with me on this side."

"I will when I come back."

She's not showing me to Sunderland. She's trying to convince me not to go. And failing.

I kick a dirt rock to the side of the road. "I spent all that time not remembering what you looked like. Feels silly, now. It's hard to believe I forgot."

Her hand is at her mouth, as she's deep in thought. The clap of the sandals against her heels. "We're made from the same thing."

"Isn't it that we're more sisters?"

"I was made to be your mother. You my daughter. And you had the last say, although you don't completely remember. It's still perfect that way. You don't have to like your creator to respect what they've done."

My philosophy on it: I forgot her face when she stopped using it. We don't need to talk about it. I don't need to understand it to have it be so. You can tell what a picture is by the result, not always by dissecting the process.

"There were several of them with their hands in how we came about," she says. "I'm proud, beyond proud that you came to remember." She keeps her eyes on the road, the wind blowing through her hair, shifting it so it waves above her ears. "You meet up with him, he's not going to allow you back. Your father is not only brilliant. He's a total dick."

"You think he'll try to hurt me? Or are you still trying to convince me to not go."

She stops and faces me. It's hard to believe I forgot this face. In a way, I suppose it's always been with me. That's why my body re-enacted the moment I helped create it. It's always been with me.

"You're the best thing he's ever done." She bats her lids. "He's not going to hurt you, by his standards."

"What does that mean?"

She starts walking again. "He's one of the few who crossed over. Unlike you and me, he was originally from this side. Now he makes people. He and those like him, we have almost no clue as to what they can really do."

I get it. She's scared. They don't know what he and others like him can do. I get it. I don't have the heart to tell her, as dangerous as he might be, he also created some beautiful things. Look at me, look at her. What he stuffed in us is as powerful and lasting as anything loved under any sky.

Checking how far we've traveled, I turn around. Not only has everyone disappeared, but the volcano is also gone. We're in a different place. I focus on the road up ahead. I bet a vehicle will come out of the horizon, if I were to guess, speeding. A drunk driver behind the wheel. It's this road and hills and trees and dark clouds crawling in. It's frightening.

For a while, we walk in silence. I think we're close and neither one of us is ready to say goodbye. Neither one of us looks at the other. Our pace slows a bunch.

The wind gains weight. It's as heavy as it's been. The dust is horrible, not that it matters. I smell rain.

"Let's stop for a while," she says. "My feet are killing me. It's not far."

"Is it a door? What am I looking for?"

"I know Sunderland is over that hill. Where over it, I don't know. I don't know what he has planned. If you're going to trust it, then go ahead and trust it." She smiles and nods. "He didn't invite me."

I bet I can make it by myself from here. She knows it. The clouds never stop rolling in, though never get to us.

She scooches closer, takes my hand and places it on her cheek. "If you come back, don't forget me."

"I'll be back."

She stands, so I stand, and then we hug. It's not a good hug by any means, but it's not nothing. We release each other, and just like that she's off the opposite direction. I think she'll turn back to take a final look at me, but she doesn't. Not yet. And she keeps walking. I imagine she's crying. That's the reason she doesn't turn around to say goodbye one last time. She's that bad at communicating. My mother—although she didn't give birth to me, she's the one who drove me to school and made me breakfast, the one who taught me fractions and how to read, the one who first drew with me and hugged me at night before bed—she's ten yards away. Twenty yards. About thirty yards away and she hasn't turned around.

"Mom!"

She swings around, plants her feet, and waves with both hands, side to side like S.O.S. I wave back. She backpedals. She stops, does like Bernadette did, does like what they all did for me. She claps and claps.

Thank you.

Thank you.

Thank you.

She claps as loud as she can above her head. She applauds.

I do the same.

At the peak of the hill, the road becomes an area with dense trees, and then the road is gone. I'm in the woods, and those dark clouds have caught up to me. A body lies near the side of this trail, no more than a few feet from me with its head missing. Everywhere my eyes go I'm looking for a head. It's a man dressed up as roadkill. Muddied jeans and boots, a red and black checkered flannel. The body lies on its side, and then it's gone. In a blink, gone.

The cycle reset.

Despite what I know and what I've seen, I still shuffle in a circle. Where'd it go? I'm still getting used to the rules, still getting used to seeing remnants of violence. It feels like I should be doing something, feeling a certain way about finding a decapitated body. What are my responsibilities? I walk forward, close to the passage or portal or wherever I need to be that's around here somewhere, miles up or something like that. Who knows what I'm looking for? A door? A clay wall? A rabbit hole?

The footsteps in the dirt behind me are like bricks falling in rhythm. I freeze, whip myself around. A person in a dirty, black hood, like a bag with holes, has his back to me. He drags the soon-to-be headless guy up this path from under the victim's armpits. If you see this sort of thing you want to hide. He senses me, yanks his head around.

For a second, we stare at each other.

He drags the body to a tree, grunting the whole time, and then sets the body down, just drops it. The person in the black hood must be a man. Look at the broad shoulders and the thick neck. Look at how wide his thighs are. The beheaded guy must weigh a few hundred pounds, and it's of no effort to this guy to move him. Through holes in his hood—a black sack with the eyes cut out—he squints. He's an animal who hasn't decided to run or fight.

"I don't care what you're doing," I say. "We're fine."

He takes one step toward the trees. He takes another step. His third step is smaller. None of them in my direction. As he's inching away, I am, too. He bends over. When he's upright again, it's with a long blade in his hand and he's after me. Dirt and leaves kick up around him, he's after me so fast.

What I didn't see when it all reset is the weapon he used to cut off that man's head hidden in the brush.

I look back and he's too fast. I already can't breathe. A few yards back, he's got both hands on the handle of the blade. The word machete crosses my mind. A squeal escapes my mouth. His breathing is steps behind. He shouts, curses at me. He calls me a bitch, a whore, a bitch. He's so angry, his voice sounds on fire. I don't need to look back.

There's a person in front of me. My father. Less than a hundred yards away, but he's also in a mirror or something that reflects the world I'm in. He's not over here. He's over there. He reaches for my hand. If I can get to him... He's reaching for my hand.

I do a little cut to my left, take a hard cut around a tree, dart to the left of another. My would-be murderer doesn't maneuver so well. I gain a step on him. He must think I saw him kill that guy. He's trying to cover up a murder by cursing at me and knifing me. I know I won't be permanently injured. I'm not *risking* injury, the pain of it all. I'm not risking being decapitated. All I need is to get to the reality that's right there.

My dad grins.

I reach out and grab his hand, squeeze it.

Instantly I'm a child. I'm in Sunderland in the familiar yard from childhood. The anxiety of being chased by a machete is gone. I'm a child. It's nice being small and protected and special.

"Let's go down to the water?" my father says. "You want to see the water?"

I can smell the water. "Yes, daddy."

Gripping his hand, we spin in the grass of the place where we took our family vacations in years and years ago. The man looking to murder me didn't make it through whatever I went through. And I can't help but to laugh, as me and my dad spin.

We Are All Ghosts

The vacations to Sunderland were mainly for my parents' anniversary. That anniversary date, I bet it's also the anniversary of us being created. It makes sense to me.

The place where we vacationed was actually a family friend's house near the water in Sunderland. It's in the backyard of the family friend's house where my father spins us in a circle, I'm so small. In my eyes, he's never been young. He's old and spinning me. I remember this moment. I was happy.

And here we are now, today. His blazer flaps in the air as he twirls, our hands clasped together. He's like a pole that I swing around, and just like that I'm not young anymore. It's odd for him to spin me in this way. In fact, he's struggling to not toss me across the yard. He lets go and I slide across the dirt of the backyard that was once so green.

How am I even here?

He walks toward me in one of his suits that he likes so much. "You made it."

"I don't know how some of this happens."

"I wouldn't have gotten you back the way I did unless we were here. This is a special place with special energy. I'm ecstatic, if you can't tell."

At best, he's content.

I stand so he's not towering over me. "Why'd you send me there?"

"I didn't. It was your time."

"There's a reason why we met here, though. I mean, right?"

He stuffs his hands in his pockets, looking me up and down. He's no longer content. I bet he's wondering what I know. I bet he's wondering who I ran into over there, who I talked to that he hadn't expected. And he circles me. I turn with him. It reminds me of when I met Bernadette, how she circled me in the street, how she had that third arm. What special feature does my dad have that he's not showing?

"I thought you would help Zarieanna," he says with a grunt.

"You'd think being made from clay is something you'd tell me about."

He stops, takes his hands from out of his pockets and shoves them back in.

"Everyone there is a ghost," I say. "What did you expect would happen to me?" What did he expect I'd do in the face of all of that?

"In many ways, we are all ghosts. Our life is one event, not the many we pretend to have. We don't change. We haunt our lives more than live them. We repeatedly return to everything that hurts us. Pain and suffering are the most durable things you'll encounter. To grow from them, it makes them a marker for us. We'll always have that reference point. We are all ghosts. I'm not wrong to think you've seen it play out on that side of things."

It's so flat how he says it, it doesn't sound rehearsed. No, that's not it. It sounds like he believes it. He doesn't have religion. He has this.

He takes a deep breath. "Zarieanna must have been a problem for you."

I think back to the man with the slashed neck and the woman hanging off the far side of the bed. "She murdered a family. She can rot. You could have told me about what it would be like. I saw a mother get shot in the face, a, uh, a drive-by shooting. I can still hear the gunshots. The little boy and his mom…"

I look away from him, focus on the well-maintained house behind him, to make sure I'm thinking right. The blue paint is newer. The windows are clean. I close my eyes and focus on the smell of nearby water. Anything besides imagining death and blood and leaving people to their deaths. Few can do what I can do. I can help the truly suffering.

I have to get back to my mom.

"It's a horrible place over there," he says. "Too many things you only need to learn once."

What I see is the stabbing in the park.

To remain calm, I think of being with my parents and crossing the water from here to get to the boardwalk on the far side of the lake. Each time we crossed made me feel small and closer to them. They surrounded me with safety and small talk. It took a while to get across and dock and tie the thing down and be careful with it. The man in front of me now isn't the same man from all those years ago. There's something different about him. Something in his tone.

He glances at my sketchbook.

"You could have told me I could do special stuff with it." I turn my palms up and shrug, like, come on.

His hands go back in his pockets. He's perplexed at something else. He's not sure about what I can or can't do, I bet. It's like he's, you know, a dad.

"You think you're better than me?"

Something happens with his eyes, something behind them. Something sinister.

"You know why we're in this particular place?" he says. "You don't remember?"

I search around.

He says, "You don't remember. Several of us worked together, we combined all we had with what's in this soil itself, the last place to find it. Underneath our feet.

I look around at the area. There doesn't seem to be anything special about it. You need to have faith that magic is all around you.

"This is the only place to create people," he says. We created your mom, you know. We had to redo her. The original version, I stored in the basement. We had to start from scratch. And as far as life went, we got it correct with you. Born right from the original dirt of the Earth. I dare say you're still not better than me."

"I didn't say—"

"I release people from their pain. I should be an example. You should help people. You saw someone in pain and walked away. Zarieanna said you walked away from her. You could have released her over there. You walked away as if you could judge her. Katy, you can do *things*, I don't completely know what."

"How don't you know? You made me."

"We made you. Gus, his wife, myself. You're an idea tossed into the air. An idea that chooses to let people suffer. I help. I use the clay itself." He bends over and snatches up a handful of dirt. Or the same clay I'm made from. "I use it to bring those in pain back to this side where they're safe. Once here they get a second chance for an indefinite amount of time. A small moment for a second chance. Sometimes it's years. They make peace with themselves, with death. They move on when it's time. I dare say that with all your gifts you're not even better than I am."

"Am I *supposed* to be better than you?"

"Tess killed herself in Zarieanna's home? Did you know that? While you were gone."

Why does he want a rise out of me? If Tess had died, I'd know about it. I'd think I'd feel it. Knowing she hasn't died doesn't stop me from looking through the back of the yard and wondering how I can get to her. This spot is the gateway back to her.

"I already received her from that horrible place," he says. "There's a strong chance she's at home with Ms. Maxine, as we speak. You can ask her all about her experience. You two will have plenty to talk about, including how you could have stopped the entire scenario from happening."

I think back to learning how to jump rope with her, going off to college with her. We even accidentally dated the same guy. I practiced my first kiss with Tess. We planned our future around each other. We didn't think we'd always be around one another. We still planned it that way.

She killed herself.

"Why'd she'd do that?" I ask.

My dad bobs his head in agreement of something. You know how it is when you're talking to yourself, like, yeah, yeah, yeah.

"You're more talented than your mother. You're not more compassionate, effective, or useful. It's all still perfect."

It's all still perfect. What does that mean?

Keeping his eyes on me, like I'm going to steal something, he strolls past me to the far side of the yard. This yard had never grown anything but patches of grass way back in the day. This backyard is dirt, and it's by design. It's the original soil. He squats, digs his hands into the ground, into the clay Earth. It's effortless how he scoops it up, how it sits in his hand and falls off the side of his palm. It's more moist than it appeared at first.

His face shifts: It blurs, smears. He stands, one hand full of what I think is the clay that makes us. He turns his back to me, squats, and again leans over. When he rises, both of his heads are demanding I don't be scared.

This is what he'd allow himself to look like if he were in my mother's and Bernadette's world. He's never shown himself to me.

His heads look like bunny ears stuffed with skulls, respectively. In either hand, there's a ton of clay.

"Come here," he says.

Hell no.

He takes a step in my direction. "This is me. We all have our differences. This is mine."

If I had expected it, it wouldn't be so frightening. He's no different than Bernadette, than my mother, than myself. He's in front of me, both heads confident in their own way, with distinctly different expressions. One face looks sad and openly compassionate, the other hinting at something sinister. He's two-faced and both faces tell a different truth.

"Let me show you what they go through when I rescue them." He takes a deep breath. "It's important for you to know what Tess and those like her went through if you're to help them from this side of things. You know there's no going back."

I find my feet curled at the sight of him. Despite his faces, it's one voice simultaneously dropping out of both mouths. Half a mouth on one head, the other half on the other head. Two small necks branched from a single one. Two small throats. One voice. A different facial expression for the same thought.

He says, "I can show you how to help them, regardless."

Sounds good. Save people from this side, be with Tess. I could be looking at this all wrong. Clay or no clay, it's not like he hasn't let me lead a decent life. He's never laid a hand on me, never asked for anything in return. He's a good dad. He's actually trying to help people. It could be that how I feel about his appearance is just me being shallow, considering the scope of everything. I need him to be a good dad and not sinister.

Be a good dad.

He packs a handful of mud on my shoulder.

"This is what I do," he says, rubbing clay up and down my arms like it's lotion. "It's less awkward than one might think. The dead and suffering don't take much time agreeing to be naked. Enough suffering and you don't worry about humiliation. Enough pain and you don't worry about the look of the person helping you. I can say that you can have two heads and they'll trust you if they've been in enough pain."

"You did this to Tess?"

"It only took a few words to convince her."

Which meant, according to him, she had been through a lot of pain and suffering. I want to apologize.

I take off my leggings and shoes and shorts. This is part of it, I suppose. I lift off my blouse and sweater. "You're smarter with two heads instead of one?"

"Love and death on one side, always separate from everything else. When you're done, you're going to be covered. From your feet to your forehead, you should be completely covered with clay."

Covering myself will be easier, less weird if I do it. I cram this mud on my breasts and private areas, speeding up the process. I feel dirty, not sure if it's at all like a suffering ghost. By the time we're done, he steps back, dips down a bit, looks me up and down, down, and up, the movement of separate heads.

He takes another step back. "You have enough creative energy. Your hands can do this." He looks proud. "I'm sorry."

"Sorry for what?" I can barely move.

"You have to stop haunting yourself. You need to change into something else."

"What the hell?"

He turns his back on me and walks away, hands in his pockets. A man simply doing business. I'm stuck in this position. It's quiet, yet not peaceful; it's insidious.

Changing into something else.

Something new.

Alone, again.

I'm a sculpture.

Why didn't my father tell me he wanted to make me into something else?

Why wouldn't he tell me?

Why didn't he tell me?

Revenge

To know about something, you don't need to have connected every single dot.

I'm in a specially made dirt cocoon. My father waits for me to change into something else. He left so he won't hear me scream. I wait for the pain. No help to look for. It's dark beneath the clay. It's like floating. I know he's still waiting.

There are things about me he doesn't know and can't see, although he created me. He has blind spots to keep himself powerful, to compete with me, despite being the reason for me. Nobody is like him. He wants more than to be the only one of his kind. He separated me from my mother. What he did to her made her not want her face, and that's why I forgot what she looked like. I don't need all the information lined up to know this to be true. She stopped using that face and therefore I forgot that face.

He has blind spots. He wasn't lying when he didn't understand me forgetting what she looked like. He basically has no idea.

My dad must think when I'm done in this cocoon, I will have forgotten everything, I will have changed. He thinks he's giving me an opportunity by putting me in this situation. He thinks we're generally all ghosts staying the same, haunting ourselves, as if it's a bad thing. I don't want to change. I kind of like being me.

Whatever result my dad wants, screw that, whatever it is.

Out of nowhere, light seeps through holes that can't be any wider than my pupils. I'm stiff, haven't left the dirt yard. I see him through the holes. He retreats enough so I can see his hands stuffed in the pockets of his clean suit. A grin spanning two heads.

"I love you and always will," is how he starts.

"You might actually believe that."

"I would understand if you were upset. I imagine you're angry. It's something we need to discuss."

There's nothing to discuss. He tricked me into this.

"When you do things while angry, you don't hear or see what's going on. When I pick and peel this from you, it's best to relax and we'll take time to get it right. This, too, we can discuss."

Rocks grind at my spine. Is he talking to me? What he said translates to being placated. Sometimes you need to be how I am now, you need to be mad. I'll stay mad, appreciate the electricity zapping me from the inside.

"What's next?" I ask him.

He ignores me or doesn't hear me. Shit, he can't hear me or a thing I've said.

"I know you think I tried to get rid of you," he says.

"I never thought you were getting rid of me. You're trying to change me!"

"Arcilla, if not at this moment, then at another moment, we can create another daughter, we can go as far as to have a son if it's something you want."

He thinks he's changing me into my mom? A, uh, another version of her. A third version. He thinks he's created another version of her with me at the core. It all adds up. It does. It all adds up. I matured, so he wanted me to get some seasoning by going through what we all go through, and the more I gain, the less he needs to create. And he thinks I'm better than my mother. He's making another version of my mother, but not from scratch. He's lazy.

I dare say I'm better than him. He can't *change* me into her if I've always *been* her. Another thing my dad doesn't know, although he's a creator and a father, is that he's speaking to me, not someone new, not something new. He looks right into my eyes and doesn't see me. He never sees me. He's never seen me. He's so confident and sad, if you saw him, you'd be convinced he loved my mother. He doesn't. Love won't make you destroy your family.

"You must be perplexed," he says. "I can give you that time. Any confusion about what I'm saying, we can discuss these things."

He's got his hands on his hips pacing in a small circle, one head deep in thought, the other, lips pursed. I laugh and laugh, tickled from the inside by what I'll describe as sunshine in my bloodstream. He can't hear me. And the rocks at my spine. That electricity. And my anger. Sadness and disappointment. Nobody has ever felt this creative.

He steps up to me and starts to peel the used clay away. "You'll notice the house. You're safe, we don't have to go anywhere you don't want to. You'll be disoriented, remembering things about your daughter that only she experienced. We can use what's here to shape and create what's needed to leave here as a family. Focus on your impulses. Everything you want, we can make from this very spot. Gus and his wife will arrive at my call."

He's so confident, and then he's not. My dad stops, recognizing his mistake. For him to be speechless enough for both of his mouths to be quiet, it must mean he realizes he screwed up.

He finally sees me.

I lash out in a maelstrom of laughter and screams. I grab his wrists. One of his facial expressions is an acknowledgment of how because we're in this particular backyard, I have the creative juice to manipulate his flesh. He can tell I mean to do exactly that. He knows this is where they make people, where they shaped me, the place with enough creative energy to make something that lasts or for me to destroy something that lasted.

He's made of dirt. Man of clay. Feeling his wrists, they're like my mother's face, how I can dig into them. I twist his wrists and peel them back, so his wrists are flush to his forearms. He yelps and howls like a grown person being ground in a woodchipper; I bend him, shape him into something broken. He screams as he shifts back to an injured human.

He headbutts me. I stagger. He tries to run away. In a step and a half, I grab him by the arms, sink my fingers deep into his clay and yank, separate his lower arms from his elbows. Like pulling apart cookie dough. One of his heads gasps so hard, it about suctions itself onto the other one. I take him apart by the handful. I can't hear him shouting over my own laughter. Inside my grip is his suit blazer and work shirt. All of it made up from the dirt up. All of it artwork made from good ol' clay of the Earth. I yank and shred it like cardboard to be recycled. I throw him piece by piece throughout the yard. Everything is clay and part of him—tie, socks, the pen in his top pocket, it's all mine to manipulate, all made from the ground beneath us.

Turning about, some of him is recognizable. His limbs. I find his trembling hands and arms and legs, and I mash them into the dirt with my foot, a lot like putting out huge cigarette butts. One head is in two pieces, attached to his branch of a neck. He's not back to his clay self so the amount of blood is crazy. Take a handful of Play-Doh and squeeze it until it oozes between your fingers and you'll see what his neck looks like, as it bleeds.

My father meant to kill me.

His other head, it's a yard away, torn into three pieces, still all connected, though flowered open like a malformed strip of metal. It's shifting to clay. It's looking like dirt. Time will do this to all of us, and I mean all of us, no matter where you sit on the Venn diagram.

Before he can get deeper into the dirt on his own, I punch this skull into the ground the same way you dream of punching the bully in the face as one of your friends holds them down.

If for some reason he's still alive, he probably doesn't realize his folly. I could be wrong. I'll wait for him to gather himself, to put all that is himself back together on his own. After he straightens himself out and doesn't act mad or too sensitive about me ripping him apart limb by limb and stomping him into nothing, we can…discuss it.

I'll wait.

My dad was a creature of extreme habit. I'm sure I can find the keys to the car on the living room table in the house.

I walk around to the front. I might as well be entering a museum of my childhood. Nothing has changed. There's carpet over the waxed, wood floors. Everything is spaced well. I remember being so damned happy in this place. My mother—even if she didn't give birth to me— was ready to love me. Why can't we die and relive *these* moments? Where is *that* place? Give me *that* death.

I grab his keys from the living room table, leave the leather wallet. Sure, I'm tempted to walk through the house, discover what memories are present. I won't. Not a good idea to focus on fond memories of the person you just killed. If the person you love is killing you, then it shouldn't be the person you love. I'm no longer captured. I step outside the house to remain free.

I killed my father.

I cross the yard, look back this one last time. I may never be here again. The sunset is beautiful, highlighting everything perfect about the house's shade of blue, about the size of it. There's something too proper about the house, something too manicured, too clean. It's probably made of clay like I am, like my sketchbook is.

An American flag hangs from the facade. For him, the flag was nothing more than an image. He shares this place, but this idea he owns. It matches the color of the house and goes well with his suit and shoes. The flag matches the idea he wants people to have of him. The bushes on the perimeter are waist high and squared off. The front yard is full of soft, neon-green grass. The backyard, where nobody sees, it's dirt.

Turning my back on all of it, I'm not done with this place. There's so much of my history in it that I'll never be done.

The road lacks a sidewalk. It's steep and angled and winding. I don't see any now, but it's not hard to spot deer. We used to hike up this hill, right down the middle of the road. Not a lot of people drive down it. Most people park their cars across the water on the opposite side of the boardwalk. It's so hilly, a car is good only for going from house to house. There's nowhere else to go. No stores or pubs. It's psychologically an island, though you can take the back way to get places, take the far side where I entered, in and out.

If I go back that way, if I can find a way to go back that way and to the other side where my mom is, I can help so many people. If I go the way I'm going, I can see friends who are happy. I can exist in new moments. I can see Tess.

But, yeah, we're all ghosts in our lives. It sounds like a bad thing. In practice, if you do it right, it's like finding a good glass of wine and sipping from it every day. It's visiting a childhood vacation home and, guaranteed, those smiles will always be waiting for you there.

We'd walk down this hill on the way to our boat. Everybody has a boat. Often, we'd talk about ice-cream and swimming and playing. My dad would chime in about doing art stuff. He liked working with clay. We'd have small talk about my drawings. They convinced me I was amazing. I feel sorry for you if you didn't grow up thinking you were amazing.

My father tried to kill me.

I dismembered him.

Across the water, on the boardwalk, there used to be a stand where they sold slush ice-cream. Lemon flavor was my jam. That side of the water is called Rowe Park. Haven't been here or there in nearly ten years.

At the bottom of the hill where it curves, I'm going to continue straight and walk across a small, sandy area that turns into a large path slicing through a row of trees. On the other side of those trees will be a rocky beach. After a few hundred yards, there's a small dock. It's where my father would wait for us and prepare to row us to the other side. I'm looking at it now. No motor on the boat. Oar power. Part of me thinks I'll tip it over and need to swim. The other part of me wants to be on this glassy lake, the mountains in either direction, the clouds dipping below them, you can see that far. The sky is orange and blue. Getting in the boat and rowing, can't you imagine me paddling to that volcano where my mom is and peering into space, looking at the sky with that black canvas atop it, those stars sprinkled like glitter.

Being on the water, my dad would have a hard time going across sometimes, in those shiny shoes of his, the wrists of the silver blazer getting in the way of things, coming close to getting caught on stuff. He's never been amazing in a boat. Sometimes he'd take off the blazer, though he always wore that same thing. He always wore that same shit and Mom never said anything. I know she wanted to. Like change your damned pants!

I dock the boat, manage to find my way over to the park. It has a parking garage across the street. He'll be parked on the second level all the way to the back near the staircase. A man of habit and routine. Every memory of him is positive. Never laid a hand on me or my mom. He paid for my school. He said it wasn't enough to explore myself. He said I needed to explore with like-minded individuals.

Walking up the parking lot steps is familiar. I feel like I'm in his skin, twirling his keys, to drive away in the same car he's always had.

You know what, though.

My father tried to kill me.

I dismembered him.

Home

Tess couldn't sleep.

She was never a reader, didn't want the television on, and as much as she enjoyed music, it wouldn't appease her mood. A good portion of what she had always enjoyed or put her time into seemed useless. Her mind kept sliding through recent horrific events with Jessica. When it stopped sliding it landed on dying. As much as she wanted to be alive, her thoughts remained on that couch with Jessica doing self-harm.

To keep her mind busy, she made chocolate chip cookies. The oven was preheated. She had the bag of pre-made and pre-cut cookie dough. One by one, she peeled the cookie dough off the card stock in the wrapping and spaced them out on a cookie sheet. She set them in the oven and stared at the timer on the microwave for a minute, then another minute. By the time the cookies would be done, it'd be 10:30 at night. By 10:45 she would have eaten all the cookies.

No way around it. She had killed herself. She imagined cutting herself with a sharp knife. She still smelled the kitchen at Zarieanna's where her suicide kept happening. If she thought about it too much, she felt blood on her hands, heard Jessica screaming, every time screaming, and neither of them could help the other.

Best to hunker down and make cookies. Best to enjoy everything in front of her the first chance she got. In no time, she'd enjoy music more than ever. She'd go buy clothes she'd always wanted and rock the hell out of them. She'd jog every day, use more curse words for no particular reason and flip more people off. She'd appreciate more of this dying world. She'd go places she never thought about going. Not far places. Close places. Parks and pools and hear people talk about nothing. She wanted to see small actions of others, see their fruitful gestures to their loved ones. She'd write about these places and people and names and styles. Her fiction would be based in truth.

All of this she'd do, precisely when her mind let her. Right now she could only focus on cookies and bleeding.

A knock at the door.

On most occasions, if someone knocked at this time, she'd make sure to answer as soon as possible. Don't wake Maxine of all things, don't wake Maxine. This time she let them knock. If Katy's father was at the door, as much as she wanted to thank him, she didn't necessarily want to see him. He could say, Tess, tomorrow is the day. She didn't want the heartbreak of it being Arcilla. Hell, it could have been Sam or Lollar. Package delivery? Salesmen? She didn't want to answer the door.

Another rap on the door. Without checking, she swung it open. To her surprise, Katy stood before her, lips pursed. Her hair pulled back in a ponytail. Shocked to see her best friend, Tess bounced on her tiptoes, allowed herself to take a moment to be speechless. They hugged. The moment felt better than eating half a plate of fresh cookies.

"Come in," Tess whispered.

"I'd like it better if we stayed outside."

Tess closed the door behind her and stepped outside. "I thought you died."

"For a minute I thought so, too." Katy looked at her as if she discovered a lie. "I talked to my dad."

"Is he here?"

"No."

"I can't explain enough of what he did for me."

"It's true?"

A wave of shame washed over Tess. "It's such a wicked, horrible, fucked up, shitty moment that I don't know if I can shake it, Katy." Her head became warm.

"Shake what?"

"That feeling. That house. It's stuck in my head. I think I'm going to go back there and do shitty shit. I can feel it."

"You're not going to kill yourself again."

"I don't know that. You don't know that." Tess slid next to Katy, rested her elbows on the porch wall. "That's all something I need to work with by myself. I want to know exactly what happened to you because—"

"You met my dad. Did you see what he really looks like?"

"God, yes."

"I was where ghosts are. Not ready to talk about it. You don't want to talk about something, and I'm not ready to talk about anything."

"I'll believe what you say about it, if that's what you're worried about."

Katy said, "I don't care to talk about it. Hey, you know what? Come with me."

"Where? Right now? Am I driving, or are you?"

"Could be two places."

She waited a beat for Katy to tell her where.

"I'll drive," Katy said.

"Far?"

"No."

Tess grabbed her phone, jacket, her wallet, and backpack. Katy had parked in front of Tess's house and had her dad's car. She never drove his car.

"Where's your dad?" Tess asked.

"No idea."

As if in a hurry, they made their way to Katy's dad's car.

Katy unlocked the passenger side, since her dad didn't have automatic doors.

Once inside, Tess locked the passenger side door. "You didn't come from your house?"

"Nope." Katy pulled away from the curb.

They drove to the Belmont area. It looked different this late in the evening. The route Katy took to wherever they were heading reminded Tess of the route she took to Zarieanna's the other day. "Wait. Where're we going?"

"Hopefully somewhere that will make you feel better."

They pulled up in front of Zarieanna's home. A for-sale sign stabbed through the ground in the front yard, just as she and Jessica had left it. The trust Tess had for Katy kept her from kicking and screaming. The trust came from more than knowing her for a lifetime. She respected Katy's untold story of traveling through where the dead were. Twice she heard her on that side. Tess trusted her, respected her, but why were they here after what she had told her.

"I can only be here for the minute it's going to take for you to make me feel not so shitty about this place," Tess said. "That's what you're trying to do? No more than—screw it—thirty seconds. I can't be here."

Across the street, Tess figured this could be a safe distance from that hell house.

"Did you guys leave Zarieanna there?" Katy rolled down her window and hung her arm out.

"I'm not going to find out."

Katy smacked the steering wheel. "I understand what you went through. I think I do."

"What happened to you?"

"You know my dad isn't human."

"I know."

"I'm not either."

"I know."

Katy said, "I can do everything he can. You'll be safe with me, is the point. I want you to know you'll always be safe. You don't have to worry about being a ghost when it's your turn to go. No matter what, I'll be there for you. My dad thought Zarieanna was too dangerous for him to bring her to this side. He was right. He's so right. It's why I'm going to release her on the other side. That way she can leave the house. She won't be a problem to the living folk, not like she is now."

Tess imagined the ghost of Roger broken and leaving the house. If she thought about it hard enough, she thought she could see him. "Roger is in that house." She found herself squirming in the seat.

Katy said, "I found Roger on the other side. His suffering has stopped. He had something in him that I don't know what it was. I shouldn't have said he was always going to kill himself. That was wrong."

"He wound up being a piece of shit."

"Hold on. I shouldn't have said he was always going to kill himself. I should have said, or I meant to say that I didn't feel like I knew him. That's the truth. I didn't feel like I knew him so I made up a story about Roger that I could believe. That's my judgment on all of us. I didn't think I knew him so therefore I pushed him away. I didn't know him, so I pushed him away. When I saw him shooting himself, I knew it was my fault. I stayed and I listened, trying to get to know him, but Tess, he was already dead. It had already happened. I thought I knew how to help him. We walked out of there together, healthy and ready."

"I heard that. I saw that." Greta had seen it, Tess thought. Too bad Roger couldn't have seen Greta care for him like Greta never had when he was alive. "I heard you at his house with him. I heard you in Zarieanna's."

"Hold on." Katy pondered something. "Feeling good about what you're doing and helping aren't always the same thing. It's not bad that he's gone. No different than Zarieanna needing to be gone, he needed to go. He needs to have faded away by now. Not a bad thing for him or anybody. He had something nasty in him."

Tess thought of, not only the abuse he unleashed on her and Jessica, but of how he talked to her, how much disrespect he showed. "Maybe I didn't know him enough to actually judge him. Fuck him, anyway," she said, the words scratching her throat on their way into the air. "As long as he's gone, I don't have to hate anybody."

Katy set her hand on Tess's lap. "He did something to you in that house?"

"Your dad saved us from him."

"I think he said something like that. I thought of you and your situation and what you must have gone through. It sounds worse than what I thought. I'm so sorry."

"That's your thirty seconds," Tess said.

"You're here and you're safe, is what I want you to know. I mean, you're at this particular place and you're safe. You're safe even here."

"You're going to free her on the other side?" Tess asked of Zarieanna.

"Come with me."

"You're not being real, are you?" To anybody except Katy, being on the other side meant being dead. You shouldn't need to die to hang out with someone. "Are you threatening me?"

Katy chuckled at the sarcasm. "I think I found a way where we can walk right in."

Then she started the car and pulled away from the curb.

Physically, the next morning, Tess watched television while eating cookies. Mentally, she prepared herself for Katy's departure.

After they said their goodbyes last night, they decided it would be better for Katy to stop by the next morning and honk when she was ready to leave. If Tess wanted to go with her, she'd hear the honk and walk out her front doors and meet Katy at her car. According to Katy, Tess wouldn't need anything. Make like the Mayans and just walk away.

She had burnt the cookies from the night before, which didn't matter due to the cookies this morning being perfect. She set them on a plate and munched on them while watching television. Half done with the plate of cookies, she clicked off the TV.

If she decided not to go with Katy, it'd feel like breaking up. There were some decent reasons to go with her. The first was *screw this world and its' dying*. Why not skip the rest of all this living and head there now? How many people would do what she had been offered? No pain. Just pick your day and leave. Instead of going to the beach, go die. No skeleton left behind. According to Katy, finding food on the other side wasn't a problem. She could even choose the weather. The argument against was she had to watch all the death. As horrible as that would be, she could also be with Katy as she helped all those people.

Maxine sat next to her on the couch. "Here you are, going to eat every cookie. Give me at least one." Maxine bit into one, smiled in approval. "I raised you well, yes, I did."

"You did." Tess could say goodbye right now. Maxine of all people would understand with little explanation.

Could she still write stories on the other side? Would they make sense? On the other side, would they need to make sense? She wouldn't have a purpose. Did she need a purpose?

Maxine asked, "Do you mind if I turn on the TV?"

Tess did mind. She wanted to be able to hear when Katy pulled up. Although it'd be easier to wait outside, they had already said their goodbyes the previous night. Tess didn't want to risk the pain of saying goodbye again. Katy would honk, and if Tess didn't go out to greet her, she'd just drive away.

"Can we talk for a moment?" Tess grabbed the remote and set it in her lap so Maxine wouldn't reach for it. "You're not going to deem it time to go on your own, are you?"

"I'm outliving you."

"What if I'm not here?"

"We already decided to not talk like that."

Tess waved at her, a gesture saying, no, no, no. "If I'm gone, I need to know you're looking after yourself."

Maxine's nostrils flared. "I take care of you. You don't grant permissions to me. Just 'cause you make a good cookie doesn't mean you have something sweet to say."

The squeal of brakes meant a car had pulled up out front. Tess went to the door and looked through the peephole. Katy's father's old Riviera was parked in front. Katy in the driver's seat, not honking. Tess eyeballed the room for her phone. What if Katy was calling her for some reason? She had left her phone upstairs. Stick to what they had agreed on. Wait for the honk.

"What are you doing?" Maxine asked.

Then the honking of Katy's horn, the signal Tess had been listening for.

She took a final gaze at Maxine. "It's Katy. I gotta go."

Maxine sighed the word, "Okay," as they hugged.

Tess ran out of the house, not wanting to give Katy any doubt.

During the first hour of the drive, they listened to rock music too loud to talk over. They still hadn't talked about where they were going, as they switched who was driving at the gas station. Tess would drive for a while instead of Katy. Tess bounced in her seat and tapped the wheel, swerved a little. Holding the wheel, her hand shook in her nervousness and curiosity. Seeing they'd be there in not too long, she felt pressured to ask questions. She already knew it would be scary, already knew she and Katy wouldn't have the same experiences there, and she already knew it would be plenty like being married, as they tried to not grow apart. In the meantime, they had almost unlimited music thanks to commercial-less, gorgeous technology.

According to Katy, they were on their way to Sunderland, to where she and her parents vacationed back in the day.

Tess turned the music way down. "What's it like crossing over?" Would there be a whoosh of wind? What would they see? What would it feel like? "It's scary, huh."

"I've never done it. I imagine it's terrifying."

Not the response she thought she'd hear. "Are you sure it's possible?"

"It's possible. I've never entered going that direction on my own. I can see being scared. I'm scared so you can be scared. Don't be. There's so much clay there, and I have so much creative energy while there, I'm certain I can get you through in a similar way to how I got Roger from out of his cycle."

"You don't know where your dad is? If I could, I'd thank him every day for the rest of my life."

Katy turned the music up and faced the road.

They stretched their legs at a rest stop. Leaving the entire world didn't seem real to Tess yet, although there were no obstacles. This world had a clear sky and offered no reason to stay. Whatever issues Tess might have come across in her future life, it wasn't going to happen. The horizon seemed farther away. *Take a look at this beauty of land one last time, through this lens one last time, in this time and space one last time, every moment one last time, in a journey to meet me and you in a new place for the first time, one last time, like no other time.*

They arrived in Rowe Park, stranded the car on the second level in a nearby three-story parking garage, and then they headed for the boardwalk.

"It's a rowboat," Katy said. "Across the lake is where my house is."

A sense of worry invaded Tess's mind. She had thought of leaving—which would be done easily enough. She hadn't really thought of not coming back. Up until now she hadn't been close enough to the edge to look down.

Katy ran through the park and found the swings. To Tess it was too dark with those dimmed orange lights. She followed anyway. Get used to following Katy. There'd be a lot of that coming up. Tess often used the word "agency" when she spoke about her characters. In this case, it applied to her. If she followed Katy, she'd lose agency. Katy might have seen starting this new life as them going somewhere together. Tess saw it as Katy needing to be her light to stand behind. She'd need to follow. If she did follow, on the other side, were there people to read her stories? Having someone care about her stories seemed childish. In this rare scenario, her inner child mattered.

"When's the last time you played tag?" Katy wanted to know.

"We're not playing tag."

Tess finally broke down and was "it". Katy could seriously run and jump, stop and dive and go underneath things. It wasn't long before they wore each other out. Sitting on the swings, Katy didn't look at her. Said nothing. Katy abruptly got up and began her trek to the pier, waved for Tess to follow, wordlessly made her decide if she wanted to continue the journey or not. She did follow.

Although the wind had increased, Katy stopped at a closing ice cream shack. Despite the teenage employees performing closing duties, Katy begged them to not only make a lemon slushy but to dump blue flavoring stuff over it as well.

The shadow from the hills on the opposite side of the lake were nothing more than scribbled lines in the middle of the sky. Orange illuminating from the lamp posts along the pier reflected off the lake.

Tess and Katy strolled down the pier toward the boating dock, with Katy slurping her blue slush with lemon flavoring.

"It doesn't make you chilly?" Tess said, staring out at the lake.

"It makes me lemony-blue."

They strolled down the gangway. Not even a dozen feet up, Katy stopped and stepped into a rowboat. Its oars were lying on top of each other in the shape of an X.

"Come on," Katy said, waving for Tess to follow her lead.

"I can't."

"Really? There's more to worry about here than there, I promise."

"I know."

"Then, what?"

"I. Just. Can't."

Katy pursed her lips. "Okay. That's fine." She sat there for a moment before grabbing the oars and taking the initial stroke to the other side of the lake, half of the lake obscured by night.

"Not being dead doesn't make you alive," Katy said, lifting her voice.

Living wasn't Tess's goal. After watching Katy row farther out, Tess acknowledged she wanted to be dying, wanted to experience death the same way her peers would experience it; the opportunity to properly die would happen only once in this lifetime. It should be both special and familiar, and with people who understand. As much as she loved her, Katy didn't understand, because Katy wasn't human. With that acknowledgment, Tess understood that this was their final moment together. She shoved aside the impulse to dive into the water, to stop Katy's boat, and persuade her to stay.

Katy would soon be at the edge of the orange-yellow lamp post light that glistened in a crooked line on the water. That crooked line seemed to partition the present moment from the future. Katy would soon go beyond the lights and into a shapeless, seemingly forever darkness. Near that forever darkness, Katy stood in the middle of her wobbling boat. She waved both arms above her head, like over here, over here, over here. She whooped and yelled. Katy clapped, and she clapped, in an almost desperate celebration.

"Tesla!" Katy shouted, smacking her hands above her head. "Tesla!"

If Tess saw it right, Katy was disappearing—a sliver of light fading into the darkness, all the while Katy was giving her a standing ovation. Tess responded in-kind by smacking her hands together, by clapping at Katy in recognition of the only person who would surrender her own life to risk living beyond the deepest of shadows. Tess clapped and hollered in honor of all those she met, and had yet to meet, who were somehow living in darkness—Faceless, Roger, Greta, Sam, Lollar, Jessica, Ms. Maxine, and those like them who Katy committed to rescuing. Tess finally applauded herself for even daring to step as far out to the edge as she had. Finally, she waved goodbye, as Katy floated into that darkness, to exactly where her light needed to go.

About the Author

U.L. Harper writes literary fiction that teeters on the edge of fantasy, magical realism, and horror.

Originally from Long Beach, California, he now makes his home in Tacoma, Washington, with his wife and daughter.

Keep in touch by joining *The World of U.L.* at ulharper1.com

www.ingramcontent.com/pod-product-compliance
Lightning Source LLC
Chambersburg PA
CBHW021117110726
47900CB00007B/2218